Big Girls Drama:

Carl Weber Presents

Big Girls Drama:
Carl Weber Presents

Tresser Henderson

www.urbanbooks.net

Urban Books, LLC
97 N18th Street
Wyandanch, NY 11798

ISBN 13: 978-1-62286-747-9
ISBN 10: 1-62286-747-5

First Trade Paperback Printing September 2016
Printed in the United States of America

10 9 8 7 6 5 4 3 2 1

Distributed by Kensington Publishing Corp.
Submit Orders to:
Customer Service
400 Hahn Road
Westminster, MD 21157-4627
Phone: 1-800-733-3000
Fax: 1-800-659-2436

This book is dedicated to all my BBWs.
(Big Beautiful Women)

Books by Tresser Henderson

My Man's Best Friend

My Man's Best Friend 2—Damaged Relations

My Man's Best Friend 3—Severing Ties

The Johnson Sisters

Acknowledgments

First, to God be the glory. God has blessed me with a true gift. I'm so thankful for what God has done, what he is doing, and what he will do in my life. I want to thank all of my family and friends for always supporting me. Thank you to all the bookstores, retail stores, and libraries that carry my books. Thank you to the book clubs who chose my books to read. Thank you to every individual who has supported me since day one.

Vivian

1

I was excited to finally have a little mid-day romp with my husband, Sheldon. *Husband.* I still found that weird to say. And it was harder remembering I was Vivian Garrison now instead of Vivian Johnson. Hell, I thought I was going to be the last one of the Johnson sisters to get married, even though I was the oldest. But God saw fit to send me the right man to spend the rest of my life with.

Moving from Virginia to North Carolina was a big deal for me, especially since I was moving away from my sisters. As much as I was happy about Sheldon's fantastic job opportunity and living the life with the man I loved, I still missed my sisters a lot.

The last time I saw my sisters was three months ago when they came down for our housewarming party. Sheldon and I invited our family and had dinner catered in our new home. From our living room which was bright and contemporary with its coffered ceilings to our traditional kitchen which was inviting with its muted tones and a kitchen island large enough to easily seat five, we were happy for our family to be a part of this transition.

Sheldon tucked his button-down shirt back in his pants trying to gather himself to look like we hadn't just finished fucking all over the desk in his new office.

Everything that was on his desk was now scattered about. I hurried to pick up each item so we could get it back in order before someone came knocking on his door.

With a flirtatious glint he said, "You are going to get me fired."

Organizing the papers I'd just picked up in a neat stack, I placed them on his desk saying, "I couldn't wait until dinner tonight to see you. Plus, I wanted to surprise you with lunch."

"Lunch wasn't the only thing you surprised me with."

"You didn't like?" I teased.

"Oh, I liked it. I did more than just liked it. I loved it," he said buttoning the sleeves of his white button-down shirt.

I stared at my husband feeling like I'd just cheated on him with another man. The reason why I say this is because the man I married was different than the man that stood before me now. Those once-full flowing dreads were now a thing of the past and had been replaced with a smooth fade with a tight edge-up. His jeans and Tims were now replaced with tailored suits and wingtip oxfords. His once-threatening demeanor had now been transformed into an approachable businessman. I found his new look sexy, but I still loved to see him in his jeans and fitted tees. Regardless of what this man wore, he still was fine as hell.

"We haven't done anything crazy like that in a while," Sheldon said, looking at me.

Who was he telling? I was starting to think my husband wasn't feeling me anymore. I heard people say once you get married, things changed. I was hoping they were wrong, but unfortunately, they were right.

Sheldon walked up behind me and wrapped his arms around my waist. He nestled his clean-shaven face in the crook of my neck as I leaned back enjoying his loving embrace.

"I love you so much, Viv."

"I love you too, babe."

"You did a brother well."

"Round two is later. Do you think you can handle me?" I teased.

"Me? Handle it? I was *born* for this," he joked.

I could feel his semi-hard dick grow to his maximum length as it poked into my back. I reached around and stroked it through his pants.

He moaned saying, "Don't make me have to go for round two now."

"You just got this job, babe. I can't have you losing it over my ass."

"But what a fabulous ass it is," he said smacking me on my behind.

"Trust me. I will tame that dick later. I'm going to leave so you can get back to work."

I patted his hand as he let go of me; then I turned and kissed him.

"We still on for later?" I asked.

"Yes, dinner tonight. I've already made the reservations. Seven, right?" he asked sliding on his suit jacket.

"Yes, that's fine. I'll meet you there."

I wished we didn't have to drive separate cars, but Sheldon was coming to the restaurant straight from work. He had another late night, and I hoped his work wouldn't make him forget about our dinner date.

Walking around his desk, he asked, "So what are you going to do now?"

"I'm going shopping."

Eyebrows raised, he said, "Oh, really?"

"Yes, I have to find something nice to wear for my man."

"Your birthday suit would suffice," he said giving me a mischievous grin.

"I don't think the restaurant would allow me to enter wearing that suit."

His phone rang, and Sheldon went from husband to corporate man in two point five seconds.

"Sheldon Garrison speaking."

He looked at me as the person on the other end spoke. I gathered the basket I had filled with food I'd prepared for this lunch date. I made his favorite, gumbo. I wanted to bring some wine also but knew he couldn't drink on the job. I looked around and everything seemed back in order. I wanted to spray some air freshener just in case the scent of our sex was in the air, but I figured that would be a dead giveaway for what we'd done.

"Okay. I'll be right out."

Sheldon hung up the phone saying, "I'm sorry, babe, but business calls."

"It's okay, honey."

He walked around the desk to kiss me good-bye when something caught on his foot. He reached down to see it was my pink lace panties.

"I forgot I didn't have them on."

He smirked as he brought them to his nose and sniffed.

"You are so nasty."

Chuckling, he stuffed the thin material in his pocket saying, "For later. Call it foreplay."

Kellie

2

Today, I worked half a day, and now I was in the doctor's office waiting to get the results from the testing Dr. Hoffman suggested I get due to the abdominal pain I'd been experiencing for the past few weeks. I thought it was cramps at first, but when the pain persisted, I knew I had to find out what was going on with me. For a brief moment, I thought I could be pregnant and excitement filled me. I've always wanted children, lots of them. But being the negative Nancy I was, I immediately wondered if I could be miscarrying the baby, which was the reason why I was experiencing so much pain. As quickly as my enthusiasm settled in, so did grief.

To hear my doctor suggest getting tested for sexually transmitted diseases was devastating, especially since I was married. I knew I hadn't stepped outside of my marriage, which could only mean my husband had. I thought my husband and I had gotten past his adulterous behavior, but if my doctor came back with positive results showing I had a sexually transmitted disease, all hell was going to break loose.

"God, please let me hear some good news," I prayed, looking up to the ceiling.

My cell phone rang, which caused me to jump, and for a split second, I wondered if it was Jesus calling to answer my prayers. I giggled knowing I was losing touch with my reality. One thing was for sure, Jesus himself would not be calling me on my phone. I looked to see it was my big brother. I knew he was calling to see how my doctor's appointment went since I'd told him what's been going on with me.

"Hey, Vic,"

Vic, short for Victor, was four years older than me. Even with this age gap, we grew up like Siamese twins. We've been connected at the hip for as long as I could remember.

"Girl, why haven't you called me to tell me what the doctor said? I've been waiting all day to hear from you," he said worriedly.

"Boy, my appointment wasn't until 12:30 p.m. I'm sitting here in the examining room waiting on my doctor to come in."

I told my brother about the pain I'd been experiencing but neglected to mention my doctor tested me for sexually transmitted diseases. I knew if I told him that, this would be a different type of conversation. Especially when I knew my brother didn't care too much for my husband. I guess that was my fault since every time I needed to vent about my husband, I picked up the phone and called Vic. I told him the good, the bad, and the ugly regarding my marriage.

"You could have informed a brother. I need to know what's going on with you."

"Stop it, Vic. You're making me nervous, so chill. My anxiety level is already at a seven, and you making it go up to a ten."

"Kell, I'm just worried about you," he said, using the nickname he gave me when we were younger. "You are the only sister I have. If you ask me, I think you're pregnant. I'm going to be an uncle. I'm so excited."

I chuckled, saying, "We don't know that yet."

"I'm claiming it, honey."

Changing the subject, I asked, "Have you spoken to Mom lately?"

"You kidding, right?" he said, tone flat and despondent.

"No."

"Kell, it's been four years since I heard that woman speak to me."

"That *woman* is our mother."

"Well, she has a funny way of showing it."

"Call her, Vic."

"For what? So she can preach the Word about how my soul is going to burn in hell forever for being a gay man?"

Growing up with a mother who kept us in church, Vic learned early on men and women were supposed to be together. This started him down a road of pretending to be a heterosexual man knowing our mother's view about gay individuals. It wasn't until Vic was eighteen years old when he realized there was no reason to continue to hide who he really was. It was that, and the fact he fell in the love with the man of his dreams.

"Give her time," I urged.

"You don't think four years has been enough time? Hell, I've finally got past some of the hurt feelings I have toward her."

"That's a step in the right direction."

"But I can't be the only one going in that direction, Kell. You know as well as I do one person can't make a relationship work, and that goes for family too."

"You're right," I agreed.

"My heart still yearns to have a relationship with Mom, but she doesn't want to have anything to do with me."

"She still loves you, Vic."

"She has a weird way of showing it," he countered.

"I'm going to continue to talk with her."

"Why waste your breath? Mom is a lost cause, especially when it comes to two men being in love with each other. Of all people, you should know how stubborn she is."

"You're right about that."

"I want to tell her so bad God made me who I am. If he created me, then how can I be a mistake?"

"You aren't."

"Try to convince her of that."

"I have. There is no talking to Mom. I'm still trying to not hold a grudge with her for withholding our father from us for as long as she did."

I loved my mother, don't get me wrong. She did the best she could raising us as a single mother. The thing of it was, she didn't have to raise us alone. It wasn't until I turned fourteen and Vic was eighteen that we found out who our dad was.

Come to find out, our mother was intentionally keeping us from our father because he left her for another woman. She used us as pawns in her revenge, not caring that keeping us from him not only hurt him, but it hurt us as well. From that day on, we vowed to get close to our dad, which we did; that is, until he died a few years ago.

"Are you okay, Kell?" Vic asked, breaking me out of my thoughts.

"Yes. Just thinking about Dad. I miss him so much."

"I miss Pops too. It's good to know where we got our light skin and this good hair from, because for years, I knew our dad was mixed with something."

"And Mama wonders why I have trust issues," I quipped.

"Speak it, Kell. That woman lying to us all those years was enough to screw us up. I feel cheated out of all the years I could have spent with him."

"Me too. That's why I'm trying so hard not to have ill feelings against her."

"I should because maybe Dad could have helped me early on to understand the feelings I was having."

"He loved us so much."

"He loved us unconditionally. Even when I came out of the closet, Dad didn't flinch. You would expect a father would have an issue with his son being gay, but here it is our mother. Dad loved me until the day he died. I know that's why I keep pushing forward because he told me don't let no one make me feel bad about the man I am."

"He's right, Vic."

"I know that now, which is why I'm not in a hurry to talk to Mom. As much as she thinks I can get over being gay, she needs to understand gay is not a cold you can take medicine for and it goes away."

My brother was a very intelligent person and didn't have a problem speaking his mind. I guess years of holding back who he was changed his perception of how his life should be lived now, and I was happy for that. Vic stood in his truth, and there was nothing stronger than that.

"Chile, I have to get off this line before I lose my job. I'm talking like I'm at home. A couple of people looking at me crazy, and I don't feel like cussing nobody out because they all in my business."

"Then you better get off the phone," I said, chuckling.

"You call me when you know the real, okay?"

"I will. Love you, Vic."

"Love you too, Kell. And don't forget to call me."

I hung up with my brother, still beaming from speaking with him. I truly did love him. He always knew how to put a smile on my face.

Kellie

3

When Dr. Hoffman entered the examining room, I tried to read her expression but couldn't. I guess being in her profession for as long as she had, she'd mastered holding a poker face so no one would be able to tell what she was going to say, and this made me more nervous.

"Kellie, your weight is good, 129 pounds, which is great for your height of five foot five. Your BP is great, and vitals are good. Your temperature is normal as well."

I felt like she was telling me all the things that were good before she was going to drop the bad news on me. Nothing could have prepared me for what she told me next.

"What did you just say to me?" I asked in disbelief.

"I'm sorry, but you have Chlamydia," she repeated slowly, looking at me with compassion.

I couldn't say anything. I shook my head with a pained expression on my face as she gazed at me sympathetically.

"You told me you didn't have any other sexual partners, correct?"

"I don't. Jeffrey has been the only man I've been sleeping with."

"I hate to say it, Kellie, but this means you had to get this STD from your husband."

I shook my head, knowing my husband wouldn't dare cheat on me again.

Dr. Hoffman continued by saying, "You really need to have him come in and get treated for this condition as well."

"He's cheating on me," I whispered to myself, trying to make sense of this entire situation.

"Kellie, there is something else."

I looked at her like I didn't want to hear anything else. This news was enough to annihilate me. Even though her face couldn't be read, the way she spoke was enough for me to understand the next bit of information was not going to be any better. I dropped my head as I reached down and gripped both sides of the examination table as hard as I could. I think I was trying to hold on. Was I trying to hold on so I wouldn't hit the floor? Was I holding on for hope for better news? Or was I gripping this table so tightly because I felt a rage build within me that I'd never experienced before. Whatever, none of this was good.

I looked at Dr. Hoffman waiting for her to drop the next misfortune on me. She took this as her cue to proceed.

"With you being diagnosed with Chlamydia, I suspect you could also have a condition known as PID."

I frowned as I asked, "What is PID?"

The doctor smiled warmly before saying, "I'm sorry for using abbreviations. PID stands for pelvic inflammatory disease. It's an infection of your female reproductive organs."

"Is it serious?" I asked frantically.

"It can be. This condition could lead to irreversible damage to your uterus, fallopian tubes, and other parts of your female reproductive organs."

"So this could be why I have been having this pain?"

"The pain could stem from this or the fact you have this STD," she answered. "More likely than not, I think it's the beginning stages of PID."

"You said there could be damage to my female organs. Does this mean it could affect me having children?" I asked fearfully.

"Unfortunately, yes."

And there was The Catastrophe. I sucked in a breath, shocked at her answer.

"In many cases, women who get this condition become infertile," she responded honestly.

I began to weep. I couldn't take this news. I'd rather hear my husband was cheating than the fact his deceitful actions could have affected my chances of ever having children.

My doctor rolled her chair closer to me and began rubbing my leg lovingly.

"I can't believe this. I thought my marriage was great, but I guess I was wrong, especially if he's cheating."

"Please understand I'm not saying you have PID, but unfortunately, the signs are there. What I want to do now is do further testing."

"I'll do anything. I want to have children."

"Okay. I'll send you to the lab today to have blood drawn to see if there is evidence of an infection. Then I'll set up another appointment for you to have an ultrasound done to have your reproductive organs examined. I'll see if they can get you in as soon as possible. These things will let us know the severity of your condition. Once I have your results, I'll give you a call to come in for your findings."

I nodded, feeling numb to all of this. Jeffrey promised me he wouldn't cheat on me again. So not only did I have the burden of knowing my husband was back to his old tricks again, I had to deal with the revelation I was infected with an STD that could possibly ruin my chances of ever having children.

"I've sent over a prescription to start treatment for the STD, but please understand, if you continue to sleep with your husband who's not being treated, then you are taking the medication in vain."

Oh, she didn't have to worry about me ever sleeping with him again. This news was the wake-up call I needed. As much as I wished I'd never come to see my doctor, I knew it was in my best interest to do so, in more ways than one. Just like that, my entire world was ripped from under me again. I never should have trusted him. I should have left when he stepped out on our marriage the first time. Hell, the second and third time! But I loved him enough to give him chance after chance. Shame on me for making such a terrible decision, because now, my choices could have affected my chances of ever having children.

Vivian

4

I found this cute upscale boutique I'd wanted to come to ever since I'd moved here and decided today was the day I should go and see what they had to offer. I wasn't in the shop five minutes before one of the salespeople approached me.

"Can I help you?" she asked as I scanned through some clothes.

"No, thank you," I answered smiling graciously at the middle-age woman. I thought my answer was enough to make her move on to the next patron, but she continued to linger by me.

I hoped this was not another moment in my life where racial profiling was taking place. I really didn't want to be that stereotypical black woman, but if I had to, I would. All I was trying to do was look for something sexy to wear for my husband.

"Did you need something else?" I questioned with narrowed eyes, hoping she understood I didn't appreciate she was still standing near me like I was going to steal something.

"Oh no."

She said this, but she still didn't bother to budge. Now I was getting irritated.

"Then why are you still hovering over me? I hope you don't think I'm going to steal anything. I can't help but notice I'm the only woman you are watching. Is it because I'm the only African American in this establishment?"

"No, ma'am, but . . ."

"But what?" I asked in irritation.

"We . . . we don't carry many clothes in . . . in . . . your size," she stuttered.

No, this bitch didn't. I gawked at her wondering if she was serious right now. Whether there was one or one hundred pieces of plus-size clothes in the place, I had the right to look. Besides, I could have been looking for something for someone else.

I turned to face her full-on, linking my fingers together in front of me. I knew if I put my hands on my hips or folded my arms across my ample breasts, I would have probably been labeled the angry black woman. I hated to think this way, but per my experience, this was the exact way it was.

"And what size is that?"

Shifting uncomfortably, the woman knew she'd upset me. She cleared her throat as she placed a nervous hand to her chest and replied with, "Plus size, ma'am."

"So you are calling me fat?"

"No, not at all but . . ."

"But what?"

"All I was trying to say is this store doesn't carry many pieces of clothing in your size."

It was one thing to come to me thinking I was being racially profiled, but it was another to be insulted about my weight. Hell, I think I would have preferred she thought I was a thief. I was angered by her statement but couldn't do anything but chuckle.

"Do you inform all of your plus-size customers of this?"

"Um . . . Well, no, not all the time. I just thought I would save you some time."

"So you want me to leave?" I asked.

"No, that's not what I was saying," she stammered again.

"So you just do this to black women?"

"No."

"So you do this to white women also?"

"No. Yes, ma'am."

I held my hand up stopping her ignorant banter. All she was doing was stumbling around her words when I knew damn well just like she did that she was coming at me like this because she saw me as a fat black woman who probably couldn't afford a thing in here. Maybe I was out of line for my thoughts, but this had happened to me way too many times for me to not come to this conclusion.

"Is your manager here?" I asked.

"No. She's at lunch."

"Okay, then, I will sit and wait for her to return, if that's okay with you," I said smirking at the nervous woman.

"She just left. I'm not sure when she'll be back."

"That's okay. I have time to wait," I said finding a seat next to the dressing room.

I smiled flatly and watched as the scrawny brunette woman sauntered in the direction of the checkout counter where another worker was ringing up a customer. She whispered something to the coworker and both looked my way. I waved and both turned away quickly when they noticed I was glaring at them.

Ten minutes later, a curvy Caucasian woman approached me with a huge smile on her face. She was quite attractive and looked too young to be a manager of this establishment. I looked to my right to see the lady who made the rude comment watching from afar.

"Hello, my name is Julia, and I'm the manager here," she graciously greeted as she held her hand out to me. "How can I help you?"

"Yes, I would like to file a complaint against one of your employees."

"Sure. Follow me to my office and we can discuss this matter further," she said leading the way.

Miss Julia was not only a curvy woman, she had a behind on her as well. I wasn't into women, but I admired when a woman carried herself as well as she did.

We entered a room painted in stark white. It was so white the room looked sterile. I felt like I was waiting for a physician to come in and examine me. There was nothing on the walls, and her desk was in front of a huge window covered with plantation shutters. I did notice some boxes in a corner with items which consisted of some picture frames so maybe she was in the process of decorating this space.

"Please, have a seat," she gestured toward the black leather chair across from her, and I sat down.

"So what happened?"

"First, this woman stalked me throughout your store like she expected me to steal something. Then when I addressed her, she proceeded to insult me further by informing me this store doesn't carry many clothes for women my size."

The woman's brows rose at my statement, and she immediately went into apology mode.

"I am so sorry for that. We do not tolerate such behavior here. And I'm so sincere when I say this. I mean, look at me. I'm not a size two," she said chuckling.

"It just gets tiresome dealing with individuals like this woman."

"Trust me, I understand."

I wanted to ask her how could she. We may have our curves in common, but at the end of the day, I was still a black woman, and she wasn't.

"May I ask which employee was rude in this way?"

"It was the older brunette woman."

The woman dropped her head as she shook it before saying, "Meredith." She inhaled a breath before continuing. "It is not our intention to make any patron who attends my store be addressed and berated in such a manner. She will be dealt with."

I was hoping she wasn't just telling me this to make me feel better. Often in this type of situation, when you returned to these stores, that same ignorant person was still employed and still acting ill-mannered.

"Thank you for letting me know. I can't afford to lose business because my employees are not acting according to our policy. All business is welcomed, and I mean that. Meredith is basically out the door. That woman has caused me more business than anybody. The only reason why I've kept her on for as long as I have is because she's my aunt."

I chuckled, surprised Julia was even kin to this woman. But you can't choose your family.

"Thank you for allowing me to talk with you," I said, standing. "I really need to get going to find something to wear tonight."

"Please feel free to look around," she stood.

"Unfortunately, I will be taking my business elsewhere. It's nothing against you."

The woman looked taken aback before asking, "Are you sure, because I would be happy to assist you personally? I have some fabulous new pieces in the back that haven't hit the floor yet."

"I don't know."

"And I'll give you a 25 percent discount on your entire purchase as well."

She was really buttering me up to make this purchase. This was unusual. I thought she would have told me she understood how I felt instead of sweetening the pot for me to purchase from her establishment.

"Sold," I said with a smile.

"Fantastic. I can't wait to show you what we have. I've been working hard to get more curvy pieces of clothing into my store. I want to be an equal opportunity merchant. When I first opened this place, the only thing I could wear was the jewelry and the shoes."

"So you are not only the manager, you are the owner as well?" I asked in amazement.

"Yes, I opened this boutique five years ago. I'm happy it's done as well as it has, especially in this economy."

"Please don't take this the wrong way, but you don't look old enough to own this store, much less manage it."

"I'm going to take that as a compliment. Would you believe I'm thirty-seven?"

"No, I thought you were in your early twenties."

"Thank you. I try very hard to take care of myself."

"You've done an amazing job."

Once we were in the back I saw many pieces in my size that I absolutely loved. When she said she was trying to get more curvy pieces in her boutique, she wasn't lying. The first thing that caught my eye was this metallic knit sheath dress with a side knot at the waist.

"This dress is absolutely gorgeous," I said holding the item up.

"Isn't it sophisticated? And guess what?"

"What?"

"We have a matching jumpsuit."

I loved the jumpsuit more than the dress.

"Both of these are beautiful. What would make them look even better is a pair of metallic strappy heels."

"I could tell by what you are wearing today you have a nice sense of style."

"I love fashion."

"It shows. Is that what your career is in?"

"Unfortunately, no. I'm looking for a job right now since I'm new to the area."

"Where are you from?"

"I'm from Virginia."

"Well, welcome to North Carolina."

"Thanks."

"You know, I can sweeten this deal even more for you," Julia said, looking at me sincerely.

"How?"

"Would you like to work for me?"

Was this woman serious? I came in here to find something to wear to my dinner with Sheldon tonight only to file a complaint on her uppity aunt no less, and here she was offering me a job. Look at God.

"Really?"

"I'm serious. I can tell you would be a fabulous asset for my business. You dress amazingly. You are curvy just like me, and we need more of that around here. And who knows, maybe you'll be the one to help me launch my plus-size clothing boutique I've been thinking about opening."

I looked at her in amazement, not being able to say anything.

"I am not a person who's at a loss for words often."

"Think about it. Here's my card. Call me once you mull it over."

I took her card, still speechless at how this all went down. I knew in this moment this was not happenstance. This was God.

"Now that we got that out of the way," Julia said, "let's see what else we can find for you to purchase."

Monica

5

Jumping to the workout DVD, I came to the conclusion it was kicking my ass. I knew that's what it was supposed to be doing, but damn . . . I was already sweating like a whore in church, and I had only been working out for ten minutes of this thirty-minute video. My lavender workout top had dark purple circles beneath my armpits. I thought by the fourth day of doing this, it would have gotten a lot easier, but it hadn't. I was worn out, and I had just got started. I marched in place awaiting the next move from the man on the 52-inch flat panel when my husband walked into the living room.

"Hey, baby," I spoke, panting and reaching to the ceiling. Right then left. Then right, then left, going to the beat of the music they were playing. I noticed Devin never spoke.

"Hey, baby," I said again waiting for him to respond.

He walked by gawking at me asking, "What's for dinner?"

"You can't speak. All you can ask is what's for dinner?"

"Hey, Monica. What's for dinner?" he responded tersely.

"Did you have a bad day at work?" I asked, noticing his obnoxious mood.

"Let's just say it wasn't the best day," he answered. "Now, are you going to answer my question?"

I stopped, trying to get some reprieve and said, "I didn't cook."

He frowned saying, "What do you mean you didn't cook?"

"Don't you remember, we're supposed to go over to your parents' house for dinner tonight?" I reminded him.

He closed his eyes and sighed in frustration. I knew from his reaction he didn't feel like going there. Especially since he said he didn't have the best day. Hell, I understood. I worked today also. All I wanted to do after this workout was take a shower and crawl in my bed to relax for the rest of the evening.

"You still could have cooked," he spat.

"The last time I cooked and we had to go over to your parents for dinner, you got upset because I prepared food, knowing we were going there. So now I don't cook at all, and you telling me I should have? You need to make up your mind," I said smartly.

"I don't have time for this," he murmured as he turned to walk away from me.

"Where are you going?"

"I'm going upstairs to get ready like you should be doing instead of wasting your time working out to that CD. All you're going to do is fix a big bowl of ice cream right before bedtime, so what's the use?"

His face was void of a smile. He was serious, and it kind of hurt my feelings. I knew Devin was not happy with my weight. He was one of the reasons why I was working out in the first place. I tried to play it off like I always did and commented in a nonchalant way, "I can work out and eat my ice cream too. And for your information, its frozen yogurt, which is healthier for you."

"Not half a gallon at a time," he replied, picking up the mail from the table behind the couch and flipping through it.

"I don't eat an entire container, and you know it," I said now doing squats. Groaning and trying to talk I said, "I don't see you pulling yourself away from drinking beer every chance you get. Ever heard of beer gut?"

Devin looked down at his stomach patting it.

"You don't see a beer gut here, do you? My beer hasn't put weight on me but that ice cream, biscuits, cakes, pasta, and whatever else you can get your hands on has. I'm the same man you married seven years ago. But look at you. How much weight have you gained?"

I was not about to answer that question as I stopped and turned to Devin, trying my best not to burst into tears. He didn't need to explain to me how fabulous he still was while he thought I'd fallen by the wayside. Hell, I was still a very attractive woman who was going through some things right now. If he only knew, but right now, I couldn't tell him.

"Honey, you didn't have to take it that far."

"All I'm saying is you are doing this for nothing. In a month, those workout CDs are going to be shelved with the rest of the DVDs we have. Hell, we have a workout room in this house that you never utilize."

I turned back to my video and started doing side kicks as I said, "Thanks for your support, Devin. I don't know why you always feel the need to put me down."

"It's called motivation. Somebody has to tell you the truth."

I stopped again, turning to him.

"Motivation, hell. Motivation is telling me to keep up the good work, or honey, you look great. Anything is better than what you are telling me now, Devin. Why can't you ever help elevate me instead of always trying to tear me down? I don't always need to hear criticism from you. If you don't have anything good to say, then keep your negative opinions to yourself."

"I knew you would turn this into something else besides me helping you."

"How is this helping me, Devin?" I questioned.

"It doesn't matter. Even if I explained it to you, you will still find a way to turn it around to fit your opinion."

"When was the last time you told me something positive?"

"This morning," he said quickly, almost cutting me off.

"What did you say?"

"I told you I loved you."

"No, you didn't. I told you I loved you, and you said, 'Yeah.'"

"Same thing," he argued.

"It's not the same thing, and you know it."

"I'm going to get ready. I don't have time to stand here and argue with you over something so petty," he said heading up the stairs.

I blinked back tears as I watched him disappear. Just because I put on this smile often didn't mean I wasn't in pain. What in the world was happening to us? Was my appearance that bad that he felt like he had to treat me like crap all the time? I was really trying hard in this marriage, but I wasn't sure how much more of this I could take.

Sonya

6

When I walked into my daughter's room, I wanted to scream. She wasn't here, but she left this room looking like a tornado just went through it. If I knew it looked like this, Ms. Thang wouldn't have been allowed to go over to her friend's house. I guess that's why she pulled the door closed so I wouldn't be able to see what a wreck her room was. No female should be this nasty. I tried to instill in Meena to be clean and pick up after yourself, respect yourself and what you have, and take pride in your appearance, but the only thing I felt like she listened to was taking pride in her appearance. My daughter always made sure she looked good at all times.

Stepping over all the clothes on her floor, I maneuvered to her dresser to put away the clean clothes I'd just finished folding. I started to place them on her bed, but I knew all she would do when she got here was push them on the floor with the rest of the clothes. What was the point of me washing them if she was going to mix the clean with the dirty?

Opening the top dresser drawer, I went to put her socks in it when something caught my eye. I pushed a few items of her clothes aside to make the object visible and was stunned when I saw a plastic sandwich bag filled with marijuana. Adrenaline now pumping, I quickly moved more of her clothes around to see if there was anything else she was trying to hide from me. Nothing else was in that particular drawer, but I began to search the rest, and to my dismay, I found something else unusual. In the bottom drawer was a white envelope. I pulled it out and opened it to find money in it. Counting it, I saw Meena had $260 in her possession.

All type of scenarios ran through my mind as I tried to think of the reasons why my daughter would have this weed and money in her possession. Just five minutes ago, I was mad because she couldn't keep her room clean, and now, I was facing the fact my fifteen-year-old daughter was involved in something much worse. And the only conclusion I could come up with is that my daughter was a freaking drug dealer.

I rushed out of Meena's room and retrieved my cell phone. I needed to talk to her ASAP. I dialed her number, but Meena didn't bother to pick up. This frustrated me. I knew this girl's cell phone was constantly glued to her hand, so I know she saw me calling. She just chose not to answer.

Not willing to let this go, I decided to call her friend Shannon's home.

"Hello."

"Hello, this is Ms. Gordon. Is Meena there?"

"No, she isn't."

"Then where is she?"

"I just dropped her and Shannon off at the mall. I hope that wasn't a problem. Meena said it was okay with you."

"Meena told me nothing about going to the mall."

"Well, I'm sorry. I should have checked with you first."

Maybe you should have, I thought.

"Who's picking them up?" I asked, ignoring her statement.

"I'm picking them up at seven. Do you want me to drop her off then?"

"Please, because I need to have a serious talk with my child."

After hanging up with Ms. Brooks, I couldn't do anything but pace the floor waiting for her to arrive. I didn't think this day could get any worse, but I should have known not to think such a thing. First, I got an invitation to my ex-fiancé's wedding, and now this.

I looked at my coffee table to see the invite I'd just retrieved from my mailbox, cordially inviting me to the nuptials of Kegan and Imani. He didn't waste any time wanting to make this woman his wife. I kept thinking receiving this invite was a joke because Kegan and I did not break up on good terms. As a matter of fact, he cheated on me with Imani. I was supposed to be the woman he was marrying, not her. Funny how things can change in such a short period of time.

My stomach began to churn at the thought of another woman having what I worked so hard to achieve for myself. But this whore swoops in and gets the marriage while I got the daunting task of molding him just for her for six years.

I plopped down on the sofa and leaned back, sighing. I was stressed to the max and would have given anything for a bottle of liquor right now. I swear if I had it, I would down it right here. Right now. A tear streamed down the side of my face as I thought about how bad things were at this time. I knew it was nothing but the devil. The more I tried to do better, the more he threw obstacles in my path to make me stumble, and he knew my biggest stumbling blocks were my daughter and my ex. Right now, the devil was winning. As much as I hated giving him any victory in my life, I couldn't help but feel helpless in this situation. I've prayed. I've cried. And I've prayed some more for my life to turn around somehow. And it's not that it hasn't. It has. I had a house for me and my daughter. I had a job to pay the bills and put food on the table. I had great friends. But even in having all of those things, I felt like I had nothing. I felt alone.

When I heard a car door shut, I ran to the window to see Meena waving bye to her friend and mother. It was right at seven thirty. When Meena entered our home, she looked like she didn't have a care in the world.

"Were you looking for me, Mom?"

"Who gave you permission to go to the mall, Meena?"

"You told me it was okay."

"No, I didn't. I told you it was okay to go to Shannon's house. Not the mall."

"Sorry."

"And why didn't you clean that room before you left?"

"I didn't feel like it."

"I don't feel like doing a lot of things, but I still have to do it, Meena. I don't like to work and pay bills and buy you these clothes you beg me for, but I do it."

"Okay, Mom, chill," she grumbled.

"Don't tell me to chill! I'm your mother, and you will *not* speak to me like that."

"I'll be in my room," she said flippantly, attempting to leave the room but I quickly stopped her.

"Hold up, wait a minute. I didn't dismiss you."

"What, Mom? Dang," she said, her voice vexed with attitude.

"Don't what me. I swear you are going to make me slap the taste out your mouth."

"All I'm trying to do is go to my room. You do want me to clean it, don't you?"

"Are you going to clean it? Or are you going to look for this?"

I held up the bag of weed and the envelope filled with money.

"Why are you messing with my stuff?" she said nastily as she walked up to me trying to snatch the items out my hand, but I jerked it back before she could. "Give it to me, Ma."

I pushed her in her chest asking, "Where did you get this from?"

"A friend," she stated, face twisted in annoyance.

"What friend?"

"You don't know him."

"Who is he, and why is he giving you weed and money. Are you selling drugs?"

"No, Ma."

"Then why do you have this in your possession?"

"Because I wanted it."

She was saying this like it was normal for a fifteen-year-old to have drugs in her possession. Hell, I knew I hadn't done drugs around her. I can't say I haven't smoked weed before but never in the presence of my child.

"Are you using drugs now, Meena?"

"No."

"You know you are not making any sense, right? Either you're smoking weed or you're selling it. Which is it?"

"Just give me my stuff and I'll give it back to my friend."

"I'm not giving you anything," I retorted.

"But it's mine. I bought it."

"With what? You don't have a job, and you damn sure don't get an allowance that's over $200. If you think I haven't notice the new clothes you have been wearing, I have. Look at you. You have bags in your hands now, and I know I didn't give you the money for it."

"It's none of your concern," she said like she was undaunted.

I sighed feeling my chest tightening. This girl was taking me to the place that was going to make me do something I may regret. Lately, these feelings of anxiety were happening to me more often than I'd like to admit.

I knew it was because I was holding back from going the hell off. No one knew how much on edge I was. I was really trying not to lose it on anybody, especially my daughter. But she was pushing the right buttons that were moving me closer to the point of exploding.

I don't know what happened to Meena. Ever since Kegan . . . And then I paused, knowing ever since he left, she's been acting out. Kegan was not Meena's biological father, but he definitely played the role of one for her. He was the only man she knew that really loved her. Her real father was nowhere around. He disappeared soon as I told him I was pregnant, and I hadn't seen or heard from him since. Like most men, he said the baby wasn't his, and I can't say I wasn't hurt by this. I never understood how a man could walk away from someone he helped create and was supposed to love. I guess I could blame myself for choosing the wrong man to father my child because now, Meena was paying the price.

Unfortunately, since we broke up, Kegan hadn't been by to see Meena, which I found disrespectful. She didn't do anything to him. What happened with us was between us and us alone. He didn't have to abandon my daughter in the process. He promised her he would be in her life no matter what, but unfortunately, that was a promise he hadn't kept.

I looked at Meena as I felt myself calming down.

"You are bringing drugs into my house, which made it my concern once they crossed the threshold of what is my property."

"Then I'll take it out," she said, holding her hand out for me to give it to her.

"And do what, smoke it?"

"Mom, I've only smoked weed once or twice. That's it," she finally admitted.

"And the money?"

"It's mine. My friend paid me to hold on to his stash for him, and I'm doing that."

"What else are you holding?"

I hoped this was it. I searched her entire room but didn't find anything. Still, children had a nifty way of hiding things.

"This is it, Mom."

"So you making my house hot by holding some drug dealer's stash. Did you ever think why he couldn't hold it himself?"

"No."

I shook my head saying, "I raised you better than this, Meena."

She exhaled, crossing her arms as she always did when her attitude set in.

"You know I have every right to go into your room and tear it up."

"How is that fair?"

"Because I run this. I run you. Until you get eighteen and out of my house, you do as I say. Do you got that?"

"I hear you," she said smartly.

"Don't make me smack the crap out of you, Meena."

"I said I hear, you. Dang. What else do you want me to say?"

At this point all I wanted was for this child to get out of my face before I punched her in it. I was so sick and tired of her attitude, like I was always bothering her when all I was trying to do was take care of her and be the best mother possible.

"Can I go now?" she asked.

"No, you can't."

"Why?"

"Because you are going to take me to this boy's house."

"But, Mom," she said, now looking frantic.

"Not buts," I said, grabbing my keys. "Now get your behind in the car and let's go meet this boy who thinks it's okay to give my fifteen-year-old daughter drugs to hold for him."

Meena didn't budge for a moment, but when I opened the door, she knew I was serious. That attitude was gone now. She may have thought I let her get by with that smart mouth, which I had, but now I was going to show her. I was going to have her take me to this young man's house. I needed to put a face to the drugs and possibly inform his parents the type of illegal antics he was up to.

Vivian

7

I was still thinking about my encounter with Julia today wondering how I ended up getting offered a job in her establishment. Not only did I walk out of her boutique with the dress and the jumpsuit, I also purchased two pair of distressed jeans, three shirts, and three pair of shoes. And she kept her word giving me the discount of 25 percent. So what turned out to be an unfortunate event with her employee ended up turning into something fantastic for me. I was still unsure if I was going to take the job. The money was nowhere near what I was used to making, but I would be doing something I loved, and that's working with clothing. I told her I would call her in forty-eight hours with my decision. Right now, I wasn't working at all so something was definitely better than nothing. I still wanted to talk to Sheldon before I made my decision. If I only had my sisters here to talk to about this . . .

"What are you thinking about?" Sheldon asked, sitting across from me in a quaint corner of the restaurant.

"I was thinking about my sisters," I said smiling.

"You miss them, don't you?"

"I really do."

"Do you regret moving here with me?"

From the expression on his face, he was hoping I would say no, and that's the answer I would give him, even though a part of me did regret moving away from my family.

"Of course not, Sheldon. You know I will follow you to the ends of the earth," I told him, reaching across the table for his hand. He placed his hand into mine and smiled.

"I'm glad. Because all I want to do is make you happy."

"Well, this evening is a great start."

"Did I tell you, you look amazing?" he complimented.

I actually felt amazing. I was wearing the jumpsuit I purchased with a metallic strappy heel. Once in a while, I would put something on that would make me feel like the most beautiful woman ever.

"I know I've been working a lot lately, Viv. I feel like we haven't spent much time together."

"That may be true, but I know you need to do what you got to do to prove this company chose the right man for this job."

Sheldon smirked humbly as he brushed his thumb across the top of my hand.

"So do you still love the job?"

"I do, but like most jobs, you're going to have your haters."

"Don't I know it?"

"Another downfall is not spending as much time with you as I would like. I feel like I'm neglecting you. Hopefully, that will change in the near future."

I smiled encouragingly as a silence fell between us. Sheldon gazed at me. Each time his eyes stared into mine, I fell in love with this man all over again. I wondered how I got so lucky. He was the only man who could make me leave my sisters.

A cute brunette walked over to our table infringing on our moment together.

"Good evening. My name is Hailey, and I will be your waitress for the evening," she greeted gleefully.

She had the most striking blue eyes I'd ever seen. She made it a point to greet both of us, but, of course, most of her attention was directed to my husband.

Here we go again, I thought. I swear every time I went out with Sheldon there was some thirsty-ass chick raring to take him away from me. It was always the same thing. They always gave me this look like I didn't deserve to be with a man as handsome as Sheldon. I knew I was a plus-size sister, but come on. I deserved respect. It wasn't like I was going to lie down and let some trick come in and take him away from me. I wanted to say *Bitch, he chose me, so step the hell off*. But I never reacted that way for fear I would bring embarrassment not only to myself but to Sheldon. This was getting tiresome, however. If this kept on happening, I was going to lose it on one of these women.

"Can I start you out with something to drink?"

Sheldon was too busy looking at his menu to notice this chic's infatuation with chocolate. I knew she couldn't help herself because my husband was fine. He didn't have to try at all to be sexy, because he just exuded it.

With narrowed eyes, I watched this woman drooling over my husband. Instantly, my mind went to her eagerly wanting to please him by sucking on his very laudable chocolate bar. I mean, that's what white girls were known for, right? See, I shouldn't go there. Here I was stereotyping, when I knew damn well everybody, and I mean every race, sucked dick.

Regardless, any woman wanting to be with my husband was a problem. I was tired of them looking at me like I sat in bed all day eating Debbie Cakes and washing them down with a two-liter Pepsi. I needed to get my mind right. I was so paranoid that I was stooping to levels of stereotyping when I knew how that felt being the plus-size sister I was.

I don't know why I punished myself with thoughts like this. I knew it was my insecurity rearing its ugly head, but I couldn't help it. I was frequently ashamed of my size, and when skinny women like Hailey came along, I always wondered if she could do a better job at pleasing my husband than I could. I knew how ridiculous this was, but it was something I did quite often for fear someone just like this skinny heifer could possibly succeed in taking my one true love away from me.

"I would like to order a bottle of your Dom, please," Sheldon told her.

"Nice choice," she said like she was impressed. "I'll get that for you, and when I return, I'll take your order for appetizers."

The trick bounced away just a little too much with her double Ds jiggling. I stared at Sheldon who looked at me with an inquisitive gaze.

"What?"

I shook my head saying, "You never notice these desperate women?"

"Babe, I don't care about any other woman but you. I've told you this."

"I'm just tired of this happening all the time."

"I can't help your man is handsome," he said tugging on his collar like he knew he was cute.

Smiling flirtatiously, I admired him in his black suit with a white button-down shirt. He'd removed his tie and unbuttoned the top two buttons for more comfort.

"Here's your bottle of Dom." The waitress returned, placing a bucket of ice with the bottle of wine in it by our table.

She made sure to lean forward just a little too much so Sheldon would notice her now visible cleavage. This trick had unfastened three of her buttons trying to get the attention of my man. He noticed but quickly averted his eyes, looking at me like he saw what I was talking about now.

"Do you know what you would like to order for your appetizers, sir?"

She gave me a quick glimpse I guess to acknowledge my presence but turned her full attention back to Sheldon. I exhaled deeply to control my temper as Sheldon nervously spoke.

"Um, I'm sorry. I still haven't decided."

Sheldon may be a bit rough around the edges and came from the streets, but he also knew I could get hood real quick. I knew that's why he stammered to answer this woman because he knew if she kept this up, I was going to check her quick, fast, and in a hurry.

Tumbling from my husband's mouth, he said, "I . . . I would like the seafood cocktail."

This trick probably thought he was stuttering over her ass. Little did she know I was seconds away from jumping on hers.

"Sweetie, what are you having?"

He made it a point to reach across the table again and take my hand into his. I loved when Sheldon let these tricks know I was the only woman he had eyes for. This didn't sit well with Ms. Trying to Seduce My Husband. The trick actually looked like she got jealous. Sheldon wasn't even hers to get jealous over. She shifted from one foot to the other like she was bothered by his act of love for me.

Gripping his hand into mine I said, "I'll take the mixed salad."

The patronizing sneer she gave me ticked me off even more. I didn't know if it was because I was holding my husband's hand or the fact I ordered a salad. Hell, skinny women weren't the only ones who enjoyed the green leafy appetizer. Either way, I didn't like the way she was looking at me.

With a forced smile I said, "We would like to place our entrée order as well."

I was trying to eliminate as much contact with this woman as possible because I didn't want to use her face to wipe these floors with.

"Okay," she said grinning sardonically but disrespectfully turning away from me to ask Sheldon what he wanted first.

No, this heifer didn't. I gripped Sheldon's hand unknowingly. He knew what was about to happen if this woman didn't get the hell away from our table.

I was so sick of being treated like a second-class citizen from these skinny women who thought they were better than me. I dealt with someone like her way too many times to count, and I was getting sick of it. What was getting ready to happen was I was going to jump on her and make an example of her for all the other women who thought it was appropriate to treat me like I was unworthy and who had the audacity to come at my husband all types of wrong. It was enough to make me want to snatch people up on a regular, but I knew I couldn't do that without catching a case.

"Please, take my wife's order first," Sheldon gestured toward me.

Smiling sheepishly, Hailey turned her attention back to me and asked, "What would you like, ma'am?"

"Ma'am," I murmured as I giggled to myself. I looked over at Sheldon whose eyes were pleading with me to keep my cool. I let go of his hand and picked up the menu to decide what I wanted.

"First, I would like you to button your blouse back up and stop throwing your breasts along with yourself at my husband because he doesn't want you. He wants me."

"Um, excuse me?" she said as confusion blanketed her face. She gripped her blouse in befuddlement. Her breathing was uneven, and it was then when I came to the conclusion this woman had never been addressed about her sexual antics before. There was a first time for everything.

With an expression devoid of emotion I continued.

"Second, if you continue to disrespect me like you have been doing, I will have no other choice but to turn those pretty blue eyes black. Please feel free to use your imagination on how I will make that happen."

"Honey . . ."

I heard Sheldon calling my name, but I wasn't done with this trick.

"And third, I would like filet mignon with lobster butter on the side and the tempura asparagus."

I graciously closed the menu and handed it to Hailey for her to do her damn job. The woman appeared shaken by my words but knew better than to say anything sideways to me. I'm pretty sure the menacing glare I was giving her further let her know I was serious and had no qualms about backing my words.

I grinned ruefully as I turned to Sheldon and asked, "Honey, what are you going to have?"

Kellie

8

I had been in a daze ever since Dr. Hoffman told me the devastating news. I had an STD which could have possibly ruined my chances of being able to conceive a child. I was only twenty-eight years old. I still had so much life ahead of me, and that journey going forward always had children in it. But that portion of my journey may have been derailed . . . all because my husband chose to cheat on me again.

I sat in the parking lot of the clinic not able to move. With my head leaned back on the headrest, I contemplated calling him. I knew something like this couldn't be discussed over the phone, but a part of me wanted to ruin his day like I'd had mine ruined. So I picked up the phone and dialed his work number.

"Jeffrey Woods's office. This is Bridget speaking. How can I help you?" his secretary greeted.

"Hi, Bridget. This is Kellie. Can I speak to Jeffrey, please?"

"I'm sorry, Kellie, but Jeffrey is at a lunch meeting. I can take a message if you like."

A lunch meeting, huh? I thought.

"Kellie?" Bridget called out.

"No, that's okay. I can wait and talk to him when he gets home."

"Are you sure?" she asked.

"Yes, I'm sure," I hesitated.

"Kellie, are you okay?" she asked.

Tears formed at her simple act of caring. I tried to gather myself because I didn't want her to know how upset I really was.

"I'm okay, Bridget. Thank you for asking."

"Okay. I'll tell Jeffrey you called."

I hung up. A part of me wanted to drive over to his job and confront him, but I knew I was going to cause a big scene which could potentially cause him to be fired. Look at me. Here I was thinking about him and what was best for him. He didn't bother thinking about me when he was screwing some other whore and how his cheating could jeopardize my life.

I began to weep uncontrollably. Now the realization had set in as I thought about Bridget being nice enough to ask me how I was and the man who supposedly loved me didn't give a damn about my well-being. Not sure why that question from Bridget was the tool needed to break through this barrier of pain I was feeling, but now I couldn't stop. I needed to talk to somebody desperately, and the first person I thought of was my brother Victor.

I was supposed to call him with the results, but I couldn't tell him this. I couldn't even talk to him because I knew he would figure out something was wrong. As much as I wanted to speak to him, I knew now was not the time. Hell, I didn't know when there would be a good time. As soon as Vic heard this news, he was going to get in his car to come down here just to beat Jeffrey down. I wasn't about to risk my brother's well-being, knowing he would speed down the highway to get to me. So I decided to wait.

Then Mom came to mind. I wasn't sure if calling her was a good idea either, but I needed someone to talk to. I could call Monica or Sonya, but they had their own things going on, and I wasn't ready to unload yet another chapter in the life of how mine was so bad. So I decided Mom was who I was going to call.

"Hello."

"Hi, Mom."

Hearing her voice caused me to break down again, but I managed to keep my sobs under control.

"Hi, honey. How are you?"

Mom sounded happy, which made me even sadder because I knew what I had to tell her would change her mood. I knew I could pretend like everything was okay, but she would figure it out. So I might as well go with my original plan by talking to her about this. I just hoped I wasn't making a big mistake by doing this.

Most kids usually could talk with their mother about anything, but in my case, I couldn't. My father was that person for me, and he was no longer here. My mom always seemed distant in a way, and I never felt that mother-daughter connection I thought a daughter should have with her mother.

"Mom, I'm not doing so good."

"Why, Kellie? What's going on?"

I couldn't say anything as I heard the concern dripping from her words. Even though Mom got on my nerve at times, she did have a tender side. To hear her worried about me caused me to hesitate for a moment.

"Kellie, are you there?"

"I'm here, Mom," I struggled to answer.

"What's wrong?"

"I found out today that I have a sexually transmitted disease."

"What?"

"And as if that's not bad enough, this disease could have caused damage to the point I may not be able to have children."

"Lord, have mercy. The devil is sure doing his job, ain't he?"

I was waiting for her to say I told you so, and my mother didn't disappoint.

"So I take it you got this disease from that Jeffrey?" she asked.

"Yes, Mom."

"I knew it. I knew nothing good was going to come from you marrying that man. I tried to tell you."

"Mom, please. I don't need to hear this right now."

"Well, somebody needs to tell you. You're a big girl wanting to live this life with a man way too old for you, if you ask me. That man has done nothing but bring drama to your life."

I almost hung up on her. I'd done it before but quickly apologized knowing it was disrespectful. But sometimes Mom never said what I wanted to hear. Why couldn't she just say it's going to be okay, or she was here for me? That was what I wanted to hear.

"Mom, I'm married, so it's done. Can you just please be a mom for once and console me without telling me what I've done wrong?"

"If I don't tell you, then who will?"

"So is that what we're doing?" I asked.

"What do you mean?"

"My life may not be perfect, Mom, but the one thing I haven't done is turn my back on my family."

Mom said nothing.

"When was the last time you talked to Vic?"

"I don't know who you are talking about," she replied in a disdainful tone.

"He's your son, remember?"

"Victor is dead to me, Kellie."

"How can you say that?"

"No son of mine is going to live his life being in love with another man, do you hear me!" Mom yelled.

"Oh, I hear you. I just can't understand how you can call yourself a Christian woman and turn your back on your fellow man, and this man happens to be one you gave birth to. Are you trying to say God made a mistake blessing you with him?" I asked.

"The Bible says—"

I interrupted responding with, "I know what the Bible says, Mom. You've shoved that scripture down our throats so much that it's burn into our memory."

Mom quoted anyway, *"If a man lies with a male as with a woman, both of them have committed an abomination; they shall surely be put to death; their blood is upon them."*

I rolled my eyes knowing I had to get off this phone before I disrespected her, but I had some scripture to quote to her as well.

"First Timothy 5:8 says, *'but if anyone does not provide for his relatives, and especially for members of his household, he has denied the faith and is worse than an unbeliever.'*"

"Kellie," she called, but I ignored her.

"First Corinthians 13:13 says, *'So now faith, hope, and love abide, these three; but the greatest of these is love.'*"

"I love Victor, but I don't—"

I cut her off again saying, "Luke 6:37 says, *'Do not judge, and you will not be judged. Do not condemn, and you will not be condemned. Forgive, and you will be forgiven.'*"

Mom was quiet now.

"So as much as you would like to claim Christianity, no matter what, you should still love your child. The only person who can judge is God, and the only one that can pay for the sins we commit is ourselves. So you have no excuses, Mother."

"You will never understand until you become a mother yourself."

Her words caused me to stiffen. I'd just told her I may not be able to have children, yet, she throws this in my face. She was so busy trying to be right that she completely ignored the reason why I even called her in the first place.

"Well, I may not get the chance to have children, Mother."

The line went silent, and I used this as my opportunity to get off the phone with her.

"Mom, I have to go. You have a good evening."

I didn't bother to hear her respond before I hung up the phone.

Sonya

9

As soon as we started driving in the direction of this young man's home, I knew his family had to have money. The congested street we lived on quickly turned into tree-lined roads with houses separated by acres of land in a beautiful subdivision. Why would this boy need to sell drugs if he was living large like this? It boggled my mind. Now if he was in the hood and needed money to provide for himself and his family, then I could understand that because I grew up in the hood myself. And the Lord knows I've done plenty of things I'm not proud of. But this didn't make any sense to me.

I was even more amazed when we pulled up to this palatial two-story brick home with a three-car garage located by a community lake. I felt like my Mazda wasn't even welcomed in a neighborhood like this. To say I was a little intimidated was an understatement.

"That's his car," Meena mumbled, and I looked at a cherry-red BMW sports coupe with tinted windows and chromed-out rims. I admired the car then turned to Meena wondering who this kid was. Yes, I couldn't understand why a boy with a blessed life like this would want to play himself by selling drugs.

"Mama, please don't make me do this," my daughter pleaded one last time.

"I'm not changing my mind, Meena."

"But this is embarrassing."

"Good. Maybe it will teach you to make better decisions so you won't have embarrassing moments like this again. Now get out of the car. We need to get this over with."

Hesitantly, Meena exited my car along with me. She lagged behind me as I made my way to the massive double-door entrance. I started to knock but saw the button to ring the doorbell. I pushed it. I could hear the bell-like chimes, alerting them I was here.

I looked at Meena who stood with her arms crossed tightly across her chest. She was so worried and pivoted from one foot to the other like she was trying to walk out her nervous energy.

I could hear footsteps approaching and moments later, a young man greeted us.

He smiled warmly at me. Then he looked at Meena, and his smile widened even more.

"Yo, Meena, what are you doing here, girl?"

"Hi, Corbin."

The child with the smart mouth and eye rolling was now looking shy and timid. I almost had to do a double take to make sure this was my daughter.

"So, you are the one who gave my daughter weed to hold for you?" I asked, getting straight to the point.

Corbin looked over his shoulder before stepping outside with us and pulling the door behind him. He eyed Meena nervously, like he was checking with her to see what was going on.

"There's no need to stare at her. I'm here to find out why you feel the need to involve a fifteen-year-old in your drug transactions."

"Look, yo," he smiled coyly.

"Yo? Son, I'm *not* one of your friends. You better look like coming at me correct," I advised.

"Ma'am. I'm sorry. I didn't mean to come at you like that."

"Good."

"I needed a favor, and Meena was willing to help. That's it."

He said this like they were exchanging video games or something. This shit was something that could land both of them in some serious trouble.

"Why couldn't you keep it here? It definitely looks like this house is big enough for you to find enough hiding spaces for it."

"I didn't have time to swing by the house to drop off my merchandise. I had to go see an officer, so I asked Meena to do me a solid. That's it. I even gave her money to do me this favor."

"How old are you?" I asked him.

"I'm nineteen."

"Are you sleeping with my daughter?"

"Mom," Meena called out in embarrassment.

"Well, are you?" I continued.

"No, ma'am. We're just friends," he replied.

I looked at him skeptically, not believing a word coming out of his mouth. There was no way Meena would be stupid enough to do something so idiotic over a friend. He had to be sleeping with her, but I wasn't going to push it. Not right now anyway.

"Look, ma'am, you can give me my merchandise, and I promise I won't get Meena involved again."

"If the *merchandise* you are referring to is the weed, it's gone."

Both Corbin's and Meena's eyes bulged.

"Gone where?" she asked.

"I flushed it down the toilet."

Corbin rested his hands atop his head in frustration, saying, "Please tell me you didn't."

"Yes, I did."

"Mom, I can't believe you did that. You could have just given it back to him."

"For what? So he could play some other unsuspecting girl. When that merchandise crossed the threshold of my home, it became my property."

"Well, I hope you're willing to pay for it," Corbin said seriously.

I chuckled at his audacity saying, "Like hell I am. I'm not paying for shit."

With his eyes narrowed in anger, Corbin began to pace.

"Why are selling drugs anyway? It's evident you have money."

"I need some extra cash sometimes so I hook my friends up. Plus, I like to smoke myself. There's nothing wrong with that."

I shook my head in astonishment. He had money, probably. I guarantee you he hadn't worked a day in his life because his mommy and daddy gave him whatever he wanted. Yet, he still disrespects them by stooping to the levels of slinging drugs. Talk about too much time on his hands.

The door to their home opened, and a petite woman with an olive skin tone and jet-black hair pulled up in a neat bun greeted us.

"Corbin, what is going on out here? Your dinner is getting cold," she said. Her expression softened when she noticed us.

The woman was very pretty and seemed well put together. My first impression was that she doted on her son. This explained his arrogant demeanor, like somebody owed him something. His mom had to be responsible for that.

"Mom, this is my friend Meena, remember? Her mom brought her over here to talk about this project we're working on together," he lied.

Meena stepped up to speak to the woman.

"Hello, Mrs. Bennett. It's good to see you again."

Again? I thought. *How many times has this woman seen my daughter?*

Meena continued, "This is my mom, Sonya Gordon. Mom, this is Mrs. Bennett."

"Please, call me Leann. It's a pleasure to finally meet you," she said courteously. "Meena is such a wonderful young lady."

"Thank you," was all I could say as I watched my daughter do some of the best acting I'd ever seen. *My daughter, a wonderful young lady?* I thought. She was when she wanted to be, but here, lately, we were bumping heads like crazy. The young lady she was referring to was a disrespectful teen in my eyes. I guess my child knew how to act with other adults, so that was a plus.

"We're sorry to stop by around dinnertime. Forgive me for that. I just needed to talk to him about this project because you know we are trying to get a good grade on it," Meena continued.

"Your dedication is refreshing. I hope it rubs off on my son," she said, playfully hitting him.

"Ouch."

"Corbin, you know I raised you better than this. You could have at least invited our guests in," his mom reprimanded.

"It's okay. We have to get home. It's getting late, and I need to get back to working on our project," Meena lied. "It was good seeing you again, Mrs. Bennett. Corbin, I'll see you at school."

"No doubt," he replied.

"It was a pleasure meeting you, Ms. Gordon," Mrs. Bennett said to me.

"Likewise."

"Maybe next time, you can come in and sit for a bit."

"Maybe next time. You have a good night."

Mrs. Bennett smiled, tenderly grabbing her son by the hand and walking him into their home as Meena linked her arm with mine and led me to the car.

"I know you did that so I wouldn't put your boy on blast."

"Mom, please. Just leave this alone. I've learned my lesson. There was no need to get him in trouble."

I didn't know about that. As a parent, I should have brought this subject up to his mom, but I didn't. I guess I was too amazed at how the two of them finagled the conversation to fit their needs. Then again, maybe it was because I didn't want her being disappointed in a child that was obviously unappreciative of what his parents were doing for him. The news of him dealing drugs would have devastated her. She was so gracious, and I didn't want to bring that heartache to her. So the incident would remain between the three of us. I hoped I wasn't making a mistake by not saying anything. As much as Meena told me she learned her lesson, I wasn't sure exactly what lesson was she referring to. All I knew was the lesson that she learned from me today was that I wasn't a parent who would always let things slide. She may get smart and roll her eyes sometimes, but today, she learned I was a tad bit crazy and had no qualms about embarrassing her if the need came up. So for now, I'd won this battle, but little did I know the war that was coming soon.

Kellie

10

This had to be the worst day of my life. I mean, seriously, I didn't think my day could get worse, but I was wrong. When the pain from my nail digging in my skin let me know I was indeed up and wasn't dreaming, I knew the scene unfolding before me was actually happening. There sat Jeffrey on the edge of our bed, leaning back on his elbows with head back as far as he could take it, enjoying the lips that surrounded his dick. My mint-green silk curtains were pulled closed like he was trying to hide his indiscretion, as my aroma therapy candles flickered in the background.

I don't know if I screamed, yelled, called his name, or just cried out in anguish because all I heard was the ringing of dead silence in my ears. I knew I said something because Jeffrey was struggling to pull his pants up as the lips surrounding his dick unlocked from around him. The man on his knees and in-between my husband's thighs didn't bother to budge. If anything, he looked upset that I interrupted what he was doing to Jeffrey.

He smiled at me confidently as he dabbed at the cracks of his mouth with his manicured fingers. He acted like he had just devoured a full-course meal.

His eyes spoke volumes as they gloated saying, "I got your man, bitch."

"Baby," Jeffrey called to me. "What are you doing here?"

"In our house, Jeffrey!"

"I thought you were at work?"

"I thought you were too," I glared.

"Look, let me explain."

Why did all cheating-ass men say that, like an explanation was going to do them some good when they were clearly caught in the act? Maybe they felt the details were warranted so their significant other wouldn't kill them, because that's what I felt like doing to Jeffrey right now. I wanted to commit first-degree murder.

"It's not what it looks like," Jeffrey floundered to say.

"Really? So this . . . this . . . person wasn't sucking your dick?"

"My name is Kyle, and, yes, I was sucking his dick, bitch, and I did it real good too, right, baby?" the tall, lanky man said running his hand down Jeffrey's leg as he continued to kneel before him. Jeffrey jerked away, looking at him with a scowl.

Eyes narrowed in anger, I looked at Jeffrey waiting for him to say something. My husband understood my hardened expression and began quickly explaining.

"Baby, this is Kyle. My . . . my lover."

"I don't give a damn who this is. You're introducing us like I'm supposed to reach out and shake his hand or something. All I want to know is what the hell is he doing here, in *our* house, and in *our* bedroom, no less."

"Isn't it obvious, boo boo?" Kyle deduced.

"Shut up, Kyle," Jeffrey said through gritted teeth.

"And it ain't my first time here, bitch."

His man whore stood upright as he shifted his weight more to his right foot as he stuck his ass out. The man's ass was bigger than mine, and I knew then who was the penetrator and who was the penetratee.

"Kyle," Jeffrey snapped, shooting daggerlike stares at him. Kyle retreated. He wasn't a bad-looking guy. He was shorter than Jeffrey with dark coppery skin, a clean-shaven face, and brows arched to perfection. This man's face was beat to flawlessness. For a moment, I was jealous because he did look good. As sad as it sounded, I could see what Jeffrey saw in him. But, it was still a man. Jeffrey was not gay, or at least I never thought he was.

"Baby, I never meant for you to find out like this. I thought you were coming home later."

"Excuse me from coming to my home and interfering in you getting you dick polished off by *that*."

"Bitch, don't get smacked."

"Kyle."

"But she—" his whore began to say, but Jeffrey cut him off.

"Kyle, please leave. I need to talk with my wife."

"Oh, so it's like that," he said, looking at me sideways.

Jeffrey glared at him but said nothing.

"Okay, then, I see how you going to treat me. But don't come begging me back so you can get some more of this good old ass," he said, turning his ass to Jeffrey and smacking it.

I closed my eyes in disgust as his friend exited our room. Eyes locked on Jeffrey, it wasn't until I heard the front door close before I spoke again.

"Do you know where I was today?"

"I thought you were at work."

"No. I got off early to go to the doctor."

"For what?" he asked like he was concerned.

"I found out I have Chlamydia."

Jeffrey stood, stunned by my words.

"I wondered where in the world I could have gotten this from, because I knew I wasn't cheating. I hoped my husband hadn't cheated on me again, but then I come home to *this*."

"Kellie."

"The STD is not the worst part. Because of your inconsiderate actions, I may not ever be able to have a child of my own."

"What?"

"That's right, Jeffrey. This STD may have affected my chances of ever having kids."

"Baby, I'm sorry."

I chuckled as I said, "And for the life of me, I can't understand why I'm not whooping your freaking ass right now. I mean, really," I said stepping closer to him. "Why am I not tearing this house up? Why am I not trying to kill you right now?"

"Kellie, you need to calm down."

"Don't you think I've done an amazing job at that already? Haven't you wondered why I haven't jumped off the deep end, like I did before?" I asked, still walking toward him.

Jeffrey was now backing up slowly.

"Kellie, we are not going to do this today."

"Why not? I mean, I did find out my husband is not only an adulterous bastard, but he like's fucking men in the ass too."

"I'm not gay."

"Oh really?" I said coming to a halt as I looked at him with a confused expression on his face.

"Him sucking me doesn't make me gay."

Jeffrey seemed to be getting angry, and this actually amused me. My husband was telling himself anything to convince himself he wasn't gay, or at least bisexual.

"Right. That's what all African American down low brothers say."

"I'm not a down low brother."

"No, you just like to dip your dick down low in his ass."

Jeffrey rushed toward, me but I didn't bother to flinch. He stood nose to nose with me, heaving like he wanted to hit me. But I didn't care. I actually wished he would. It would really give me a reason to kill his ass. Then it would be self-defense.

Monica

11

When we walked into the dining room of Devin's parents' home, all eyes settled on us. I made sure to look the picture of elegance and grace because I knew how his parents, especially his mother, felt about me. For some reason, they didn't think I was good enough to be with their son. And the reason for them thinking this way was sitting at the table. My confident demeanor dissipated when my eyes skimmed the room and landed on the last person I expected to see at this dinner tonight.

"Son, you are late," Mr. Woods admonished. With forehead creased, his father looked sternly at both of us. One of the things his dad didn't like was *un*punctuality.

"My apologies, Dad. I had to work late," Devin responded as we leisurely walked deeper into the room. I hoped my dissatisfied expression wasn't noticeable to everyone as his mother spoke.

"It's okay, son," Mrs. Woods said warmly.

"Isabelle, no, it's not. That boy is working himself to death. He needs to understand family overrides any job he is doing."

I could feel Devin tense as I held his arm. I knew he was not happy hearing what his father was saying to him. We hadn't sat down yet, and his father was already getting on his case. Unfortunately, this was the typical thing my husband had to deal with when visiting with his parents, or should I say, his father.

Mr. Woods could be a very intimidating individual. His six foot one, 190-pound stature was brawny for a man who was sixty-three years old. His face was clean-shaven, and he still had all of his hair, which was salt and pepper in color and neatly trimmed, making him look quite distinguished. He kept a suit on. It was rare that we saw in him in jeans and sneakers. His version of dressing down was a pair of slacks and a Polo shirt. To me, it always looked like he was running for senate.

I gently clutched Devin's arm, letting him know I was here for him. He looked at me sincerely before turning his attention back to the dinner table, which sat ten people, including his parents. I knew he hadn't notice the individual who didn't belong, and that was good in my opinion. I just wanted to revel in this moment, which was the first time in a long while Devin looked at me as lovingly as he did. I felt like he knew in this instant, despite what we were going through in our marriage, I was here for him always.

"Devin, honey, don't mind your father. He's just been in a tizzy since he got home from the church. Please come to the dinner table and join us."

Devin led the way as I continued to hold on to him. He pulled out my chair, allowing me to sit before he settled next to me. His mother was on the other side of him. And strategically placed across from my husband was his ex-fiancée Georgiana Jacobs. I couldn't believe his parents had the audacity to invite her to this dinner, knowing the history she and my husband had with each other. I knew Mrs. Woods didn't like me, but this act of disregard further let me know this woman was dead set on ruining my marriage to her son.

"How are you, Monica?" his mother finally greeted.

Trying my best not to defiantly stare, I responded with, "I'm fine, thanks. And you?"

"I'm wonderful," she answered, smiling sheepishly as her eyes bounced from me to Georgiana.

I knew this was only a show Devin's mom was putting on for the men and women who were also staff members at the church Devin's father preached at. And she wondered why I didn't like attending church? When the pastor and first lady made you feel like you were insignificant, then why would I want to go hear the Word from a family who were hypocrites in my eyes? No need to pretend you loved me in the Lord's house when you couldn't stand me outside of it.

"Hi, Devin," Georgiana gushed. "It's good seeing you again."

"It's good seeing you too," he responded.

What in the hell did that mean? *It's good seeing you too*. Was he glad to see her sitting at this table across from him? I shot a disapproving gaze at my husband, but he never noticed. His eyes were affixed on his ex. I detected a small inkling of affection twinkling in his eyes for this woman, and I became furious. I knew this look all too well because it was the same steely gaze Devin gave me when he told me he loved me for the first time. Now he was gaping at this woman with the same admiration, and it ticked me off.

I wanted to get up from this table and leave them all to enjoy their dinner, but my pride wouldn't allow me to do so. That was too much like giving up, and I'd be damned if I gave them the satisfaction of knowing they'd gotten to me. Plus, I wasn't going to make it easy for my husband to possibly be taken from me by a woman who lost her chance to be with him. She needed to know her position and stay there—as his ex.

"Hi, Georgiana. I didn't expect to see you here. Are you part of the church committee now?" I asked.

This let his mother know I recognize the people here, and Georgiana was an extra distraction that didn't belong. They wanted to play games with me . . . then, game on!

Shifting her gaze to Mrs. Woods, Georgiana cleared her throat as she said, "Um, no. I'm not part of the committee."

"Oh, I thought you were since everyone here is part of the board. Forgive me for assuming," I said smiling coyly.

Devin reached under the table and gripped my leg gently, signaling for me to let this go. I gave him an icy glare before picking up my napkin and draping it in my lap. I hoped he understood my expression. Try me if you want to. I will turn this dinner out.

"Honey, please, fix your plate. You look like you need to eat. Is Monica feeding you?"

Shade thrown and I caught it. It was subtle, but nonetheless, it was still there.

"Mom, Monica cooks for me all the time."

"Well, I can clearly see she's eating. Is she gaining the weight you are losing?"

This was her way of criticizing me and my weight without coming out her mouth and calling me fat. She was real good at dancing around things she didn't like, and right now, she was fox-trotting all around me.

"Mom," Devin called out.

"Honey, I'm just worried about you is all."

Shade thrown again. I pursed my lips as I looked at the various guests around the table who also understood the shade thrown but knew better than to say anything to the first lady.

"I'm fine, Mom. I'm eating very well," Devin countered.

"If you say so. But you do look a few pounds lighter."

Devin passed me the dishes after placing food onto his plate. I felt like all eyes were on me to see how much food I was going to put on my plate after the shade Isabelle threw. I didn't know why they were paying attention to me because a few of them weren't lean themselves. A couple of them were bigger than me. Unfortunately, Mrs. Woods was an elegant, tiny woman. I had to give it to her, for sixty years old, she was a beautiful woman. Her nut-brown skin was flawless. There wasn't a wrinkle in sight. Her hair was cut in a pixie style, making her look twenty years younger than she was. She was about five foot two and couldn't weigh any more than 110 pounds. She could stand to eat a bit more herself, but I guess the first lady needed to maintain her image of what she considered perfection.

Georgiana was a very pretty woman also. Her shape could easily be compared to that of Beyoncé. Her skin was a golden brown, eyes catlike, giving her an exotic appeal, and her hair was cut into an edgy layered bob which had pops of red making her more alluring. To say I was jealous was an understatement. As much as I didn't like her, I could see what my husband saw in Georgiana. I just hoped his feelings for her would remain in the past.

"Well, son, I was telling everyone about how excited I am about the church anniversary celebration we are having the Sunday after this one coming up. I can't believe it's been twenty-five years already."

"We are so excited about it too," Deacon Jackson stated.

"We all are," his wife added.

"We have a choir coming all the way from New York to sing the Lord's praises that day," Secretary Annabelle stated.

"And they are wonderful. They really know how to get people on their feet. It's sure to be a magnificent church service," Devin's mother said.

"Son, I know you are going to enjoy yourself," Mr. Woods stated.

Devin swallowed hard as his body became rigid. He placed his fork on his plate as he cleared his throat before saying, "I'm not sure I'm going to be able to make it."

An awkward silence filled the room. Everyone's gazes shifted to his dad who picked up his napkin and dabbed at his mouth as he chewed the remainder of the food in his mouth.

Forehead creased, his father leaned forward, placing his elbows on the table. Hands now in the steeple position, his stout voice broke the stillness as he asked, "What do you mean you are not going to be able to make it?"

My heart galloped for my husband. Mr. Woods wasn't my father, but he was definitely an intimidating individual.

Shifting nervously, Devin said, "I have to fly out to California on business."

"Honey, you sure you can't reschedule? You know we would love to have you there. You are our only child, and this event is very important to us," his mother chided.

"You see, Isabelle, this is what I'm talking about. This boy chooses work over God all the time, not realizing it's God who's blessing him."

"Dad, that's not what I'm doing."

"Then what do you call it?"

"Everson, not here in front of our company," Mrs. Woods pleaded.

"They understand what I'm talking about," he pointed to the guests, and most of the deacons nodded in agreement. "Your place is supposed to be with your family on that day. It's bad enough you hardly come to church any longer. You supposed to be there every Sunday. But now, one of the biggest events we have during the year and you have to go out of town on business? What is the congregation going to think? Half of them are forgetting I have a son at all."

"Dad, I don't care what the congregation thinks," Devin countered. "The congregation doesn't pay my bills. You do want me to use that college education you paid for to further my career, don't you?"

"If I knew paying for your college was going to cause you to choose career over family and church, then maybe I shouldn't have paid for it at all," Mr. Woods deduced.

"Everson," Mrs. Woods called.

"No, Mom. Dad is telling the truth. He paid for my college, hoping I would follow in his footsteps."

Mr. Woods's jaw tightened as Devin continued.

"But I disappointed him. When I told him I wanted to be in the corporate industry, he was not happy about it. He should be happy I've made a name for myself and be proud of what I've accomplished. All he chooses to do is put me down because I didn't follow in his seminary footsteps."

"A son is supposed to want to be like his father."

"Who says I'm not?" Devin addressed his dad. "I'm successful just like you. I'm smart just like you. I'm talented just like you. But what, just because I'm not preaching just like you, that makes me a failure?"

"Honey, that's not what your father is saying," Mrs. Woods said, trying to calm the conversation.

"Then what is he saying, Mom, huh?"

The room remained silent, and to my surprise and utter dismay, Georgiana began to speak.

"Mr. Woods, can I add something please?"

Devin's father nodded.

"Devin is right. I mean, look at what your son has accomplished. Just because he's not going to preach doesn't mean you have failed as his father. You and Mrs.

Woods have done a marvelous job raising a wonderful, respectful young man. You have a lot to be proud of regarding Devin. And most of all, you have instilled God in him. Just because you don't see him every Sunday doesn't mean he's not praying and giving God the glory. And that's because of what you and Mrs. Woods instilled in him. Why do you think he is as successful as he is? It's God, and I know Devin knows where his blessings are coming from," she said, looking at Devin lovingly.

Devin looked at her for a long moment before she turned her attention back to his dad.

"You work hard with the church because that's your calling. Devin works hard in business because that's what he wants to do. Both of you are successful in your own right. Who's to say that one day you two won't be working side by side? Yes, there's a possibility that day may never come, but if it does, and you two ever get together, you would be a force to be reckoned with," Georgiana concluded.

"Amen," Isabelle said, smiling from ear to ear and the guests around the table shouted amens as well.

I was speechless because I felt like, as Devin's wife, those should have been the words coming out of my mouth, *not* his ex-fiancée's.

I looked at Devin who was still staring at Georgiana like I wasn't even there.

"Mr. Woods, I hope I didn't overstep my bounds and disrespect you in any way because that was not my intention. But I know Devin wants to be there for you and Mrs. Woods. But please look at his accomplishments and know if it wasn't for you guys, he wouldn't be the great man he is today."

Devin's father paused as he looked at his wife and said, "No, you didn't disrespect me at all. In fact, what you said made a lot of sense. I never looked at it like that before. I was so busy feeling bad about my son not wanting to be a preacher like me that I totally overlooked what he has accomplished."

"Your son is a very successful man and that comes from the examples you have set for him. I'm pretty sure Devin can make other arrangements to be there for your church anniversary celebration because he has it like that. At the same time, you have to make him feel happy to be there. You know, as well as I do, pushing your son never works," she chuckled. "He tends to run in the opposite direction."

There was that damn eye contact again. Georgiana looked at my husband once more in that loving way that I knew was melting Devin's heart.

Mr. Woods chuckled, saying, "You got a point there. That boy didn't even like when I used to push him on the swing. He always wanted to do it himself."

Laughter erupted around the table, and Devin even chuckled himself.

"You see, Devin wanted to be independent back then, and that was because he wanted you to see he could do it," Georgiana added.

Nodding again, Mr. Woods said, "Son, I want to apologize for what I said and how I came off earlier."

"It's okay, Dad. I should have taken your feelings into consideration about a day I knew was very important to you and Mom. I promise I'm going to try to rearrange the trip for another weekend."

"Amen," Mrs. Woods said, smiling as she reached over and grabbed her husband's hand. She then reached out and grabbed Devin's hand as well. "God is so good."

"Yes, he is," Georgiana agreed, along with the other guests around the table.

"Thank you, Georgiana," Mr. Woods said. "You always knew how to come to my son's rescue."

"That's because she knows him," Mrs. Woods declared.

"It's not a problem. You guys know no matter what, Devin will always have a special place in my heart."

Out of my peripheral, I could see Mrs. Woods glaring at me as Georgiana again gazed at my husband. She shifted her look to me but kept that same kind smile on her face . . . like she'd won. And I guess in a way, she did. She definitely won his parents over, and now I thought she was winning with my husband as well.

"Now, let's get back to eating some of this good food I prepared," Mrs. Woods gushed.

Chatter filled the room as eating resumed. Needless to say, my appetite was ruined. Georgiana's presence overrode mine, and if I didn't know any better, I was the freaking extra here. It was evident his family wanted Devin to get back with Georgiana, and from the subtle glances they kept giving each other, I wondered if my husband wanted to get back with his first love as well.

Vivian

12

I lay in my husband's arms hearing the rapid beat of his heart after I'd just finished sucking him to a blissful end. I was happy I could bring him to this brink of pleasure since most times when I sucked him, he refused to climax, always wanting to get inside me to reach his pinnacle. I found it extremely gratifying to bring him to a level of exploding without him even entering me. He was always disappointed, but he truly didn't understand the fulfillment I got from pleasing him orally.

I knew I had to do something. It had been close to two weeks since Sheldon and I did anything sexually. The only thing we did was kiss when he was on his way out the door to his job. As fine as he was and as horny as he stayed, I couldn't understand why he wasn't interested in having sex with me as much anymore. In my eyes, we were still newlyweds. Just having celebrated our first-year anniversary, I thought we should still be at the stage of not being able to keep our hands off each other. But, boy, how times had changed.

"You okay?" he asked tenderly.

"I'm good. Why do you ask?"

"Because you are not saying anything."

"What am I supposed to say, babe?"

"I don't know. I just wanted to make sure you were good. You seemed troubled about something."

I was, but I couldn't bring myself to tell him how I felt. In the darkness, he couldn't see my grim expression. As much as I would like to think things were okay with us, I honestly didn't feel good about us at all. We were living an amazing life in a new city and a fantastic home, but for me, I felt like if the sex wasn't present, then things were critical.

I still couldn't get over the fact I couldn't reach over and touch him in the middle of the night without him jumping up and acting like he wanted to attack me. The first time he reacted like that, it scared me. I didn't think wanting to hold my husband was a bad thing, but from his reaction, evidently it was. He explained that I frightened him, but he always had this same reaction when I tried to touch him. A few of those times he got mad at me for waking him. What man didn't want to be awakened by his wife holding his dick in her hand, ready to please him?

I asked him about his reaction to me touching him in the middle of the night, and he basically brushed it off like it was no big deal. But I could clearly see it was a big deal. The one thing about being his friend first and now his wife was that I could see when something was up with him. Why he wasn't telling me bothered me. Maybe I was overreacting. I tended to read too much into things sometimes. Besides those incidents and the decrease in our sexual activities, Sheldon wasn't acting any different. He was working more but seemed to love his job. At home we talked and laughed like we always did, but I knew there was something he was not telling me, and the fact he felt like he couldn't tell me bothered me.

I wondered if us getting married was a mistake. I loved him, but I loved the friendship more. It was so effortless. Marriage made things more complicated. The excitement of us being together was no longer present. I felt like somehow, it was my fault, and maybe he came to the conclusion I wasn't the woman for him after all.

This was what I hoped would never happen with us. Sheldon was my best friend for years before that one night that changed everything. It was after a nightmarish dinner I had with my sisters. Sheldon ended up coming over, explaining how he had the same type of awful night himself with some blind date he went on. We sat up laughing, eating, and watching television until we both drifted off to sleep. The next thing I knew, he was nestled up behind me with his arm draped around my waist. I could feel his erection poking into my backside, and it felt good. I knew this was a line I shouldn't have crossed, but that night, we stepped over the line. We damn near erased it, in fact, and it ended up being one of the best nights of my life because Sheldon rocked my world.

That sexual encounter ruined our friendship for a while, which was the main reason why I never wanted to go there with him. I didn't realize I was pushing him away because I wasn't happy with myself, especially my body image. I was a plus-size sister weighing 225 pounds at five foot five. I felt like Sheldon was the type of man that should be with someone half my size and as gorgeous as he was. I wondered why he would want me when there were so many other women that would look better on his arm.

"Viv, you know I love you, right?" Sheldon asked, breaking me out of my thoughts.

"I know, babe. I love you too."

"Do you?" he asked.

"Of course, I do," I said lifting my head to look at the outline of his face in the darkness.

"I understand things have been a little weird lately, but please understand it has nothing to do with you."

I wanted to ask him what it had to do with, but I didn't want to ruin the tranquil moment we were in right now. So I just listened.

"Did you hear me?"

"I did, Sheldon."

"Do you believe me?"

Exhaling, I said, "Yes."

"I know you have a lot of fears, Viv, and I don't want our relationship to be one of them. Like today at the restaurant, I know that bothered you."

"What made you think that?"

He chuckled.

"What you fail to realize is women like that waitress Hailey are always trying me. They are wondering how a woman like me managed to snag a man like you."

"A woman like you? What does that mean?" he asked.

"Come on, babe. I'm a plus-size sister, and you cut to the max. Hell, you can be Morris Chestnut's body double."

"First of all, Morris Chestnut is bald, and I have dreads. Second, I think I'm better looking than him," he joked.

"You are right."

"You're just agreeing because I'm your husband."

"You are my sexy husband who I adore."

"I adore you too."

As much as I would like to think I got over my insecurities about being the size I am, I wasn't past it at all. If anything, being married to such an attractive man made me feel even more insecure about myself. I didn't know what I needed to do to change my perception of myself, but I knew I needed to do something quickly before I allowed my insecurities to ruin my marriage. I'd pushed him away before. I didn't want to do that again now that I was his wife. I had to understand he chose me, and this was an equal exchange of love and affection. But deep down, I couldn't help but wonder if he ever believed he was doing me a favor by being with me.

"You are a very attractive man, Sheldon. You can't tell me you haven't been hit on since we've gotten married."

"I'm not interested in any other woman, babe. I've told you that."

"I hope not."

"What do you mean? You're saying that like you think I have some side piece or something."

"Do you?" I asked.

"Hell no. Do you have another man?" he retorted.

"Of course not, Sheldon."

"Okay, then, this subject needs to be squashed."

"I know you love me, but I'm always scared someone else will come along and take you away from me. And, of course, I'm going to think it has to do with the way I look."

"There is nothing wrong with the way you look. I hate that you are always so down on yourself. If anything, that makes you unattractive."

His words hurt. Was it already starting, me pushing him away by my negative opinions of myself?

"Society makes me put down myself."

"But you don't have to feed into it. You need to love you. You don't need to worry about society, babe."

"That's easier said than done, Sheldon."

"I'm trying to love you for the two of us. If you can't love you, then I'm going to love you more than ever, because then, I will be loving a woman who's grown to understand her value. You are worth so much, babe. You just need to see that within yourself," Sheldon said thoughtfully.

I smiled at his empathetic words.

"I'm sorry I've been feeling this way. We've seemed distant lately. Our communication has been less, and our sexual connection has been damn near nonexistent.

Of course, I'm going to fear you finding someone else. Especially with your high sex drive."

He chuckled as he said, "Believe you me, Viv, I've wanted you. I mean, I want to get all up in that ass. But, babe, I've been tired as hell. There is no other woman, I promise. I told you I would never do you like that. You are my world. I've loved you for years before you agreed to be my wife. No woman—and I mean *no* woman—compares to you."

Sheldon rubbed my shoulder as I smiled down at him lovingly.

"Thank you for that."

"Thank you for being my partner for life because without you, I would have nothing."

I leaned down and kissed Sheldon deeply. His tongue explored mine as we enveloped each other. There was the Sheldon I knew. Then I reached down to caress his manhood.

Disconnecting, he asked, "Are you going to ride it for me?"

Smiling devilishly, I said, "I would be happy to."

The sex was absolutely amazing. I know I'd climaxed several times to the point of wanting to pass out and was happy because my body needed the release. When I looked over at my husband, he was sound asleep.

I was happy we'd talked and had this moment with each other. Still, I felt like he wasn't saying something to me. I was going to leave it alone for now. Sheldon could brush it off all he wanted to, but eventually, I was going to get to the bottom of what I was feeling. I just prayed it wouldn't have a devastating impact on our marriage.

Monica

13

The ride home was a quiet one, and it was no different when Devin and I climbed into bed to go to sleep. He seemed exhausted, but I was still seething from the show his parents and ex put on for me and the church committee. It upset me more that Devin didn't bother to see how I was doing with what happened. I guess he was so deep in his own thoughts he couldn't worry about my feelings. But I bet you his behind was wondering about Georgiana and how *she* was doing.

Before we left his parents' home, his mother asked to speak to him for a moment. They went in the direction of the kitchen as everyone remained seated around the table. Georgiana was still in our presence, which meant his mother wasn't trying to let the two have a private moment together. Every now and then, Georgiana's and my eyes met. Mine was telling her she better back off, and hers were telling me, game on, bitch.

Mr. Woods laughed and talked about church and visits he'd had with some members of the congregation as we sat and listened. I didn't want to hear any of this. If anything, I was ready to go home. So I decided to excuse myself and find my husband so we could leave.

I noticed Devin and his mother in the direction of the kitchen, and that's where I heard them talking. I stood at the corner and waited as I listened to what they were talking about.

"Mom, please. I want you to stop this," I heard Devin say.

"Son, you know Georgiana is the woman for you."

I knew that's why she invited her. She wanted them back together. This infuriated me. It was one thing to think I knew, but to hear it come from the horse's mouth pissed me off. I almost walked in to lay his mother out, but that would have let them know I was eavesdropping on their conversation, so I remained still and continued to listen.

"We are over. We had our chance."

"Then give her another one."

"Mom, I'm *married.* You of all people should understand the vows I said before God. How are you asking me to betray that?"

"That marriage is the devil's doing. You know I never wanted you to marry that woman."

"It's not about you."

His mother ignored what he said and continued like he said nothing.

"That woman was nothing but a rebound. The only reason why I went along with it was because I wanted you to be happy. You know as well as I do you married Monica to get over Georgiana."

Devin said nothing to defend his love for me, and that upset me. Why wouldn't he speak against what his mother was saying . . . unless what she was saying was true?

"Mom, I'm married."

Was that all he could say? *Mom, I'm happy*. Why not give her reasons why you married me and why you loved me?

"Devin, are you happily married?" she asked.

I waited with bated breath to hear the answer to this. I hoped his answer wouldn't be I'm married again because that wasn't enough to suffice.

"You see, you are not. That's why I said this is the devil's doing. Why are you settling, son? You only get one life to live, and until you come to the realization she's not the one for you, your life will never be complete."

"I love her, Mom."

Finally, he said he loved me, and this caused me to breathe a sigh of relief.

"Do you?" his mother asked. "Do you love Monica as much as you love Georgiana?"

I waited to hear Devin say yes, and that he loved me even more, but again, he said nothing. It was like he was just trying to shut his mom down subtly but really believed in what she was saying.

"You see, you don't love her as much as Georgiana. You know you still have feelings for that woman."

"Mom, what can I do about that?"

He did love her more than me. I braced myself against the wall as my knees buckled beneath me. I clinched my stomach as I leaned my shoulder against the wall to steady myself. Here I was fighting for a marriage I longed for, and my husband wasn't in love with me as much as he claimed. Was our marriage a farce?

"You need to ask that woman for a divorce."

"I can't do that."

"Then you will be unhappy for as long as you are married to that woman. Son, please think about this. You deserve greatness. You deserve happiness. You deserve true love, honey, and your true love is Georgina."

A hand on my shoulder caused me to whirl around, and to my dismay, it was Georgiana.

"Are you okay?" she asked with a look knowing she'd caught me eavesdropping on my husband's conversation with his mother. Her voice interrupted the conversation Devin was having with his mother as they walked out to see both of us standing there. Mrs. Woods gave me a look like she hoped I'd heard the conversation, because in hearing it, I now knew I was second best and the first-place winner for Devin's heart was standing next to me.

"Honey, I'm ready to go home. I'm not feeling well," I said.

Now I was lying in bed next to my husband who had his back to me. He didn't even bother to say good night to me.

"Devin," I called out to him softly.

"Yes, Monica?"

"Are we okay?"

"Yes."

I paused to see if he was going to say anything else, but he didn't. I knew when he didn't feel like talking, but I needed some answers. Pulling the covers further up, I held them like it was my shield as I began to speak.

"I heard the conversation you and your mother had tonight."

He sighed, turning on his back to look up at the ceiling. As much as I wished he would turn and look at me, I was happy that I wasn't talking to his back anymore.

"So you were eavesdropping?" he asked.

"Yes."

"Why?"

"I don't know. I heard your mother talking about us, and I wanted to know what she was saying about me."

"You shouldn't have heard any of that."

"But I did and . . . and . . ."

I choked on my emotions thinking of the next thing I wanted to say, and I knew I had to be prepared to hear the answer, whether it was good or bad.

"And what?" he asked.

"Am I the rebound?"

Devin heaved another sigh as he said, "No, Monica."

My stomach relaxed at his answer, happy that he didn't say yes. I asked, "You can understand why I think this, right?"

"I can."

"When you got with me, it was right after your breakup with Georgiana. I know losing her was devastating, but I thought you would be past that by now."

Silence filled the room. Devin saying nothing was like him saying everything that needed to be said. My once-relaxed stomach quickly tightened.

"So you do still love her?"

"Yes," he answered.

I was caught off guard. I really hoped in my heart he would say no. Was this *really* happening right now?

"Did you say yes?" I asked to be sure I heard him correctly.

"Yes, I still love her."

"Do you love her more than me?"

"Yes," he said again, and with these answers, I could feel my stomach churning. I felt like the dinner I'd consumed was going to come back up and choke me. Did he realize he'd just stuck a knife in my heart and twisted it?

"Do you want to get back with her?"

He paused for a moment before saying, "Yes."

My breath caught in my throat as my heart slammed in my chest. This meant he didn't want me anymore.

"I'm sorry, Monica, but I do want a divorce. I've wanted one for quite some time, but I just didn't know how to ask you for one."

"How long have you known?"

"At least eight months," he answered.

"I feel like I've been jumping through hoops for you, Devin."

"I know, and I'm sorry."

Did he think just saying those words to me was going to make everything okay? For goodness' sake, he'd just told me he wanted a divorce and was not in love with me but still in love with his ex who decided to call off their wedding two weeks before they were supposed to walk down the aisle. Yet, he still wants her.

A hundred things raced through my mind. I cook, I clean, I work and contributed equally to this household. I loved him. I sexed him. Hell, I even licked this man's ass before, and he wanted to be with the bitch that basically dumped him.

I erupted.

"Sorry? You're sorry, but you want a divorce," I said with a raised voice.

"Monica, calm down."

"How in the hell am I supposed to calm down when my husband wants a divorce from me so he can be with his ex who left him crushed."

"You see, I knew I should have just had you served with the papers."

"What?" I said in astonishment.

Devin threw his legs over the side of the bed and sat there saying, "I have already filed. You should be receiving the papers next week."

"You lying next to me like we good, and you've already filed the papers?"

"I should have told you sooner."

"You *think?* Is that why Georgiana was there tonight, to be with you?"

"No."

"Were you hoping I wouldn't go so you could be with her?"

"I didn't know she was going to be there."

"We've been married for seven years, Devin. You mean to tell me you didn't know when you married me you were still in love with her?"

"I knew but—"

"You knew?" I said throwing a pillow and hitting him in the head with it.

Devin stood and looked at me with darkened eyes.

"I'm going to leave before this goes too far."

"It already has," I yelled. "I was supposed to have your whole heart. No wonder we've struggled in this marriage. You haven't been fully present."

"I know I hurt you."

"Why did you marry me? Especially if you didn't love me."

"You were there for me in a time when I felt like I had no one to turn to."

"So a rebound chick, just like your mother said."

"At the time, I didn't see you that way."

"How did you see me?"

"I thought I loved you. I guess I loved what you were doing for me."

"Wow. I can't believe you. Seven years later and *now* the truth comes out."

"I thought being with you would help me forget about Georgiana, and you did. But tonight, seeing her brought back feelings that help me know I've made the right decision in filing for a divorce."

"Have you thought about her since we've been married?" I asked.

"Yes but—"

"When we had sex, did you think of her?"

He hesitated before saying, "Yes, Monica but—"

"You *are* a preacher's kid, right?"

"You know I am."

"Isn't there a scripture that says honor your wife and your marriage?"

"Monica."

"Your parents are the exact reason why I don't go to church. They smiling in everybody's face every Sunday playing the perfect Christians when your trifling mother is trying to tell you to abandon your marriage for another woman."

"Don't call my mother trifling."

"Would harlot or hypocrite suffice? Or how about heathen?"

"Monica, that's enough."

"Come on, honey. Quote the scripture for me. I know you know them all. Tell me the Lord's words that coincide with you breaking your marriage vows to me to be with another woman."

"I'm not doing this with you," he said picking up the pillow I threw at him. "I'm going to sleep in the other room."

"What? You can't stand the heat? You might as well get used to it because you are going to burn in hell for what you have done to me."

Devin opened the door to our bedroom to leave.

"If you think I'm going to agree to this divorce so you can make Mommy and Daddy happy and so you can be with that woman, you got another think coming."

Devin halted with my words but then disappeared into the hallway.

"You better lock the door," I yelled. "Your ass might not wake up in the morning."

My mother used to say you can't do people wrong and expect that wrong is not going to come back and bite you in your ass. As much as I was angry with Devin, I understood in this moment I was getting back what I deserved.

Devin still loved Georgiana, and his secret feelings were now out in the open. I had a few secrets of my own, and I knew that's why this was happening to me. But I was happy no one knew mine. Not yet anyway. I might as well get ready for more bad karma to come my way because the revenge I was going to bestow upon my so-called husband was going to be sweet as honey. And as mad as I was, I didn't care what the repercussions were going to be for what I was about to do to him.

Kellie

14

Jeffrey was gone. I made him pack his belongings and get the heck out of our home. Of course, he didn't take everything, saying he was going to do whatever it took to get our marriage back on track. Evidently, he didn't understand he was the one who derailed it in the first place. I was tired of dealing with his disrespectful ways. He must have thought since I was younger than he, I was going to be gullible enough to deal with his bull. But he was sadly mistaken.

I sat on the couch, listening to the soothing sounds of the late Luther Vandross. I was already in my fleece pajamas as I thought back on how awful of a day this had been. I chuckled to myself because if it wasn't for having bad luck, I wouldn't have any luck at all.

There was a knock at the door, and I picked up my cell to see it was after midnight. I knew it better not be Jeffrey trying to crawl his trifling behind back up in here because it wasn't happening. I didn't care if he didn't have anywhere to go. He could sleep on the front lawn as far as I was concerned.

Peeping through the peephole, I was surprised to see it was my brother, Victor.

Opening the door, I said, "Boy, what are you doing here?"

He grabbed his chest and blew out a sigh of relief.

"Girl, I'm mad at you," he said pushing his way past me.

I closed the door behind him and watched as he walked in with a suitcase. He dropped it to the floor and turned to face me with his hands on his hips now.

"You can't answer your phone?" Vic asked.

I did see he'd called me several times, but I wasn't in the mood to talk. I should have known my brother would eat up the highway to find out why I wasn't accepting his calls.

"I thought something had happened to you," he said, walking over and giving me a strong, loving embrace.

"Vic, I'm sorry."

"I'm just glad you're okay. Now, I should whoop your ass for scaring the hell out of me."

I giggled as I said, "Come over and sit down."

I took my brother by the hand and led him over to the sofa. We both plopped down, him harder than me since he looked exhausted. I knew he was. Especially since he'd just driven six hours to get to me.

"Your ass owes me some gas money, a trip to my therapist, and a spa day for the years you aged me thinking something had happened to you."

"It's been a day," I said taking a sip of my wine. Before I knew it, my eyes began to water. Just the thought of my brother being here was enough for me to cry uncontrollably because I knew I was with someone who truly loved me.

"Sis, no. Don't do that," Vic said scooting closer to me. I fell into his embrace as he asked, "What happened?"

"It's bad, Vic."

"What do you mean? Do I have to kick someone's ass?"

"He's not worth it."

"By he, do you mean that husband of yours?" he asked.

I nodded.

"Kicking his ass would make me feel better," Vic said.

With eyes still brimming with tears, I sat upright. Vic took his hand and wiped my tears away as he looked at me with concern. I smiled warmly at my brother, happy he was by my side.

"I'm glad I came."

"I'm glad you came too. Jesus must have known I needed you."

"Well, I hope Jesus intervenes before I kick your husband's ass. Where is he anyway?" he asked looking around for him.

"I kicked him out."

"Good, because if you hadn't, I was."

"You are so crazy," I said giggling.

"You damn right I am. Now get it together so you can tell me what happened."

I explained to Vic everything that I'd been through today, from my doctor's appointment, to my conversation with Mom, to finding another man sucking my husband's dick. Vic looked on like he was not surprised, with his lips twisted up and forehead creased with frustration.

"I rebuke all this nonsense in the name of Jesus."

"Amen to that," I said.

"I can't believe you've been dealing with all of this and you didn't bother to tell me."

"I knew you would come running to my rescue."

"And why shouldn't I?" he asked.

"You have a life of your own. I don't want you always rushing to my rescue every time bad things happen to me."

Tilting his head he said, "Kell, I'm your older brother. That's what I'm supposed to do."

"But what about your boyfriend? I know he gets tired of you coming to me."

"Well . . ."

"Well what?" I asked looking at him suspiciously.

"Aaron and I are over."

"What?" I said in disbelief.

Aaron and my brother had been together off and on since he came out. He was his love that gave him courage to stand in his truth. So to hear they were no longer together surprised me.

"Me and Aaron have been over for about two months now."

"Two months? Why didn't you tell me?" I asked.

"Probably the same reason your behind didn't tell me what was going on with you."

He had a point there. We held each other's gaze before both of us burst into laughter.

"I guess we are more alike than I thought," Vic said.

"I think so. Here we are trying to deal with our own drama, and we still end up by each other's side in the end."

"I guess the lesson is we need to start telling each other everything because we will always be here for each other."

"That's true. As much as I'm not happy about you flying down the highway to get here, I'm glad you are here, Vic."

I leaned over and hugged my brother again.

"I hope you mean that."

"Of course I do."

"You sure?" he asked.

"Vic."

"I'm just asking because your brother needs a favor."

"Anything. You know I got you. So what do you need from me?" I asked.

"I need a place to stay."

Sonya

15

Sitting in the kitchen at the table, I stirred my coffee with a spoon thinking about everything that happened yesterday. I still couldn't believe my daughter would be so gullible to hold drugs for some punk who didn't give a damn about her. All she could see was *I* was the enemy. If she knew like I knew, she would know I was the number one person in her corner rooting for her to be successful in this cruel, cold world.

A tear formed as I thought about my own mother. Today was her birthday, and she would have been fifty-four. And as much as she wasn't a mother to me, I still loved her. Any issues I had, I had to thank my mother for. We were close at one time, but it was in the friendship sort of way and not in the mother-daughter way that it should have been. Growing up with my mother only made me want to be the best mother I could be to my own child.

I was always put in situations which made me question the type of love my mother had for me. No child should ever have to figure out if the love they are receiving was right or wrong.

A lot of it started when I found out later in my childhood my mother cheated on my dad. The way I found out about my mother cheating, Daddy was at work one day and Mama decided to invite over her “friend.” And I use “friend” loosely. Mama’s “friend” ended up wanting to see her bedroom. Not only did he want to see her bedroom, he wanted to see her bra, her panties, her sheets, and he also wanted to see how good my parents’ bed was to sleep on. Only, they didn’t do any sleeping.

Mama had the door pushed closed but not completely. I was able to watch them through the crack in the door. To me, it looked like wrestling. I was too young to understand what was really going on. This was why I didn’t think there was a problem mentioning it to my dad. Needless to say, he lost his mind. My parents argued for hours while I sat in my room crying and thinking it was all my fault. Dishes were thrown as explicit words followed. The next thing I heard was the slamming of the front door, not knowing that was my father leaving us.

From that point on, Mama acted like I didn’t exist. Daddy left me with someone who didn’t want to acknowledge me as her daughter, and that hurt me tremendously. She fed me and clothed me, but no mother-daughter affection occurred between us. So I blamed myself for the outcome of not having a mother or a father.

A few weeks later, Daddy came back. They were hugging and loving on each other again, and Mama started talking to me more. I was happy, but Mama was never satisfied with what she had. Mama ended up cheating on Daddy again. And again. And again until I lost count. The sad part about the whole thing was Mama was dumb enough to allow them in our home again. It was like she wanted to get caught. She almost was when Daddy arrived home not even ten minutes after one of her men left. That let her know she needed to take her cheating elsewhere.

Mom used me as her alibi, taking me with her as she did her dirt with all these different men. She gave me this long talk about how I could never tell Daddy because he would leave us again and we wouldn't be a happy family anymore. She would leave me in the car to read or listen to the radio while she went in and did what she had to do. On most occasions, she forgot I was still in the car. Or maybe it was that she didn't care. A few times I had to knock on the door to tell her I was ready to go home. A man usually came to the door with no shirt on, looking sweaty and nasty talking about she'll be out in a minute. A couple of times, her conquest had the nerve to come to the door naked, with his manhood pointing directly at me. The look they gave me still gave me chills. Lucky for me, she was a selfish mother and didn't allow any man she was messing with to touch me.

When I reached sixteen and was interested in boys myself, she pushed me into dating. I did, thinking this was what I was supposed to be doing. When I got a boyfriend, she would go pick him up on her way to her rendezvous and have him be my company in the car. Of course, I loved this because I didn't have to be by myself anymore. She always told me it was okay for me to "do it" in the car if I wanted to but to be careful and don't get anything on the seats. Never once did she mention protection. She was worried about the seat of the car.

My boyfriends at the time thought Mama was the coolest woman ever. I did too for a while . . . until I was thirty men deep into sleeping around just as much as she was. I started to be known as the girl with the mother who was cool with her daughter sleeping with men in the car. Each relationship, if you can even call it that, was tainted by the boys bragging about being with me. My title as a whore was stamped and approved, and the only person I could blame was myself.

Dating quickly became no longer fun. At eighteen, I was ready to move out on my own. This was due to my now-growing belly. I became pregnant, and the father of my baby denied it since I was the slut around the streets. Hear anybody tell it, this baby could have been anybody's child. This devastated me. I considered having an abortion, but knew I couldn't because I really didn't believe in it. This baby didn't choose to be born and shouldn't have to die due to my reckless behavior. This child was a gift, and I had to cherish it. My father was not too happy about this but eventually accepted my pregnancy and supported me as much as he could.

So I cleaned my act up, stopped sleeping around, and concentrated on graduating from high school, which I accomplished. I soon had Meena, who I was determined to be a better mother to than my own mother was to me. I got a job. I got my own place, and I applied for college and went on to get my associate's degree in the health industry.

Mama still thought I could be her alibi, and she could use my place to have her fun, but I quickly nipped that in the bud. Mama wasn't happy, but I didn't care. I was trying to get away from her and her trifling ways. It was bad enough I had to keep her secret rendezvous away from my dad for years. I felt like I was betraying him. It always crossed my mind to tell him, but I was afraid it would ruin the relationship he and I had with each other, so I continued to keep my mouth shut.

Mom only cared about herself. She didn't truly love my dad, and it was her fault I was as promiscuous as I was. She didn't teach me to value myself, but I guess she couldn't when she too didn't see value in herself.

My life was just beginning, and I was not about to have my mother's twisted behaviors come upon my child like it did me. She didn't have enough love and respect to not involve me in her philandering, so I was not about to allow her to be disrespectful around her own grandchild.

It wasn't long before Daddy found out again about her cheating. He left her soon after I left home. I feel like my father knew what she was doing but was waiting for me to get out on my own, and I appreciate the sacrifice my dad made for me. My mother never knew the damage she did to me emotionally—if I could call her a mother at all. She was a woman who only cared about herself. And by herself she was when she died. All those men and all those so-called friends were ghost when it came to her passing. Thinking about that always made me feel bad for her. At the same time, I knew she reaped what she'd sown.

As for my dad, he passed away when Meena turned eight years old. I'm glad she had some memories of her grandfather. She definitely had a bunch of pictures with him so where one grandparent failed, her grandfather took up the slack.

Meena was the reason I pushed forward and made something out my life. She didn't have a clue the sacrifices I made for her. I was a mother, and I was going to show my daughter more love than a child could handle. She didn't understand it now, but I knew the day would come when she would see how much I truly loved her.

Monica

16

I thought it was about time for this conversation I was about to have. I figured I had some time to spare before meeting with my friends for lunch so now was as good a time as any to confront the woman who was causing so much dissension in my marriage. I didn't know why I was so nervous. As I stood at her front door, a part of me wanted to turn and walk away. But I knew this was long overdue, so I rang the doorbell and waited for someone to open the door.

"Monica, what are you doing here?" Isabelle greeted with rigidity. She looked as flawless as ever, wearing a belted yellow, white, and tan floral print fit and flare dress with a soft yellow cardigan.

"Good morning, Isabelle. I was wondering if I could speak with you for a moment."

She seemed skeptical as she asked, "Why didn't you call first?"

"I did, but no one answered."

Her expression let me know she knew I called. She just didn't pick up. I should have used my home phone because she would have answered thinking it was Devin. But since I called from my cell, she deliberately ignored it.

"Can I come in?" I asked, still waiting for her decide.

"Well, I guess since you're here," she said tersely as she stepped to the side, allowing me to enter.

"Please, follow me to the kitchen," she commanded, and I did as she asked.

When we entered her kitchen, I had a seat at the kitchen table and watched as Isabelle went over to the cabinet to retrieve a mug. Pouring herself a cup of coffee, I wondered if she was going to be hospitable enough to offer me a cup. But when she sat down across from me placing the ceramic mug in front of her, I knew this was just another way she was letting me know she didn't like me. Again . . . church people.

You would think since I'd been married to her son for seven years, she would have come around already. But the conversation I overheard the other night let me know she still felt some type of way about me. It was time to get our issues out in the open once and for all.

"Okay, Monica, what is it that you need to speak to me about?"

"I want to know why you have so much animosity toward me."

"Excuse me?" she asked like she didn't know what I meant.

"I know you don't care for me. I want to know why," I said.

I looked Isabelle squarely in her eyes awaiting her answer. She returned the glare as she stirred her coffee before taking a careful sip. Placing the mug down, she began to address me.

"You are not the woman Everson and I wanted for our son."

She was straight and to the point as she looked impassively at me. I nervously shifted in my seat before responding.

"I get that, but Devin chose me. Isn't that enough of a reason for you to at least try to get to know me?"

"Monica, you are Devin's rebound. You know it. I know it. Everyone knows this," she responded coldly. "So to me, there is no reason to get to know you any better because I think it's a matter of time before my son comes to his senses and moves on to someone more fitting for him."

More fitting I thought. Did she just say that to me? Yes, she did. You know why, because there is no one around for her to hold back her negative comments. I had to inhale before continuing to speak to her because I knew if I didn't, this conversation was going to take a turn for the worse, and I was going to be the one who took it there this time.

"Regardless of what you and others think, Devin still chose me. He saw something in me that he loved enough to want to marry me," I spoke firmly.

Isabelle picked up her cup and took another sip before leaning back assertively. She asked, "Monica, who are you really?"

This question caught me off guard.

"What do you mean?" I asked with a frown.

"Seriously, who are you? As long as you've been with my son, we haven't met any of your family."

"I know he's told you I had a brother who died. My parents are no longer living."

"We know that's the story you told our son."

"Story?"

"Monica, I've had you investigated, and it's almost like you never existed."

My heart began to beat rapidly at the mention of her investigating me. You would think I wouldn't be shocked by anything this woman did, but I was. The mischievous look she was giving me made me wonder if she found out about my past. Was this a game of who was going to break first? Maybe she had nothing and was waiting for me to spill my life story to her, but that was never going to happen. If she was a real woman, she would have asked me about my past before having me investigated. I would have respected her more for it.

"Why would you do that?" I asked coolly.

"Mr. Woods and I are prominent figures in the community and have a reputation to uphold. More importantly, you are with our only child, whom we love dearly. Knowing whom my son is married to is understandable, don't you think?"

"What I think is you had me investigated to see if you could find out some dirt on me."

"So dirt *does* exist on you?" she asked with a raised brow.

"Everyone has dirt, Isabelle. So, please don't sit there like your past is pristine. As I recall this happily ever after marriage you and Mr. Woods are portraying is not so happy since it rumored he's had numerous affairs on you."

Her condescending gaze quickly changed to anger at the mention of her husband's "indiscretions." She was so busy trying to dig up dirt on my past, she needed to use that same private investigator to find out what her husband's been up to lately.

Clearing her throat, Isabelle leaned forward, resting her elbows on the table as she clasped her hands together.

"Monica, if you want the real, here it is. I don't like you. You are an okay-looking woman, but you need to pull away from the table. I'm still trying to figure out how my son could stomach laying up with you. Now, Georgiana, she's beautiful and a model."

"Excuse me?"

"I think you are an opportunist who took advantage of my son during a difficult time. You dug your claws in him as soon as you got the opportunity and ran with him to the alter. Georgiana is the love of his life, and I think you know that already. You are nothing to my son, and the quicker you get that through your head, the better we will all be. Now, as for my marriage, my husband and I are happily married. Believe the rumors all you want, but the fact still remains, my son does not love you, not like he loves Georgiana."

A seething hatred rose within me as I absorbed this "Christian woman's" words. I watched as she confidently picked up her coffee again and sipped it like we were having a pleasant conversation.

"Devin does love me," I insisted.

"Keep telling yourself that, honey. I know my son, and it's only a matter of time before he divorces you."

"Do you really think I'm going to give up that easily?"

"It's in your best interest to," she said sharply.

"Why? So Devin and Georgiana can get back together, and you all can play the perfect church family?" I asked angrily.

"Exactly. You *are* getting the picture already. I'm *glad* we had this talk."

I couldn't believe Isabelle was sitting here talking to me like I was going to actually walk away from my marriage. I married Devin because I loved him. We'd had our trying times, but what marriage doesn't. When I said I do, I meant that for a lifetime—not until his ex decided she wanted him again.

"If you think I'm going to divorce Devin, you have another think coming."

"Honey, stop torturing yourself. I know my son has already filed the paperwork. He's already informed you he wants to divorce you. So please, save yourself the trouble and heartache and sign the papers so we all can move on with our lives."

How did this woman know about the divorce and him asking me? I guess my husband went running to mommy, telling her what happened last night. Or maybe it was her idea in the first place, and she helped him file the papers. Knowing this conniving woman, she's behind why Devin has been pushing me away.

"Isabelle, you better get on a move if you don't want to be late," a familiar voice said entering the kitchen. And to my dismay, it was Georgiana fastening a bracelet around her wrist. And closely following behind her . . . was my husband.

"What the hell is this?" I yelled, shooting up out of my seat.

Georgiana looked back at Devin, who seemed stunned by my presence. I didn't recall seeing his car outside, but he did park it in the garage many times when he came to his parents' home.

"Monica, what are you doing here?" he asked nervously.

"You asking *me* what *I'm* doing here? What the hell are *you* doing with *her?*" I pointed.

"I'm not with her," he retorted.

"Your ass walked in here like you with her," I yelled.

"Don't curse in my parents' home, please."

"I can't curse, but you can cheat on me with your ex?" I shot back.

"I'm not cheating."

Ignoring him I asked, "Is this why you left this morning without saying anything to me? You had to get over here to your whore."

"Monica, I haven't disrespected you, so please don't disrespect me," Georgiana defended.

"How did I disrespect you?" I asked, taking a couple of steps toward her. Devin stepped in between us.

"You called me a whore."

"You cheated on Devin with his cousin, right?"

All heads dropped at the mention of her “misdeed.” As much as Isabelle would like to think Georgiana was the perfect woman for Devin, Georgiana was also the one who broke her son’s heart.

“Oh, everybody quiet now. That’s what you did, right? Isn’t that the actions of a whore?”

“I made a mistake,” she said regretfully, cutting her eye at Devin.

“One that cost you the love of your life who is now the love of mine. So stop creeping around trying to rekindle a love you never respected anyway.”

“I will admit, I hurt Devin,” Georgiana said. When she said this, she peered into Devin’s eyes.

“I’ve apologize over and over again for my actions. Not only did I ruin our future, I caused friction in your family and humiliation in the church. Devin has been wonderful enough to forgive me and remain friends with me.”

Devin dropped his head at her words before looking back at me.

Turning to me, she continued.

“He’s a friend who I love dearly. The one thing you will never take from me is the love I have for this man, Monica. So, think what you want. Little do you realize your own actions are probably what’s ruined your relationship.”

“Are you done? Because I don’t need someone like you giving me advice about my relationship when you clearly don’t have one and couldn’t keep one of your own.”

“Monica, please.”

“No, Devin, she had her chance with you, and she ruined it. Don’t allow her to come in now and ruin what we have,” I pleaded.

“You see, this is why I don’t deal with ratchet women,” Georgiana murmured.

“Ratchet?” I roared.

"You are in a minister's home acting like this," Georgiana stated. "You're yelling and not giving Devin the opportunity to explain to you what's really going on."

"I *see* what's going on."

"What you *see* is a son at his parents' house."

"A house that happens to also be occupied by his ex-fiancée. If you were me and walked in on this situation, what would *you* think?"

Georgiana had nothing to say now.

"Exactly. So please exit left so I can talk with my husband alone."

Devin's forehead creased at my words. I looked at his mother who gloated with a pompous sneer.

"So this is how church people do. They break up marriages. Should I go to the alter tomorrow and confess what is happening? What will the congregation think when I tell them your parents are helping in the demise of our relationship because they are busy trying to reconnect a past love with their *married* son?"

Isabelle's superior grin was quickly replaced with a fearful one.

"Oh, now I got a reaction out of the first lady. Just like I suspected. The church and your precious appearance is what's more important. You know just like I do people wouldn't be happy about you breaking up the sanctity of marriage."

"Devin, please escort your Monica out of our home," his mother demanded.

"I'm his *wife*. You can say it. And as long as I have breath in my body, I will *always* be his wife."

"Come on, Georgiana. Come help me finish getting ready. We don't need to continue to listen to this woman."

I watched as both of them exited the kitchen, leaving me standing with my husband who looked dumbfounded at what was going down.

"Really, Devin? *This* is how you do me?"

"Monica, I told you, nothing was going on."

"I'm supposed to believe that when you asked me for a divorce? To me, it seems like you are not wasting any time. You are already attaching yourself to another woman when we are still married to each other."

"You can take it how you want. It's evident I can't change your mind," he said.

"I'm *still* your wife. And being that I am, you will respect me as such. We are *not* divorced. I'm *not* giving up on us. Not like this."

"I'm done with this conversation. I'm done with you. I don't know how many times I have to tell you I don't love you anymore," he said sternly, and my heart broke again.

Giving him a disapproving gaze, I nodded, knowing I had no more words to say to him at this time.

"Can you please leave?"

Eyes skimming over the man I loved, I searched for an inkling of emotion to let me know this man still loved me . . . but I found none. For a moment, we held each other's gaze. My eyes pleaded with him to stay with me, but his yearned for me to leave. Blinking back the tears that threatened to escape, I brushed past my husband, thinking this was not the end of us.

Vivian

17

When I walked into the restaurant, the first thing I noticed was how bright and airy the space was. The floors were a honey-blond hardwood, and everything within the space was white. White walls. White tables and chairs. There were even white curtain drapes hanging from the floor-to-ceiling windows which overlooked a garden. As if that wasn't enough to cause me to be in awe of this space, the main feature was this magnificent wall of branches sculpted to look like circular waves. It took up the length of the space and was something to look at.

As a hostess greeted me to ask me how many would be in my party, I saw Monica waving her hand for me to come over. I told the woman I saw my party and smiled as I walked over to meet Monica.

"I'm so glad you could make it," she said standing to embrace me.

"Thank you for inviting me. I hope I'm not late," I said sitting next to her at the table.

"You are right on time. I just got here myself."

"I probably need to spend a few minutes taking this space in. This place is spectacular," I said still taking in the scenery.

"I'm glad you like it. I love this place. It's nicknamed the Museum Restaurant. My husband and I used to come here all the time."

"Used to?" I asked curiously, wondering if it was too soon to get all up in her business. Coming here I was a bit nervous because I'd just met Monica a few months ago and we seem to hit it off. I didn't make friends easily because I was so used to dealing with my sisters. They were my friends, and I missed them tremendously. At the same time, I knew it was time to find other ladies I could hang with, and Monica, so far, seemed like the type of camaraderie I needed in my life. And being the open book she was, she graciously answered my question.

"Devin works a lot. It's been hard finding time to go out like this, you know."

"I do. Sheldon has been working like crazy as well. He's working today, as a matter of fact. I know it's for our benefit, but sometimes you just want to be with your man."

Monica smiled but seemed a bit down from some reason. It wasn't until we brought up our spouses that I noticed the change in her mood.

"Are you okay, Monica?" I asked sincerely.

"I'm trying to be. It's been a rough day already for me," she sighed.

"Not already?"

"I'm having some marital issues. Devin and I not coming to this restaurant anymore is nothing compared to the other issues we are dealing with," she revealed with a worried look on her face.

"All marriages have their fair share of difficulties, trust me. I'm dealing with some in my own marriage. But we will be okay. We married our husbands for better or worse. We just weren't counting on having as many worse moments compared to those better moments," I said chuckling.

Monica smiled warmly, like she appreciated what I said.

"I knew I liked you for some reason. We truly have a lot in common," Monica expressed.

That we did. Monica was a plus-size sister also who carried herself very well. Like today, she was rocking a cute yellow and white chevron striped maxi dress that looked great on her. I could tell she was the type of woman who embraced her curves, and I yearned to have the confidence she portrayed. I didn't look bad in my blue denim jumpsuit with a studded belt and tan espadrilles.

"You look good today too, girl. And, yes, I'm trying to change the subject," I chuckled.

"Thank you. You looked great as well. Where did you come from?" Monica asked.

"Well, I went by this boutique to meet with this manager who offered me a job."

"That's fabulous. Did you accept?" she asked with excitement.

"I did. That's why I was running behind. I was coming from there."

"Congratulations. I'm happy for you."

"Thank you."

"What will you be doing?"

"She actually wants me to manage a new plus-size boutique she's in the process of opening," I explained.

"Well, look at you."

I couldn't believe I'd accepted, but I was excited. I couldn't stop smiling at this opportunity that fell into my lap. As much as I wondered if moving here was a mistake, God kept revealing to me that my husband and I were exactly where we were supposed to be.

"Oh, I see, Sonya," Monica said as she waved her hand for her friend to come over.

This was my first time meeting these ladies, and I hoped we'd hit it off as much Monica and I did. Moments later, another plus-size sister approached our table dressed in a pair of red fitted pants and a sheer tropical print top which was cute.

"Sorry I'm late," she apologized. "I had to make sure my daughter was good. It's sad when you can't leave your teenage daughter at home by herself."

"You got her a babysitter?" Monica asked.

As Sonya lowered herself in the chair across from Monica, she explained, "I should have, but I allowed her to go over her friend's house for a little while. She really needs to be grounded for how she's been acting, but that's another story for another day. I'm just happy to be here because I really needed this girl time."

"I'm glad you are here," Monica added.

Looking at me, Sonya said, "Oh, I'm sorry. I've rattled off at the mouth before I had a chance to introduce myself. I'm Sonya."

"I'm Vivian. And it's okay," I said as I shook her outstretched hand.

"It's finally nice to meet you. Monica has told me a lot about you. I promise you I have better manners than this."

"Do you?" Monica asked jokingly.

"Well . . . some," Sonya quipped. "I'm a work in progress. But anyway, Monica said you are new to the area."

"I am."

"Do you have any family here?" Sonya asked.

"Unfortunately, I don't. It's just me and my husband, Sheldon."

"Well, I'm glad you two have decided to make Greensboro your home. I know you will enjoy it here."

So far so good I thought. Sonya seemed great. She reminded me a lot of my sister Shauna which I found comforting. As she continued to talk, I knew she was going to have me laughing or feeling uneasy because Sonya seemed like the type of woman who said whatever came to her mind.

"And where's this heifer?" Sonya asked, pointing to the last seat at the table.

"Girl, I don't know. You know Kellie," Monica chided.

"Yeah, young and dumb."

"Sonya!" Monica belted. "She's not that young, and she's damn sure not dumb."

"Maybe I shouldn't say it quite like that. All I was trying to say is I know she's going to burn our ears up with some type of problems she's been having."

"Don't we all?" Monica replied.

"Yes, we do, but, we don't unload our issues every time we get together. Sometimes you just want to laugh and trip with your girlfriends instead of talking about what's always going wrong in our lives."

There was the personality I suspected with my first impression of Sonya, and I liked it. She was the type of woman that said it like she meant it regardless if you liked it or not. I would like to think I was the same way, but I believe I was more reserved in speaking my mind than Sonya.

"You have to understand she's still learning. We are ladies in our thirties. Kellie is still in her twenties," Monica explained.

I said nothing as I listened to the two of them go back and forth wondering how old Kellie was. So I decided to ask.

"How old is Kellie?"

"She's twenty-eight," Sonya answered with her mouth twisted like it was a problem.

I nodded thinking that's not too young.

"I used to work with Kellie, and we became great friends. She may be younger than us, but she's definitely a mature and smart woman. She's been through some things, but who hasn't. She doesn't have the best relationship with her mother, and her dad, unfortunately, is deceased."

"Which explains her marrying a man ten years older than her," Sonya quipped.

"Girl, if you don't stop," Monica advised as she chuckled.

"Excuse me, Vivian. It's not that I don't like Kellie because I do. She's beautiful and intelligent. But sometimes you just don't feel like hearing that crap," Sonya explained. "I got enough going on with me and my rebellious child that sometimes I don't feel like taking on other people's problems."

I made a note to myself to never confide in Sonya. Not that I didn't understand where she was coming from because I did. I remember Mom saying a long time ago be careful taking on other people's issues because many times, those same issues would become yours.

"Speaking of venting," Monica said looking at Sonya pointedly, "how do you feel about Kegan getting married?"

Sonya's expression hardened as she gawked at Monica. If looks could kill, Monica would be six feet under right about now.

Turning her attention to me, Sonya pointed at Monica and said, "You see, it's tricks like this that get on my damn nerve."

"What?" Monica asked. "I was just wondering."

"Seriously, though, Monica, how do you think I feel about it?" she hissed. "The asshole had the audacity to send me an invitation to his wedding."

"No," Monica said as her hand covered her mouth in shock.

"Yes, and I'm feeling some type of way about it."

"Are you going?" Monica asked.

"I don't know yet. I want to, but then again, I don't. I might be provoked to object when the pastor asks if there is anyone who objects to their union, speak now or forever hold your peace."

"You wouldn't," Monica chided.

Sonya gave her a look like she would as she picked up her glass of water and took a sip.

I sat there wondering who Kegan was. Just from the conversation they were having, I rationalized that Kegan had to be Sonya's ex.

"Look, I don't want to talk about him. He and I are over."

"I know you were fussing about venting, Sonya, but sometimes, it's good to vent to each other, especially when we feel like we don't have anybody else to turn to," Monica deduced.

"Well, we need to vent to Kellie about always being late, because I'm getting tired of her always being the last one to show up. I'm getting ready to order without her."

"Look, before she gets here, let me run an idea by you ladies."

Both Sonya and I looked at Monica as excitement filled her.

"The three of us are bodacious, beautiful women," she said carefully.

"You mean plus size," Sonya surmised.

"Yes, Sonya, dag. Can't you take a compliment?"

"I can, but I also like to be real."

We all chuckled as Monica continued.

"I was thinking about having a clothing swap party."

"A what?" Sonya asked.

"A clothing swap party. You never heard of it?"

"No," Sonya answered.

"I have. I think I saw something about that on Oprah one time."

"Exactly. It's when a bunch of women get together and swap pieces of gently used clothing. I would invite women around our size and set a limit on the amount of clothing you can bring."

Monica mainly looked at Sonya probably because she would be the hardest one to convince.

"I think it's a great idea," I agreed.

"What if I don't have clothes to swap?" Sonya asked.

"You have clothes, Sonya, so stop playing. I'm pretty sure you can find several pieces you are willing to part with."

"I have been meaning to clean out my closet," she said.

"Fall is approaching. With the season getting ready to change, we can get rid of some items," Monica stated.

"Does it just have to be clothes?" Sonya asked.

"No. We can add purses, scarves, jewelry, and shoes if you want to. It's up to us. Just let me know."

"I think that's fabulous. Lord knows I need to get rid of some shoes I have. I think I have a few pair with the tags still on them," I said thinking of the massive collection of shoes I'd acquired over the years. Shoes and purses were my addiction. Well, that and food maybe.

"What size shoe do you wear?" Sonya asked me.

"I wear a size ten."

"I'm in," Sonya blurted. "If the shoes you have on now are any indication of what your shoe game is like, I want to participate. You heifers have great style, so I would love to see what you want to part with."

I took Sonya calling me a heifer as a good thing because when my sisters and I did this, it was a sign of admiration. I think she liked me, and I liked her as well.

"Did you have this little meeting now because Kellie is a bean stalk?" Sonya asked.

"Yes and no. I would love for her to participate also. Maybe she can bring items other than clothes because none of us will be able to get into hers."

"You better call her and see where she is. We are not sitting here all day waiting on Ms. Thang to show up," Sonya grumbled.

"Let me call her."

Monica took out her cell and dialed Kellie while I looked over the menu to figure out what I wanted for lunch. It felt good to get out, and I have to say I was truly enjoying myself. I needed something to keep my mind distracted from thinking about my husband and what was going on with him.

Kellie

18

"Play No Games" by Big Sean played in the background, and I thought it was fitting for the way I was feeling right now. Jeffrey was definitely playing games. I thought once I got married, the games would stop, but evidently, they haven't. I felt like I worked for Hasbro or was at least the face of their games. For real, my marriage fell into many of their game categories. Let's see, what about the game "Sorry," because I was sorry I ever married this man. He was also real good at telling me how sorry he was for hurting me all the time. Or, "Risk," which was what I took when I decided he would be the man I would spend the rest of my life with. Maybe "Clue" because I didn't have a damn clue about the man he really was. Or perhaps "Bonkers," because that's how I've felt being married to him. How about "Trouble," because that's what he would be in if my doctor told me I couldn't have children. I was still waiting on my results from the blood test and ultrasound. The longer I waited, the more stressed out I got. But right now, the best game would be "Guess Who," because I was always guessing who was going to be the next woman he would betray me for. But who knew men were part of the equation as well?

Anger simmered within me as I remained on hold waiting for my call to be the next one taken by an XM radio station I listen to quite often. I never was one to chime in on things like this because I thought it was putting too much of your personal business in the street, but today, I didn't care because today's subject was fitting for my current situation.

My phone beeped. I pulled it away from my face to see Monica was calling me. She was probably checking to see where I was because I was late. I couldn't answer her right now with me waiting to be the next caller. I thought it was my brother checking on me. When I left, he was still asleep in the guest bedroom. I told him about the lunch with my friends last night, but he decided to pass on it this time. I knew he was still tired from that drive here and knew that was the reason why he decided not to join us.

"You are the next caller in queue," the automated voice said as my heart sped up awaiting the radio DJ to pick up.

"Caller, can I ask your name please and where you are calling from?" a voice said.

I was caught off guard. I didn't want to give my real name. Bad enough I was even making this call, but to give my name . . . I had to think of one quick.

"Caller, are you there?"

"Yes. Betty," I said, giving a false name. "My name is Betty, and I'm calling from North Carolina."

Of all the names I could think of, I thought of Betty. I had an aunt named Betty, who I loved dearly, but nowadays, no one named their child Betty. Hell, my aunt was the only Betty I knew.

"Okay, Betty," he said in a tone like he knew I made the name up on the spot. "What are some red flags that your significant other is cheating?"

"Would you call getting an STD a sign of him cheating?" I said as I pulled up in a space at the restaurant.

"Whoa!" rang out as the sound effects on the other end sounded like a studio audience gasping at my revelation.

"That's a *huge* red flag if I ever saw one. Am I wrong to believe it was you who got this STD?" the DJ asked.

Silence from my end. Should I continue to talk about this? Would anyone recognize my voice? What in the world was I thinking? I never should have called in on this subject. I really didn't think this thing through.

"Caller?"

"Yes," I said nervously. "You would be correct. I was the one who got burned. As you can tell, it's hard to talk about."

"I can see why. Can I ask who gave you this STD?"

"My husband," I answered tersely.

"Damn" sound effect rang out before the DJ spoke again.

"Wow, this just keeps getting worse, my sister."

"Who are you telling?" I mumbled.

"Are you still with him?"

"I actually kicked him out last night when I caught some man sucking on his—"

"Whoa . . ." the DJ stopped me. "This is a very respectable show."

Laughter rang out like it was a joke before he continued to talk.

"So, not only did you get an STD, you caught your man with another man?" he asked.

"Yes."

"Did you know your husband was gay or bisexual?"

"Not at all. I'm still trying to understand this myself. Is something wrong with me that I didn't see my own husband had a thing for men?"

"Yo, this is crazy. You caught me off guard with this one."

"Try being in my shoes," I retorted.

"No, thank you, sweetheart. But let me ask you this. Do you still love him?"

"Of course, I do."

"Do you guys plan on working it out?"

"Right now, I don't want to. He's hurt me too many times."

"The fact you said 'right now' is an indication there is still a chance. If this man has cheated on you once, and I'm pretty sure this is not his first time, he's going to do it again. You really need to protect yourself. Men like him don't change. I know my audience is going to be mad at me for saying this, but that's what I believe. You getting this STD and catching him with another man should be your wake-up call, sweetie. The next time he could bring you something that could affect your health permanently," the radio personality said. "Once a cheater, always a cheater."

Clapping sound effects rang out as I thought about how my health may already be permanently affected, and this caused tears to form.

"Caller, think of yourself enough to divorce this man. You are worth more than you give yourself credit. Good luck to you and thank you for calling."

I hung up still listening as the DJ took the next caller who was another female who wanted to chime in.

"Caller, give us your name and where you're calling from."

"My name is Sydelle, and I'm calling from North Carolina too."

"Okay. You from the same state our last caller is from. North Carolina on fire tonight."

How ironic was this I thought as I listened to the DJ continue.

"Caller, what's your red flag?"

"I was calling about that last chick that was on the line. She needs to leave that man."

"We think so too caller, but why is that any of your concern? We wanted you to give us other signs, not talk about what another female needs to do," the DJ responded.

I thought the same thing, getting angry at the woman that didn't know me. I guess this was one of the consequences of me calling in.

"Okay. You want a red flag. I *am* the red flag," the caller declared boldly.

"What do you mean?" the DJ asked.

"I'm usually the other woman."

"Oh really?" the DJ's voice perked up as I gasped at this woman's admission.

"Uh-huh. Every man I'm with is married."

"So, I take it you are sleeping with these married men?" the DJ asked.

"You damn right I am. I only sleep with married men," the woman divulged shamelessly.

"Why do you choose to only sleep with married men?"

"Because it's easy. Yes, they hit it then quit it. I get mine. They get theirs, and they get the hell up out of my place when we done."

"So you just getting your rocks off?" the DJ asked.

"That and I'm hitting them pockets up too. Do you take me for a fool?"

"Well . . ." the DJ said and laughing effects sounded.

"I like sex, and I like nice things, and these men can provide both for me."

I couldn't believe what I was hearing. I looked at the radio like the image of this woman was going to pop up on my radio. I thought she could very well be one of the women my husband had slept with, and this frightened me. It sounded like his type . . . uneducated but willing to spread her legs for whoever could afford her. The audacity of this woman to admit to sleeping with only married men for her own pleasure and rewards. Then I wondered if Jeffrey might have paid for sex or even given lavish gifts as a thank-you for services rendered. I continued to listen as the conversation progressed.

"What have you received from these men?" the DJ asked.

"I got one paying the note on my brand-new condo. I got one keeping me in the best designer clothes his money can buy. I had one buy me the new Range Rover I'm driving. Plus, I got mad cash in the bank. I'm living the perfect life," this woman said, like she was proud of her achievements.

"You don't see this as morally wrong?" the DJ asked.

"Why should I? I'm not the one who's married. They are. I didn't say vows to no one. If they want to risk their souls going to hell, then that's on them. I'm just a woman who's reaping the rewards."

"You know you are coming off as a prostitute, right?"

"Call me a businesswoman."

"Again, prostitute," the DJ affirmed.

"That's your opinion, and trust me, I've been called worse. The fact still remains my bank account is fat, and my life is great."

"That's all well and good, but it looks like you need to be worrying about your soul being damned to hell also, sweetie. Somebody who claims life is great all the time is lying to themselves. There's a reason why you do what you do. Just from this conversation, I hear a woman who doesn't value herself, much less love herself," the DJ emphasized.

"Please, I love me some me."

"Then stop cheapening yourself by playing hooker and spreading your thighs for all these men."

"I'm not a hooker," she yelled.

"I'll say a prayer for you, caller, since you think what you are doing is okay. I can see that's the only thing that's going to help you."

The DJ disconnected the call as I sat in my ride thinking about what this woman said. I didn't know what I was going to do about my marriage. My head was telling me to file for divorce on Monday, but my heart still had love for Jeffrey. Why couldn't he be faithful and love me like he promised? I guess that was too much to ask. Men cheat on all kinds. Look at Halle Barry.

Vivian

19

Sonya felt like we'd waited long enough and suggested we all order our food. I was with Sonya, because I was hungry. I hadn't eaten anything all day as I looked forward to this lunch. Breakfast was not a meal I like to eat often, which was why I probably was gaining weight. I knew breakfast was the most important meal of the day and got my metabolism started to burn calories, but I still couldn't manage to fit it in.

I ordered a turkey sandwich with provolone with roasted tomatoes and pickles and a side of sweet potato fries. Sonya order braised beef ribs with a mixed green salad, and Monica ordered a chicken salad sandwich with a mixed green salad. It seemed like as soon as our food was placed on the table, Sonya saw Kellie approaching.

"Speak of the devil," Sonya said, and I turned to see a very attractive woman approaching our table.

"Hey, ladies. Sorry I'm late."

"It's about time you got here," Monica quipped as she stood to hug who I figured was Kellie. She spoke to Sonya, but there were no hugs for her as she sat across from me and beside Sonya.

"We went ahead and ordered our food. Nobody wanted to wait on you all day," Sonya said.

"I understand. I didn't expect for you to wait for me," she replied, hanging her purse on the back of her chair.

"Kellie, this is Vivian," Monica introduced.

"It's nice to meet you," she said smiling.

She was definitely not a plus-size sister. She wasn't even in the double digits. And to say she was beautiful was an understatement.

"Are you trying to show us up?" Sonya asked Kellie.

"What are you talking about?" she asked, pushing back her luscious curls from her face.

Kellie was rocking a pair of white deconstructed jeans with a yellow peplum top with mesh over the shoulders and around her very toned midsection. A pair of nude heels completed her look. I knew she had to be no bigger than a 7/8.

"It's not bad enough you're younger than us and skinnier than us, but you come in here looking fly as hell too?" Sonya admonished.

"Please, I'm not looking all that."

"This coming from the ultimate diva," Sonya quipped.

"You know I'm not like that," Kellie said. "You're going to have Vivian thinking I'm some stuck-up woman."

"You are."

"Sonya!" Kellie belted.

"Okay. You're not. I'm just playing."

"Thank you," Kellie said, giggling.

"But you do look nice with your skinny ass."

"So do y'all, looking all fabulous. You calling me skinny, you know I want to gain some weight, but I can't," Kellie said. "The more I eat, the more I lose."

"I knew there was a reason why I hated this wench," Sonya uttered.

"You know you love me," Kellie said, leaning over, hugging Sonya playfully. All Sonya did was roll her eyes as she placed a piece of rib into her mouth.

"I wish I had that problem," I chimed in, picking up my glass of water and taking a sip from it.

"Me too. I can just look at food and gain twenty pounds," Monica added.

"Ladies, please don't hate," Kellie said.

"We don't hate you, but we do hate the fact you can eat whatever you want to and not gain an ounce," Monica countered.

"I second that," Vivian said.

"Enough about me, ladies. I see you ordered my favorite for me," Kellie said, looking at the mango Mojito Monica order for herself and Kellie. "I need some alcohol in my life. Especially after the stressful days I've had," Kellie exclaimed.

Sonya gave Monica a knowing look, and Monica's expression let Sonya know to leave this alone, but it was quickly ignored.

"So what do you need a drink for?" Sonya asked.

Before Kellie had an opportunity to answer, a waitress came over to our table and took Kellie's lunch order. She decided to order a burger with the works and a side of sweet potato fries. When the waitress left to retrieve her food, Kellie picked up where she left off.

"I don't think I have the heart to tell you guys what's been going on with me without getting liquored up first," Kellie expressed as she picked up her Mojito and gulped it down until nothing was left.

"It's that bad?" Sonya asked, looking at her with a scowl. "Maybe we should have ordered you two."

"How about four?" Kellie groaned.

"So spill it," Sonya told Kellie not wasting any time.

"Dang, Sonya. Can I get another drink down first?"

"No."

We all chuckled as Kellie looked at all of us. Her mood quickly changed as her eyes began to fill with tears.

"Kellie, no. Please don't cry," Monica consoled.

I reached over and took Kellie's hand into mine, not knowing what else I should do. She squeezed it as she smiled weakly, and I was glad I could comfort her in this way.

"It's me and Jeffrey, of course."

"Of course."

"Stop it, Sonya," Monica scolded.

Sonya picked up her drink and looked on for Kellie to continue.

"Remember I told you guys Jeffrey has been cheating on me?"

The ladies nodded as I listened because I didn't know about anything going on.

"Well, I went to the doctor because I was having some abdominal pain. Come to find out I have an STD."

I think all of our mouths fell open at her admission. Kellie dropped her head in shame as two tears finally managed to stream down her cheeks.

"I'm so sorry, Kellie," I said, not knowing what else to say in this case.

"Did you cut his dick off?" Sonya asked.

This caused Kellie to giggle as she shook her head no.

"I would have. That bastard would have been left with a stump when I was done with him," Sonya continued.

"Something is wrong with you," Monica admitted. "Because you *are* crazy."

"Yes, I'm a little touched, but life made me this way," Sonya agreed.

I nodded in agreement, thinking back on my own life. From my father's affair which created a child outside his marriage, to my sister dying, I too had a lot of dysfunction in my life.

"If you would have dumped him when I told you to, you might not be in this predicament now."

"Sonya, stop being so hard on her. We need to comfort her, not scold her. Besides, Jeffrey is her husband, and she loves him," Monica replied.

"What does love have to do with it?" Sonya asked. "What did Halle say in the movie *Boomerang? Love should have brought your ass home last night.*"

Kellie frowned as she asked, "What movie?"

"*Boomerang*. You *have* seen it, haven't you?"

"No. When did that come out?" Kellie asked.

Sonya rolled her eyes as she said, "I forgot how old you were."

"The movie came out in nineteen ninety-two," Monica said.

"I was born in eighty-eight."

"You know what? I'm going to buy that movie for you to watch," Sonya remarked. "Then you will see what I'm talking about. Hell, you might learn something."

All of us laughed as Sonya's cell phone began to ring. At that same moment, the waitress was bringing Kellie her food, placing it down in front of her. We all watched as Sonya looked at the screen before answering it.

"Yes, Meena," she spoke.

Sonya's face went from annoyance to pure rage.

"What?" she yelled as she stood to her feet.

We all looked at her with concern.

"I'll be right there," she said jerking her purse off the back of her chair as she stumbled back.

"What is it, Sonya?" Monica asked frantically.

"It's Meena. She's been arrested . . . for shoplifting."

Sonya

20

When I walked into that Macy's office where the police held the criminals bold enough to commit a crime, I seethed, hoping I didn't put my hands on my own criminal child. I prayed to the good Lord above to give me the strength to not act a fool up in this establishment, knowing I could be the next one to get arrested for assault.

Meena was sitting in one of the chairs with two other girls by her side, one of which I recognized as her friend Shannon. She'd cut her long hair, and now it was short and dyed medium brown. Her new hairstyle accentuated her facial features. The other young lady looked like someone I'd seen before. She was also cute with braids leading up to a natural puff atop her head. Her black lipstick made her golden-brown complexion glow.

Looking at my daughter who had her head down, I said, "Don't look sad now. I can't believe you, Meena. What the hell is wrong with you?"

"But, Mom—"

I held my hand up to stop her from even talking. Before she said anything to me, I wanted to talk to the officer about exactly what happened. It was bad enough I had to end my luncheon with my friends and admit that the unlawful actions of my daughter was the reason why I had to leave them so abruptly, but the cop who was in the room with them was one of the finest black men I'd seen in a while. Talk about embarrassing. What was he going to think of me having a teen who felt entitled to taking things that didn't belong to her? Kids didn't understand when they did things like this, their actions were a representation of the parent, and I hated anyone looking at me like I wasn't doing something right. Granted, I wasn't the perfect mom, but I did my best raising Meena. And I damn sure didn't teach her to steal.

"Ms. Gordon," the very handsome chocolate man said approaching in his tailored police uniform.

"Yes, I'm *Miss* Gordon," making sure to emphasize miss so he would know I wasn't married. I couldn't take my eyes off him. His body was chiseled. He was at least five inches taller than me, which I loved. He had a low fade with waves tapered into a full thick beard nicely edged up. And his smile was radiant. I hung on this man's every word.

"My name is Officer Damon Ward. I'm sorry to call you under these circumstances."

And his voice was guttural, deep enough to make the space between my thighs quiver just from his tone. I hadn't had a man make me feel this way since Kegan.

"I'm sorry you had to call me too, but you have a job to do," I replied. "Can you please tell me what happened?" I asked, finally getting control of myself.

"Your daughter was the lookout for these young ladies who attempted to steal a few items of clothing from this store. Your daughter even brought them items she wanted for herself from my understanding. If it wasn't for one of them forgetting to remove one of the sensors, they probably would have gotten away," Officer Ward explained.

I gave all three girls a disapproving gaze as my daughter and the other girl glared accusingly at Shannon. I knew then she must have been the one to get them all caught. Officer Ward continued.

"Honestly, I think they have done this before just by the way they went about getting the items. Well, that and the fact one of them had the contraption to remove the sensor piece support my determination."

"I can't believe this," I said swiping at my hair fretfully.

I walked over to Meena who stared up at me with a bleak expression.

"Really, Meena? So, this is how you roll now. You're stealing from stores too?"

"No," she snapped.

Before I knew it, I snatched my daughter up by the arm lifting her from the seat. Her impassive eyes quickly turned to alarm when she realized I had my hands on her.

"You are the one accused of shoplifting and you have the audacity to get an attitude with me?" I said heatedly.

"Ma, I don't have an attitude," she corrected.

"You snapping at me don't show me you don't have an attitude. It shows me you think I'm going to take that smart mouth of yours because I'm in front of your friends and this cop. I had to leave my friends to come down here and pick your behind up over this nonsense, and you got the nerve to try to act hard in front of everybody? Did you forget who I am, Meena?"

I must have been gripping her too tightly because she began to whine.

"Ma, you're hurting me."

"It's better I hurt you than somebody else. Now, answer my question. Did you forget who I am?" I asked again.

"No, ma'am."

"I told you I don't give a damn where I am. If you disrespect me, I will not hesitate to let you know who's the parent and who's the child. Don't think because this police officer is here, I'm not going to act a fool because I will. I told you before, if I have to go to jail over something regarding you, I'm going to damn sure make it worth my while. And if that entails whooping your ass until they get the strength enough to pull me off of you, then so be it."

Meena shifted her eyes to the officer like she was hoping he was going to help her, but I didn't care about anybody in this room. If she wanted to act like a grown-ass woman, then I was going to beat her ass like she was a grown-ass woman.

"Ms. Gordon," Officer Ward spoke in a warning tone.

I continued to glower at Meena, ultimately letting go of her arm before I turned my attention back to Officer Ward.

"I'm sorry, but I didn't raise my child to do no mess like this," I asserted angrily.

"I understand," he responded, giving me a small smile.

"So, what's going to happen now?"

"The store wants to press charges against the young ladies to teach them a lesson."

"So now they're going to have a record?"

"Yes, ma'am, but only up until they turn eighteen. Then their record can be closed or even expunged. However, their records can be reopened if they are found guilty of a crime in the future, which can be used against them in the court of law. So, right now, it's up to these young ladies about which direction they choose to take," he graciously explained.

I was observing the girls when he explained this, and one of them had the nerve to smirk.

"Do you think this is funny?" I addressed the young lady I didn't know.

She didn't bother to answer as she gave me a look of annoyance.

"Did you hear me?"

"Yo, Meena, you better get your mom," the young girl said cockily.

I chuckled as I pointed to this little girl and asked Meena, "Who is this?"

Meena hesitated before saying, "Asha."

I stepped closer to Asha watching her smug expression change to one of nervousness. Officer Ward clasped my arm gently to stop me. He looked at me with sincerity. It was like I could hear him say I couldn't act like that with somebody else's child.

I scowled at Meena's so-called friend who didn't look too cocky anymore before saying, "Little girl, you better be glad this officer is here because I would teach you a lesson as well. Nothing burns me up more than a disrespectful child."

She must've understood the craziness that resided within me because she dared not respond.

There was a knock at the door before it opened and in walked Shannon's mom, Abigail. Even though she was dressed in a shiny gold-pleated taffeta shirt dress looking like she'd just stepped off *The Stepford Wives* movie, her face was blanketed with worry. She looked like she'd been crying. I always thought Abigail was a nice-looking woman with her olive complexion and layered bob. She was about my height, five foot five, but she was a lot smaller than I was. She appeared to be a size three. She was the same size as her daughter, even though Shannon had a model physique standing about five foot seven. I got along with Abigail, but to me, she came across a bit stuck-up.

When she saw Shannon, she beelined to her daughter and embraced her lovingly. *I guess shoplifting warranted a hug,* I thought.

"Honey, tell me what happened. Tell me you had nothing to do with this," Abigail said in a tone that would make anybody lie to her.

Shannon didn't respond. Clearly, you could tell by Abigail's demeanor she didn't believe Shannon had anything to do with this.

"Tell me who made you do this, honey," Abigail said, now looking suspiciously at Meena and Asha.

"Mom, I just want to go home," Shannon uttered glumly like she was going to burst into tears herself.

Abigail took her daughter by the hand as she turned to Officer Ward.

"Can I take my daughter home?"

"Yes, ma'am, but like I explained to Ms. Gordon, the store will be pressing charges."

"Why?" she asked in disbelief.

"Miss Brooks—" Officer Ward said before Abigail cut him off.

"It's *Mrs.*"

With a half smile, Officer Ward said, "Mrs. Brooks, your daughter was involved in shoplifting, which is a crime," he clarified with brows furrowed.

"They *made* Shannon do this," she accused. "My child has never done anything like this before. Not until she started hanging with the likes of them."

Abigail's attitude was terse and downright condemning as she pointed to my daughter and Asha, and I didn't like it. It was one thing to comfort your daughter and act like she's an angel, but it was another when she thought I was going to allow her to come at my child, and someone else's, for that matter, like they are the problem.

"Wait a minute, Abigail. You can't blame my daughter or this other young lady," I interjected. "They all did this together."

"Yes, I can, and I have. My daughter is not like . . . like *them*."

"Like *them?*" I asked, getting upset. "What in the hell does that mean?"

"Those girls are . . . are . . ."

"Say it," I dared.

"Look, I just want to leave," Abigail recoiled, evidently noticing the look of contempt I had.

"They didn't *make* Shannon do anything she didn't want to do."

Ignoring my statement, Abigail went on to say, "I was hesitant about Shannon even being friends with Meena, but I felt sorry for her."

"Sorry?" I replied defensively.

"Yes, sorry. She needed a true friend, and Shannon offers companionship wherever she goes."

She was talking like her daughter was selling friendship to underprivileged kids. Granted, my daughter didn't have as many assets as they did, but friends weren't hard to come by. Friends came a dime a dozen, and even then, most weren't friends; they were associates.

"I knew I should have gone with my gut and not allowed you to hang with them," Abigail said to Shannon, who looked pleased by her mother's behavior. Probably because her mother always cleaned up her mess for her. One day, they will realize all messes can't be straightened out. How can anyone learn anything if there are never any consequences to their bad actions?

"I'm not going to keep listening to you talk about these young ladies like this, Abigail."

"Please, I've heard what she's been up to, hanging out with kids who drink and do drugs. Shannon told me everything because my daughter and I communicate like a good mother and daughter should."

Inhaling deeply I asked, "Meena has never done anything like that. If she was doing those things, how do I know your daughter wasn't the one who introduced my daughter to it?"

"Shannon is a straight-A student with many medals and honors of achievement. She would never do what you are trying to insinuate."

"My child has good grades also. Yet, you stand here accusing her of this."

"We all know Meena is on her way to being some hoodlum's girlfriend or pregnant by a hoodlum. Both she and Asha are trouble and need some serious help."

I was getting tired of Abigail's sanctimonious banter. She could take up for Shannon all the wanted, but her steady stream of insults toward my daughter was going to warrant me beating her ass.

"How about we take our daughters together to a shrink?" I suggested with sarcasm looking at Shannon, knowing this young lady was going to need some mental help as well. I knew it was wrong to stoop to Abigail's level, but I didn't care, especially when it came to my child.

"My daughter is great and will be even better when I ban her from hanging with *them,*" she pointed, like Meena and Asha were trash. "Shannon is on the right path and will continue to skyrocket, leaving those two far behind."

I looked at the girls and saw the resentment within them. Officer Ward stepped in between Abigail and me. I guess he could sense how badly I wanted to punch this holier-than-thou woman in her not-so-holy mouth.

"Mrs. Brooks, you can't blame these young ladies without including your own daughter in this. She was the one who got caught with the stolen merchandise."

"That's because they *made* her do it," she bellowed.

"No one made her do it. We have the footage of her coming out of the dressing room alone. Meena was the lookout and wasn't even in the dressing room with them. And Asha was in a stall beside your daughter."

Giving him a look of contempt, Abigail smoothed her hair as she said, "I'm taking my child home."

"That's fine," Officer Ward retorted.

"Rest assured, no charges will be brought against my daughter. I know the vice president of this company, and I will be giving him a call on how you treated my daughter and how you spoke to me."

"Suit yourself, Mrs. Brooks."

Shannon and her mom stormed out of the room attempting to look like the victims. I looked at Officer Ward as I shook my head in irritation.

With eyes narrowed I said, "You see why I tell you to carry yourself with dignity and respect, Meena."

My daughter lowered her head in shame.

"People like her will blame you for everything just because of where you live and definitely how you carry yourself. Both of you know better than this," I addressed Meena and Asha.

"Shannon was the one who came up with the idea to steal in the first place," Asha divulged. "She's the one who gave us the contraption to remove the sensor."

"It all makes sense how she got it. If her mother knows the vice president of the company, then Shannon probably had access to get the sensor remover," Meena added.

"This is my first time doing anything like this," Asha professed.

"Me too," Meena agreed.

"And you see what happened?" I asked.

Both nodded.

"Her mother is going to pin this entire thing on both of you," I explained.

Officer Ward interrupted by saying, "We don't always have to know who came up with what because in our eyes, all of you are guilty until proven innocent."

"I thought it was innocent until proven guilty," Asha said.

"It can go both ways. When it comes to the law, you are already guilty by association, especially when you commit a crime, and especially if you are African American. I hate to say that but that's the way the world looks at us. I see women like Mrs. Brooks all the time who throw their money around and know the right people in the right places to get their children off."

"But we didn't—"

"You didn't have to do anything, Meena. That's what we're trying to tell you. If she steals and you are with her, then you go down too. Just like if she decided to commit a murder and you are with her. Then both of you would go to jail. It's that simple. That's why I've always told you to be careful about the company you keep."

"Your mother is right," Officer Ward agreed.

Our eyes locked for a moment before we were interrupted by another knock at the door. I thought it was Abigail returning to chastise us some more, but when I saw the woman who entered, I almost wished it was Abigail.

Sonya

21

When I recognized the woman who sauntered into the room, my stomach plummeted as my heart thundered in my chest. Imani's willowy frame stood before me in a pair of cargo shorts, a tank top showing off her pierced navel, and a pair of new white Nikes. Her hair was done in burgundy braids which were pulled atop her head in a neat bun. She looked like Asha's sister instead of her mother. Now, I knew why I thought I'd recognized Asha from somewhere. She looked like her mother. I had no clue Asha belonged to the woman responsible for breaking Kegan and me up.

I tightened my fist and didn't know I was doing so until I felt my nails digging into the palms of my hands.

A wicked grin spread across her face as she said, "Now, it makes sense."

"What makes sense?" I asked.

"Why my daughter is in trouble. She's hanging with Meena."

What was this—blame it all on Meena day?

"Don't talk about my daughter," I warned.

"Why? She's the reason why my child is in this predicament."

I so wanted to say the reason why her child was in this situation was because she had you as her mother and Asha only acted out what she saw in her. Underhandedness begets underhandedness. Imani was not excluded from being a criminal. She had a record also, for stealing. I guess she forgot her criminal actions were public record. As bad as I wanted to throw her past in her face, I decided that was not the right thing to do.

Inhaling, I said, "Our daughters are in trouble because they chose to do something ridiculous. There is no need to point fingers when all of them are responsible for their own actions, and each of them will have to deal with the consequences. It's as simple as that."

"Is that right?" she croaked.

"Yes, that's right," I managed to say coolly.

I was really trying not to stoop to the ghetto antics I knew Imani was all about. I could tell by the way she was glaring at me she wanted to start something. Why? She had Kegan now, even if she used her ass to take him from me. Or was that her mouth? I heard she liked to get down on her knees and blow. Nevertheless, she'd won in the end. Now was not the time for our past transgressions to play out in front of our girls.

Imani yawned, stifling it with the hand which sported the diamond engagement ring Kegan gave to her.

"Man, I didn't know I was so tired," she taunted.

I seethed, wanting to knock the condescending smirk from her face. I know she did this thinking I didn't know about their wedding. I wanted to tell her Kegan sent me an invite, but I decided against it. What better way to get under this woman's skin than to show up at their nuptials? The look on her face would be enough to make my day.

"Mom, are you okay?" Meena asked as I pulled up in the driveway of our home. She snapped me out of the memory just moments ago with Imani. The rain pounded down on the car, and for a moment, I wondered how I even got here.

I scowled at Meena until I saw the earnest look on her face. I softened my expression before saying, "I will be. Thanks for asking."

"I'm sorry about today," she apologized. "I really am."

I reached over and squeezed my daughter's hand, smiling at her lovingly before saying, "This still doesn't mean you are off the hook. You are still going to be punished for what you did."

She smiled for the first time in a long while as she said, "I know."

I patted her hand and said, "Now, I wish we had an umbrella. We're going to have to run for it."

Meena nodded, and we both exited the car and ran to the covered front porch of our home. Despite running, we still got drenched. As I fumbled with my keys to open the door, my cell phone rang and I saw it was my male friend Dempsey.

I proceeded to unlock the door and told Meena, "Go ahead in the house. I'll be there in a bit."

Meena nodded and jogged into the house leaving me to take my call.

"Hello."

"What's up, Sonya," Dempsey's raspy voice sounded through my line.

"Nothing. What's up with you?"

"I'm calling to see if I could swing through later."

I hadn't seen this man in over a month, and now he wanted to come see me.

Dempsey was, or used to be, my man since Kegan left me. Rather, he was my fallback man who helped me get over losing Kegan. I met Dempsey in a bar one night, and he offered to buy me a drink. I made sure to flirt with him openly so everybody could see our chemistry. It wasn't hard because Dempsey was a nice-looking guy, especially with his dreads and penny-colored complexion. From then on, I'd been sleeping with him. And, yes, I slept with him the same night I met him. Why not? Kegan cheated on me. So why couldn't I do it too? Granted, I didn't want to ever look like a whore again since I let go of that title when I was being used by my mother, but that night I didn't care. I was drinking down my sorrows about my relationship ending with Kegan, and Dempsey quickly became the distraction I needed to help get over my ex.

Word did get back to Kegan I was seeing someone else. The bastard had the audacity to call me and ask me about who I was seeing.

"What's it to you? You don't want me anymore, so why are you calling to ask me who I'm booed up with?"

"Don't play with me, Sonya."

"Who's playing?"

"You are."

"Does your new whore know you're calling me?" I asked sardonically.

Kegan said nothing. I knew I'd hit a nerve with him, and I didn't care. He hurt me. He cheated on me, and all I ever did was love that man.

"That's what I thought."

"I can't believe you're doing this."

"You can't believe me? What about what you did to me?" I said angrily.

"Sonya—"

"You made a clear choice, Kegan, and it wasn't me. What, you expected me to sit and wait to see if you came back to me? Or better yet, did you expect me to be your side chick like Imani was for you?"

"You know what? It was a mistake calling you."

Kegan hung up, and I hadn't heard from him since, well, not until I got that invite to his wedding. The thought of this wedding helped in my decision about Dempsey coming over.

"Dempsey, does nine sound good?"

Monica

22

The dark skies that hovered released torrential downpours. The storm came out of nowhere, much like the one that was going on in my own life. I hit the garage door button and was happy to see Devin's car was in its usual space. He hadn't left me yet. After the run-in at his parents' house, I figured he would be gone. Pulling in beside him, I was grateful on days like this that I didn't have to get out in the nasty weather.

Entering my home, I looked out the kitchen window and could hardly see the house across the street. The wind whipped the rain, making it look like sheets of water. The sky lit up from a flash of lightning, followed by a boom of thunder. I knew we needed the rain, but I hated when it came like this.

I went to my bedroom to see Devin wasn't there, but he'd been in here. The closet door was open, and I knew I closed it before I left. I walked in, noticing my husband had removed the majority of his clothes. My stomach clinched at the thought of him already packing his belongings to leave me. I walked out into the hallway and saw the door to the spare bedroom was closed. I knocked on it softly, but he didn't answer. I turned the knob and opened it to see he was not in here either. This meant he was probably downstairs in the basement.

After slipping into a pair of jogging pants and off-the-shoulder tee, I went downstairs, wanting a glass of wine. Before going into the kitchen, I peeped out the living-room window to see water running down the street like small streams flowing at a rapid pace. The large droplets continued to come down heavy and the lightning continued to light up the sky.

"Monica," I heard Devin call out to me. He was in the basement.

"Yes."

"You need to come down here."

I knew what this meant and didn't want to go downstairs, but I went anyway. Descending the stairs, I was happy to see the carpet was still dry on the finished side of our basement. *So far, so good,* I thought, but when I went to the unfinished side, I saw Devin scooping water from the basement floor with a plastic cup. He was doing this to stop the water from coming over to the finished side. We'd had this happen one other time before, and we ended up losing everything. We had to get the water vacuumed out by a company. He had to get everything treated so we wouldn't get mold. All the furniture was destroyed. That flood ended up costing us almost $10,000 with repairs and replacement of the carpet and furniture. So I could understand why Devin was working furiously to hinder that from happening to us again.

"Why didn't you bring something down here to help scoop this water up?" he asked with an attitude.

"How was I supposed to know? I was expecting to see it already flooded," I replied tersely.

"You see it's raining, right? Go upstairs and get a cup to help me. I've already put something up at the bottom of the door to help stop the water from coming in. It should slow it down a bit."

I stood for a minute watching him go back to scooping the water up. Then I turned and went back upstairs to retrieve a cup and returned to Devin still scooping water. I joined him. We were dumping it into a large thirty-two gallon trash can.

"Devin, I don't know why you don't get the problem fixed. The man told you we needed that drain at the door replaced in order for the water to not enter this basement again. How are you going to spend $10,000 for the main problem to not be resolved?"

"How did I know it was going to rain like this again?"

"This is not the first time this has happened. The first time should have been enough for you to call someone to come out and fix the problem," I retorted.

"Monica, don't be trying to tell me what I should have done. It's not doing us any good now, is it?"

"I'm just saying," I said, scooping up the water and pouring it in the trash can.

"I don't want to hear it, so just shut up," he yelled.

"I'm down here helping you, and you're going to get disrespectful? This is your domain, Devin, not mine. You wanted a man cave; you can save it all by your damn self," I said throwing the cup down and walking out of the room.

"You are such a bitch," he murmured but loud enough for me to hear it.

"What did you call me?" I paused, keeping my back to him.

"I called you a bitch," he repeated boldly.

Tears clouded my eyes as the stabbing pain from him calling me a bitch upset me. We had been together for a long time and had been through a lot and said a lot of things to each other, but never had my husband ever come out of his mouth to say that. Crazy, yes. Stupid, yes. Bitch, never. I was so taken aback I couldn't speak. I couldn't even turn to face him. It took me a bit, but I turned and walked back in the space with him. I stood there in the water while he continued to scoop the water up to save the basement. Then he peered up at me.

"Either help or get the hell out," he bellowed as he bent over again to scoop up more water.

Rage engulfed my pain. I contemplated bashing his head in with the bat that sat on the shelf we had in the unfinished room. A voice said, *"Don't do it,"* but the one that wanted to teach him a lesson said, "*Bash his freakin' head in.*"

The rational voice said, *"If you do it, you are going to have to knock him out because if you miss, this man is liable to take the bat from you and beat the hell out of you. There is no need to stoop to violence."* My rational voice concluded with, *"What if you do manage to knock him out? Will that be the blow that kills this man?"*

I didn't want to see Devin dead, but my hands tightened with the battle of fury verses common sense. I closed my eyes trying to think sensibly but *bitch* kept ringing over and over in my mind. This punk called me a bitch. What next? It was bad enough he treated me like he did. Then it was finding him with his ex-fiancée. Now this? Was his verbal abuse going to eventually turn physical? Could I continue to withstand even the verbal abuse if we decided to work out our marriage? I felt like a slap across the face would be easier to take than the words that cut to the core of my spirit. Devin was good at yielding his wounding words. His degrading remarks were starting to takes their toll on me. I was already too fat for him, which was why I was working out, but was it enough? Hell, was it worth it?

I opened my eyes to find him not paying me any attention. He looked up at me again giving me a smug look as he said, "You still here? Oh, maybe you want to use this as an opportunity to exercise and lose some weight."

Tick went my mind . . . and I lost it.

Monica

23

The rain finally stopped or at least reverted back to a drizzle. I stood in the bay window with my arms crossed, taking in the view of my neighbor's home and how green all of our lawns were. I wondered what each of our neighbors were doing. Were children playing? Were the families sitting around the table talking about the happenings of the day? Was laundry being tossed in the washing machine? Were any of the women as unhappy as I was in their marriage? Was anyone harboring secrets like I was?

The clatter of footsteps let me know Devin was coming up the stairs. Each step was slow but firm, like he was trying to keep his balance. I never looked back. I listened until I knew his measured steps brought him in eye view of me.

"What did you do to me?" he asked groggily.

I turned to see him holding the back of his head. His clothes were soaking wet, and his eyes were squinting like the light in the room was too bright for him to focus. I was surprised his ass didn't drown. After all, he did fall face-first.

"What are you talking about, Devin?" I asked as I walked over to the sofa and plopped down. I picked up the glass of wine I'd poured for myself and took a long sip. I never took my eyes off my husband as he looked bewildered at me.

"You hit me."

I swallowed the sweet red wine before saying, "No, I didn't."

"Yes, you did," he argued.

"Okay, I did. Now what?"

With widened eyes he tilted his head slightly at my nonchalant words. He was still unsteady on his feet, but the pained expression he gave me had little effect on me.

"You left me down there unconscious."

"I sure did."

"How did you know I wasn't dead?"

"I didn't," I said frigidly.

"So you didn't care?"

"Not at that particular moment, no."

"You really are a crazy—"

Expression dead serious, I said, "Watch your mouth, Devin. I hit you once. I can hit you again. Maybe this will teach you not to call me out of my name."

I meant what I said. And I think he knew it too as my dark eyes bore into him. I'd dealt with a lot with Devin, and today was definitely not an exception. But I'd be damned if this man—or any man—was going to call me a bitch whenever he felt the need.

"As long as we've been together, Devin, you have never called me a bitch. And you are not going to start now. You can call me baby, Monica, sugar, sweetie, and even crazy. But you better not ever—as long as there is breath in your body—call me a bitch."

We stared each other down. I meant what I said, and that knot on the back of his head let him know I was dead serious.

"Are there any other others I needed to stay clear of?" he asked.

"Cunt is another. Georgiana is another."

Devin nodded and understood. This was a serious hiccup, and our marriage was in jeopardy, and she was the cause of it.

"I think you did this for what happened earlier today."

"Maybe I did, in combination of you calling me what you called me. Either way, I feel empowered," I replied, giving him a bitter smile. "Now, if you would excuse me, I have dinner to make."

"Dinner?" Devin asked.

Springing to my feet, I said, "Yes. Dinner. Do you have a problem with that?"

"We are not done here," he said, finally bringing his hands down by his side, rotating his head to loosen the soreness.

"The only thing we need to discuss is how we are going to work on saving our marriage. Is that what you want to talk about?" I asked.

"I asked you for a divorce, and after what you've done to me today, this further lets me know I'm making the right decision."

"Oh, really?" I said, folding my arms across my chest.

"Really," he replied contemptuously. "People know who my heart really belongs to."

I began to chuckle as my anger began to rise within. Did Devin realize he said *people?* Now, *people* were part of this equation. Now, *people* knew he wanted to divorce me to get back with his ex. I wondered if any of those *people* were part of the congregation his parents were trying to grow. Did any of them think *those* people would be happy with him making a decision to leave his wife for another woman? Better yet, he was cheating on his wife with another woman. Whether he'd put his hands on Georgiana or not, he'd been thinking about her. He had lustful thoughts plaguing his mind, not realizing it was the affliction infecting our marriage. Or maybe he just didn't care.

"Do you think I'm going to let this go down like this?" I asked him.

"You don't have a choice."

"You think so?"

"I know so," he said forebodingly.

He began to remove his soaked clothes right there in our living room. First, it was his shirt. Then, his tank, and next, it was his socks and pants, until he was standing in front of me with nothing but his boxer briefs on. I allowed my eyes to scan the perimeter of his body as my eyes concentrated on his numerous inches. As much as I wanted to hate this man, I loved him. I loved every inch of him.

Devin chuckled bitterly as he walked around the sofa and lowered himself onto it.

"My family is very powerful, Monica."

"And?"

"And we have ways of getting what we want."

"I'm not going to give you the satisfaction of a divorce. You made a promise to me. If you think I'm going to bow down and give you what you want so you can be with your little whore, you got another think coming."

With his face hardened, Devin's voice was wicked and cold, like he had some type of ace up his sleeve. Telling me about his parents was not changing my mind. Believe you me, I'd been up against worse things.

"You will give me what I want . . . or else."

"Is that a threat?" I asked curiously.

"Oh no. I wouldn't dare threaten you. Remember, I'm the son of a preacher."

Dropping my gaze I said, "Even now, Devin, I love you."

"Too bad. I don't love you."

His words impaired me for a moment. It was never easy hearing him say this to me. I inhaled a breath to gather myself before saying, "So, are you really going to go through with this?"

"Yes. It would be in your best interest to go along with this as well. The easier you make this, the better it will be for everybody."

I nodded, saying, "I was hoping you would have a change of heart. I mean, after all, I *am* your wife."

"No change here," he declared.

"I guess it was good I took it upon myself to move some money around in our joint account."

"You did *what?*" he yelled, springing to his feet.

"I didn't want to be one of those women who go to get some money out of the bank, only to find her husband has taken everything."

"Monica, don't play with me," he heaved.

"I don't play games. That would be you."

Devin darted out of the room and to our office. I knew he was going to get on the computer to check our checking and savings account. Why this man didn't believe me was beyond me. Hadn't I proven to him over and over again I spoke truth.

I filled my glass up with some more wine. Picking up the glass, I slid back in my seat and waited for my husband to return to the room as I savored the sweet liquid.

A roar echoed throughout our home, and I waited for him to scamper back in the room, which he did seconds later.

"You had no right!" he said menacingly.

"But I did. Don't worry your little head about it. I didn't take it all. I split it down the middle leaving you half."

"Thirteen thousand dollars. How is that when I make more money than you?" he protested.

"Did you prefer I took it all?" I asked.

"I don't think you should have taken any of my money."

"Now it's *your* money. I guess you're going to say this is your house, and I'm driving your car."

"You damn right. If it wasn't for me, you wouldn't have any of this."

"Don't do that, Devin," I said leaning forward and placing my glass back down on the coffee table. "You know as well as I do I'm a woman who makes her own money."

"Then why not take your own money?" he asked.

"I think I deserve every damn dime after dealing with your BS all of these years. I had my own house before selling it to put a large down payment on this home. I'm paying for my car also, so don't stand there and act like the only money coming up in this damn house is yours."

"What? Do you want a pat on the back?"

"Yes. That would be nice for once, Devin. Why can't you acknowledge the good I've done in this marriage. I've washed your clothes and cooked your dinner. I took care of you when you were sick. I've dealt with your mother treating me like I don't belong in her family. I made sure you had your necessities down to the toilet paper you use to wipe your ass," I snapped.

"But the one thing you couldn't do for me was bear me a child."

That hurt. I think that hurt worse than him calling me a bitch.

"You knew my situation when you married me," I said dejectedly. "Is *that* why you want to leave me and get with Georgiana, because she can bear a child for you?"

"I've always wanted kids, and you can't give me any. Why should I have to suffer because my wife can't do her womanly duty by birthing me a child?"

"Wow. I can't believe you said that. *Womanly duty? Really,* Devin? Now birthing kids is an obligation?"

"I know it's one you can't give me."

"You make me sound like a recruit in your army that's supposed to perform what you want, when you want it, how you want it, when you yourself never gave me 100 percent of you. So, how can you expect so much from somebody you never gave a damn about in the first place?"

Devin said nothing. What could he say to that? He knew I was right.

"I'm finding out more about you every day. You never loved me. You are still in love with your first love, and now I'm some type of freak of nature who can't give you a child."

"That about sums it up," he said impassively.

"You are a poor excuse for a man. Here I have been trying my damnedest to please you. And for what? Nothing."

"I'm going to put on some clean dry clothes; then I'm going out for dinner. So, there is no need to prepare anything for me," he said turning and walking away from our conversation. I watched as he ascended the stairs.

"I'm not giving you a divorce," I bellowed. "You can file the paperwork all you want, but you will never marry that bitch if I have anything to do with it."

I heard the guest bedroom door slam shut. I sat defeated and feeling like maybe it was best for me to concede and give Devin what he wanted. I talked a big game when it came to signing the divorce papers, but I did have secrets that could persuade me to do so. His mother was already digging in my past, and I knew it would be only a matter of time before she came across something. This may be a battle I was going to lose; perhaps it was time for me to wave my little white flag and surrender to the demise of my marriage to my husband.

Sonya

24

Kellie was the first one who called to check on Meena and me to see how we were doing. She saw how pissed I was when I left that restaurant and knew Meena was in some serious trouble. I explained the entire debacle of an afternoon and was happy to vent about the situation. I found it ironic earlier I was talking about Kellie always venting her problems when we got together, and now, here I was doing the same. God definitely had a funny way of making me look at myself. The same situation I talked about to Vivian and Monica was the same situation God placed in my lap, and I understood the lesson.

Kellie was even nice enough to ask if Meena could come over and chill with her for a while. At first, I hesitated, thinking this was why Meena acted the way she did because sometimes, I never stuck to my guns, letting her off punishment too soon. Kellie sensed my hesitation and said Meena was like a little sister to her, and she was going to use the opportunity to talk with my daughter about what was going on with her. I appreciate that. Meena was an only child, and I thought it was nice that my daughter had someone she could turn to. Kellie may have her issues, like everybody else, but she was a good person. So, I agreed to Meena hanging out with her.

Besides, Dempsey was coming over to pay me a visit. It couldn't have come at a better time since I was already turned on by that handsome Officer Ward who, for some reason, I couldn't get off my mind. As much as I knew Meena needed to be on punishment, I needed some time to unwind.

I always anticipated that first lick, that first flicker of a man's tongue letting me know there were more of those to come. Dempsey didn't know what danger he was in playing with me like this. My mind was ready. My body was anxious, and I couldn't stand feeling the eagerness of him getting geared up pleasing me. When Dempsey's tongue finally connected with my center, I thought I would lose it. He dove deep inside me like a man doing a cannonball in the deep end of a pool. He loved to tease me, and I loved to be on the receiving end of his tongue flicking beneath the mounds of my seduction. He looked up at me smiling as he kneeled between my thighs, taunting me and asking me if I loved what he was doing to me. His voice was enticing; like the smooth music of a quiet storm that relaxed you and took you back to yesteryears. That, and the combination of what his tongue was doing to me were taking me to levels I didn't get to experience often. My breathing became shallow as the intensity of my climax began to build. I wanted to grab his head and bury his face within me, he was that good. He caressed my thighs, gazing up at me as he lapped at my sweet nectar. Craving more, I began to grind my hips into him, bringing me closer to my peak. I positioned my feet on his shoulders as I rotated my hips. I may have been a thick sister, but I was also a flexible one. I bit my lip as each second brought me closer to my eruption. My core spasmed. I reached down and gripped a handful of his dreads, pulling him into me. Like the champ he was, he continued to lick and suck until I no longer could take any more. If I didn't push him away, Dempsey would keep going, and I was already dizzy with gratification, so I pushed him away. I needed a moment to gather myself as my body continued to quiver.

I watched as Dempsey stood to his feet. He began to remove his basketball shorts. His dick bounced free from his shorts sticking straight out at me as Dempsey dropped his shorts around his ankles and stepped out of them. He was burly with broad shoulders and a somewhat flat stomach but not the six-pack I was used to when I was with Kegan. Kegan was a sculptured masterpiece of a man with abs that rippled, arms that bulged, and a chest cut to perfection. I hated thinking or comparing Dempsey to him right now, but it was hard not to. I probably would compare every man to Kegan since he had been the only man I'd ever truly loved. Hell, I didn't even love Meena's dad, and I had a child by him. But now was not the time to have all of these thoughts. I needed to concentrate on the matter at hand.

I maneuvered through the dark cobalt-blue sheets, crawling up to him until I was on the edge of the bed with my face leveled with his extension.

"My turn," I whispered, looking up at him and watching him lick his lips in eager anticipation. Before I could place my mouth on him, he was running his fingers through my kinky twist. I loved when he tugged at my hair. *Make it hurt,* I always said.

"Down boy," I spoke to his dick eager to be in something moist. "I'm going to show you some attention right now."

My warm hands instantly caused Dempsey to sigh as he looked down at me.

"Put it in your mouth," he demanded huskily. "Take all of it."

With Dempsey, I could take it all. He had a nice-size dick but not like Kegan's. Kegan had at least two inches on him, and I closed my eyes, mad at myself for thinking about him yet again. Wanting to forget about Kegan, I took all of Dempsey inside my mouth.

"Do the damn thing," he said softly.

His legs trembled with the union of my soft lips, warm tongue, and the constriction of my jaws humming a lovely tune around him. He gripped my head with both hands, pulling me further down on him. I guess with the massive dick Kegan had, taking all of Dempsey was a breeze.

There I went again thinking about Kegan. What was wrong with me? Would I ever get that man out of my system? Between the invite to his upcoming wedding and running into his soon-to-be wife, it was hard not to think of him.

I stroked Dempsey from his balls to the tip if his dick in circular movements that gave every inch of him pleasure. My thumb led the progression in every stroke. Dempsey started to join in with hip successions that sent him deeper into my throat.

"Can you handle me, baby?" I asked as I came up for air.

"Oh, I can handle you. I just don't know if I can handle what you doing to me right now . . . shit."

I smirked. I guess my cocky demeanor caused him to pull me away from his throbbing expansion. I knew he was a few strokes away from climaxing which was why he stopped me.

"Turn over," he commanded.

"Like this?" I said, getting on all fours.

"Exactly like that."

Dempsey quickly mounted me. Without any hesitation, he entered gently. My pussy welcomed him by opening wide for him. The first few strokes were slow, but each one that came brought an eagerness to speed up the tempo of our bodies making music together. I loved to face him, but if I had to choose a position, this was my favorite. There was just something about the way a man took control and pulled me into him, grabbing my waist with his big hands to plunge his dick inside me. Just the thought of this always turned me on.

Dempsey didn't disappoint. I know we went at it for over an hour before he reached his climax. Lucky for me, I'd reached mine several times over, and boy, did I need it. This was a stress reliever that was long overdue. As I lay beside Dempsey who quickly drifted off to sleep, I couldn't help but think of Kegan again and how much more I would have enjoyed this if I was having sex with him instead. He'd spoiled me something terrible, and it was then when I decided I was going to go to that wedding to see if he was going to go through with this facade of a relationship. Maybe seeing him say I do to another woman would help me get over him once and for all.

Kellie

25

Meena was knocked out as she leaned on my brother Vic's shoulder as we all cuddled up on the sofa together to watch movies. All of us were in our pajamas, and she was the first one to lose her battle to see who could stay up the longest. I'd actually had a great time with her. Vic was skeptical at first since I'd told him about why I was having her over. My brother didn't get along with kids much and probably despised teens even more. But tonight, I think we all had a wonderful time together.

Our talk went well, or I thought so at least. I asked her about what was going on with her, and at first, she was hesitant about speaking with me. I could understand since I was her mom's friend.

"Meena, what you and I discuss will be between us. I'm not going to tell your mother."

"You're not?" she questioned.

"No, I'm not. I know your mom and I are friends, but I also know you need a friend too. I told you awhile back to look at me as your big sister."

She smiled as she lowered her head.

"I have wanted to talk to you, but I never did, thinking you would talk to my mom."

I reached over, placing my index finger on her chin, lifting it for her gaze to meet mine. "Unless what you tell me is detrimental to your health, my lips are sealed."

From then on, Meena and I talked about everything from what was going on in school, to her friendship with Asha and Shannon. I basically let her vent without trying to pass judgment. If anybody could understand not being able to communicate with their mother, it was me and Vic.

When Meena and I got on the subject of sex, she shocked me when she told me she was no longer a virgin.

"Are you serious right now?" I asked in disbelief.

"Yes, I'm serious."

"Who?"

"It was with this guy I know," she divulged.

"Did he use a condom?"

I knew I was throwing many questions out there to her, but I felt like they were important things to know.

"Yes, Kellie."

"Did you see him put it on?"

"Yes," she chuckled uneasily.

"Did the condom break?"

"No."

"So you've had your period and everything?"

"Yes, Kellie. It's okay. I did everything right, including the guy I chose to lose my virginity to. I'm good. I don't have any regrets, so please don't freak out," she said calmly.

"It's hard not to, sweetie. I'm sitting here trying to figure out when you grew into this beautiful woman."

I could feel my eyes fill with tears at the thought of Meena growing up and knew why Sonya acted as crazy as she was. She was losing her baby girl.

"Don't do this, Kellie," Meena said, reaching over and rubbing my leg.

"I'm sorry. I don't even know why I'm getting so emotional about this. Seeing how fast you are growing is letting me know time is flying by. Life is on the fast track, and I pray it leads all of us to great things."

"Me too," Meena added.

Wiping at my tears, I asked, "Does your mother know?"

Frowning, she said, "No."

"That was a dumb question," I chuckled.

"You know how crazy my mom is. Just when I don't think the woman can get any crazier, she shows me she can. Like today at Macys. My mother was ready to catch a charge by beating my ass right there in front of the cop."

"That's Sonya," I mumbled with a slight chuckle.

"How does my mother expect me to come to her with anything if she's always going to overreact about everything?"

"Parents don't always know how to act. As many self-help books there are out there, I don't think there is a legit one that can tell a mom how to raise her kids. Just know your mom is doing the best she can, and she loves you."

"I know, and I love her too, but she's embarrassing."

"God placed the embarrassment gene in them to humiliate us. It's in the Bible," I said.

"No, it's not," Meena countered with a smile.

"Okay, I made that up, but what I do know is you stealing was grounds for your mother acting a damn fool."

"But I—"

"Meena, I know what you're going to say. You are going to say you didn't take anything, right?"

"Yes."

"Did you give your friend things to take?" I asked.

Dropping her head she said, "Well . . . yes."

"Then you are guilty of stealing. You knew what you friend was up to, and that's why you are guilty of the same crime. Your mother got mad because she knows you're better than that. I know you are better than that also. You are beautiful. You are smart. You don't need to waste these blessings on nonsense, sweetie."

When we felt like we'd talked enough, we switched modes and started to have some fun together. I decided it would be cool for Meena to spend the night. She didn't think Sonya would go for it, but lucky for us, she had no problems with it. That's when we decided to make it a movie night. Meena found my brother Vic to be hilarious. He kept her in stitches all evening laughing at his silliness. I know my brother enjoyed someone laughing at his corny jokes. After popping some popcorn and getting stuffed with bowls of ice cream, Meena drifted off to sleep.

"Now that was a good movie, sis," Vic said as we watched the credits to the movie *The Perfect Guy*.

"I know, right? Somebody told me it wasn't that good, but I thought it was great."

"Evidently, whoever told you that doesn't know a good movie when they see one. I don't know if the drama kept my attention or Morris Chestnut and Michael Ealy. I would give anything to spend a night with either one of them sexy men."

"There you go. You *do* know both of them are in a committed relationship and neither are gay?"

"So?"

"Vic," I said looking at him with my head tilted.

"Sis, I got skills. I can turn a straight man my way."

"I bet you can, but I never thought you were one of those men who ruined relationships."

"Oh hell. Here you go, all in your feelings."

"I'm just saying."

"Kell, I'm joking."

I scrunched my lips up at him like I didn't believe him.

"Okay, I wasn't, but . . ." he said holding up a finger, "I'm not a person who likes to ruin relationships. I know how it feels, and I would never want to put that type of pain on someone else."

I smiled at my brother as I looked at Meena who still hadn't budged from his shoulder. With all his movement, I was surprised she hadn't woken up. She was really knocked out. Vic glanced at her too and smiled.

"Homegirl is slobbing and everything. I better get her up before my entire right side gets soaked."

I giggled as I watched my brother gently try to wake Meena. This girl was a hard cookie to get up.

"Sweetie . . . Come on. Let's go to bed," Vic said, sitting her up. Meena still had her eyes closed as she frowned from us disturbing her. Vic stood and Meena took this as her opportunity to lie down where he was sitting.

"Meena, sweetie, come on. Let me take you to your room," Vic said, pulling on her. Meena sat up wiping her eyes over and over again like she had allergies. Vic took her free hand and pulled her up from the sofa. He looped her arm through his and patted her hand as he led her to the spare bedroom. I followed and watched Vic pull back the covers for Meena to climb in.

"Thank you, Vic," she murmured.

My brother beamed like a proud stepbrother and tiptoed out of the room with me.

"I just love that girl," Vic said. "And I don't get along with kids."

"It seems Meena loves you too, and she doesn't get along with adults."

We both burst into laughter as we returned to the living room to get comfortable on the couch again.

"Sis, it's close to two in the morning. If you expect me to go to church with you and the girls tomorrow, then a brother needs to get his beauty rest."

I'd completely forgot about telling Monica we would go to church with her in the morning. She called and asked, and I said yes, figuring I needed to go. But now that I thought about it, I wished I didn't make that commitment to her because I would rather sleep in.

"Now we've watched a horror movie, a comedy, and then a thriller. So we're good."

"I'm not sleepy though," I admitted.

"And what does that mean? Is that sister code for stay up with me until I get sleepy?"

I tried to give him an angelic expression, hoping he would, but my brother quickly shot me down.

"Girl, there go, using your endearing face. You know it doesn't work all the time."

"I know it's working now."

"What else is there to do? We have talked, watched damn near six hours of movies, ate all the damn snacks. It's time to go to bed."

"We can talk about taking a trip to Mommy's house."

"Oh, hell nawh."

"Vic—"

"Kell, I'm not going to see that woman."

"She's your mother."

"She hasn't played the role of one in years, not to me anyway. The woman can teach Sunday school and mentor the little children, but she ostracizes her own son. Christians don't suppose to do that."

My brother was getting very emotional, and I wished I hadn't brought up the idea. Seeing him this upset made me feel bad for him. At least I got to speak with her. She wouldn't talk to Vic, all because of the gender he chose to love. I knew now his relationship with our mother was a bigger undertaking than I thought. He'd done nothing wrong in my eyes. It was our mother who was the one wrong here.

"Can't you try one more time? You can be bigger than her."

"Why? So she can shoot me down again? For her to tell me how I'm going to hell or look past me like I'm not even in the room? Kell, that's hurtful. It's destroyed me inside. I don't talk about it, because I'm mad at myself for allowing her to make me feel so guilty about the choices I've made. I've questioned myself every single day. Hell, I've questioned God why I'm the way I am. I can't help who I choose to fall in love with, and I'm tired feeling like I have to constantly explain the fact I'm an African American gay man. Everybody knows that's the worst person to be—ever."

"That's not true," I said.

"But it is, Kell. Black society understands men who cheat, women who cheat, heterosexual relationships, abuse, lying, stealing, robbing, using drugs, prostitution, and so many more things, but accepting and trying to understand the fact a black man is gay—"

"Vic, you know we don't accept all of those things," I tried to explain.

"I was being condescending. You know damn well what I mean."

"I do," I conceded.

"I just want to be acknowledged for the man I am."

"I love you," I consoled.

My brother smiled hopelessly as he said, "I love you too."

Vic and I had this conversation many times, but I'd never seen him this emotional about it. Seeing how hurt he was pained me. I could not imagine how he was feeling with Mom disowning him. Honestly, if I was in his shoes, I'm not sure if I would handle the situation any differently. I guess the little girl in me missed the times when we were a family. I figured I would go to the person who was less stubborn to try to fix this. But now I wasn't sure if I wanted to expose my brother to being shunned again.

"I didn't mean to upset you," I said sincerely, reaching over to my brother and grabbing his hand.

"It's never you. It's the situation. Kell, I think about this all the time, wondering if I can go straight for the sake of my relationship with Mom," he confessed. "But I know I wouldn't be living in my truth. I would be living for Mom and the world, and how is that fair to me?"

"It's not. You need to walk in your truth. I'm not going to push this issue anymore. It's not up to you to try make this work when it wasn't you who walked away from the relationship," I accepted.

"Don't get me wrong, I really do want to see Mom. A part of me just wants to lay eyes on her if only one more time because I know tomorrow is not promised. I've actually had nightmares about never seeing her again, thinking I could have sucked it up and went to see her. So maybe this is God's way of telling me it's time."

"I don't want you to think I pushed you into this, Vic."

"Please, Kell. You know you can't push me into anything I don't want to do. I know in my heart I need to go see Mom even if the visit doesn't go the way I would like it to go."

"So, are you saying we are taking a trip?" I asked.

Before Vic could answer the question, there was a knock at the door. Both Vic and I just gawked at each other.

"I know ain't nobody knocking at my door after two in the morning," I said in confusion.

"You know it's for you because no one knows I'm here."

"Who could it be?" I said, standing to my feet. I can't lie, I was a bit nervous. No one ever knocked or called me this time of the morning unless something was wrong. I was glad my brother was here because I don't know if I would even check to see who was on the other side of my door otherwise.

"There's only one person I can think of," Vic said, standing with me, and he instantly got an attitude.

Swinging the door opened, I spewed, "What the hell are you doing here?"

"Whoa, whoa, whoa, hunty. Slow your roll. I come in peace."

I looked back at my brother who stood with his mouth open. There weren't many times my brother was speechless. The puzzled look on his face was one I hadn't seen before. I was embarrassed he had to witness such ghetto antics.

Turning my attention back to my husband's lover I said, "Jeffrey no longer lives here."

The first thing I noticed about him was his Chanel bag hanging from the crook of his arm. I knew it had to be fake, just like he was. He had on all-black, looking like he was about to rob the place, with huge silver hoops dangling from his earlobes. I don't know if he was trying to show me he was the better person for Jeffrey, but he didn't have to, because from where I stood, this man could have him.

"I'm not here for him. I'm here to speak to you."

"About what?" I snapped.

"Look, it's chilly out here. Can you let me in so we can talk like adults?" Kyle said.

"Oh, now you want to act like adults? Where was this maturity when you were in my house sucking my husband's dick?"

Kyle chuckled as he put his hand up to his temple like he was thinking about it. Then he sucked his teeth and continued to speak.

"Are you going to allow me to speak or not?" He said this with attitude, like he was doing me a damn favor.

"Not," and I slammed the door in his face.

I heard Kyle's gasp through the door before hearing him call me a bitch. Vic rushed to the door, but I stopped him from opening it again, knowing he was going to proceed to kicking Kyle's ass. As much as I would have loved that to go down, I didn't want to see my brother get in any trouble over someone who was not worth the time or energy. I dragged him back over to the sofa, pulling him down beside me.

"The nerve of Jeffrey to send his man whore to fight his battles for him," Vic grumbled. "I mean, what the hell?"

"My husband is a punk."

"You damn right he is. Kyle seems to have more spunk than he does."

"When I looked at you earlier, you looked like you may have known him," I said.

"What?" Vic chuckled. "I mean, I thought I may have known him too, but once he got to talking, I knew I was wrong."

"You sure?" I asked skeptically.

"Kell, just because I'm a gay man, and he's a gay man, doesn't mean we know all gay men."

I giggled as I reached over and cut the television off.

"Now, I'm tired. That confrontation was enough to sap all my energy away from me," I said, standing.

"Wait a sec," Vic said holding my hand. "If I don't say this now, I may never say it. I agree with you and think we should go pay Mom a visit."

I jumped on my brother, causing him to fall back.

"Thank you, thank you, thank you, Vic."

"No, thank you, sis. There's a reason why things are happening like they are, and I'm going to follow the path God is taking me."

Sonya

26

Someone was shaking me, and for a moment, I thought I was dreaming. I didn't appreciate being woke up because I was sleeping some kind of good. I prayed it wasn't already morning because I promised Monica I'd attend church today, and I didn't feel like getting up. When the person shook me again, I squinted and realized Dempsey was standing over me. He had his shirt off, and then it all came back to me how I invited him over to work my middle since it had been a little while.

"Man, what do you want?" I murmured.

"Sonya, you have company."

I looked up at him to see if he was playing with me, but the serious look he had on his face let me know he wasn't.

"Who? And what time is it?"

"It's a few minutes after three."

"Oh, hell no. I'm going back to sleep," I said turning away from him. "If somebody is coming by to see me this time of morning, tell them to come at a decent time to talk to me."

"Sonya, he says his name is Kegan."

The mention of Kegan's name caused my heart to gallop. I sat up abruptly, pulling the covers around me as I unconsciously began to smooth down my tangled braids.

I looked around Dempsey like Kegan was standing right there in the room and was relieved when I didn't see him.

"So, Kegan saw you?" I asked.

Dropping his gaze, Dempsey's brows knitted as he said, "He had to if I was the one who opened the door."

"Who told you to open my door?"

"Damn, Sonya. I heard the knock at your door and saw you didn't budge. Thinking it could have been Meena, I answered it, not knowing another dude was going to be on the other side."

Hearing concern in his voice and the crestfallen look he was giving me made me feel bad for coming at him like I was. The fact he thought it could have been my daughter warmed my heart. But Dempsey was the last person I wanted Kegan to see in my home this time of the morning. I know what I'd think. But why was he here anyway, and at this time? Something had to be wrong.

"He's in the living room," Dempsey told me. "Do you want me to get rid of him?"

"No, I got it."

"I told him it was late, and he needed to come back at a decent hour, but he insisted on speaking with you," Dempsey explained as I got out of bed and grabbed my robe to wrap around myself. Pulling it tightly around me, I finger combed my hair, trying to make it look better than it did when I got up. I also wiped at my mouth, making sure I didn't have residual slop present. I tended to do that when I slept extra hard.

Looking at Dempsey, his hardened demeanor let me know he was not happy Kegan was here. I'm pretty sure he was none too happy also to see me making sure I was together before I went to go speak with him. Ignoring his look of annoyance, I walked out of the room to see what Kegan wanted.

He was sitting on my couch when I entered the living room, and the pure presence of him caused my adrenaline to spike. He sensed my presence and stood when he saw me. He was more handsome than I remembered. Did he mean to show up looking this damn good? He was dressed in a black tux looking very dapper. His formal attire threw me off for a minute. Here I was looking a hot ass mess, smelling like sex, and he was looking like he'd just come from a gala event. If I didn't think it would look so obvious, I would have told him to wait a bit while I showered, changed, and made myself more presentable, but I didn't want him to think he was that important to me anymore . . . even though he was. I wished this was under better circumstances, but he was the one in my home at this late hour. There had to be a good reason why, and I couldn't wait to hear what that was.

"Hey, Sonya. I'm sorry to interrupt," he said nervously.

"It's okay," I answered leisurely, walking over to the love seat. He watched with intensity as I lowered myself, and I gestured for him to sit back down.

"So, what do I owe the pleasure of this visit?" I asked nonchalantly.

I was trying to act like his presence really didn't mess me up. I was feeling all types of emotions right now. I was feeling love, hate, rage, anxiety, fear, compassion, and even lust, even though I'd not too long ago slept with Dempsey.

"I meant to come over earlier, but it didn't quite work out like I planned," he said, looking down at his formal attire.

"You look nice."

"Yes, it was the boss's annual birthday bash."

"Oh, that's right. Mr. Chamberlin's birthday was Wednesday," I said, remembering when we'd attended this same event together last year. "How's he doing?"

"He's still kicking. I swear that man is going to outlive all of us," he chuckled.

"How old did he turn? Is it seventy-two?" I asked.

"That's right. You have a good memory."

"Mr. Chamberlin is a great man. When you see him, tell him I asked about him."

"I will," he said as he dropped his gaze.

For a moment nothing was said as Kegan looked down at the floor. That was, until the invitation on the coffee table caught his eye. He reached over and pulled it out from under the other mail that covered it. He stared at it before looking at me.

"Who sent this to you?"

"You did."

He shook his head saying, "I didn't send you this."

"You didn't?" I asked in surprise.

Then like a lightbulb went off for both of us, I said, "Imani must've been the one to send that to me."

It all made sense now, how she came at me yesterday in Macys. She purposely made it a point for me to see her ring, so why wouldn't she be trifling enough to send me an invite to their upcoming nuptials? What was more surprising to me was Kegan's reaction. He didn't seem pleased that I had it.

"I can't believe she did this."

"Why not? She was the side chick who broke us up," I said, and as soon as I said those words, I wished I hadn't because it showed how bitter I still was about what she did to our relationship.

"Sonya, I didn't come over here to discuss Imani," he said looking at me with compassion.

"So, why are you here?" I questioned.

"I came by because I heard about what Meena did."

"Your little whore couldn't wait to run back and tell you that. What? Did she tell you Meena was the ringleader?"

"As a matter of fac—"

I cut him off, bolting up out of the chair.

"If you are going to believe that bitch—"

"Sonya, calm down. That's why I'm here, to find out exactly what happened," he said, looking up at me.

"Why now, Kegan?"

"What do you mean?"

"Exactly that. Why now? Why are you worried about Meena's well-being now?"

"I've always cared about her well-being. You know I love that girl," he acknowledged.

"You have a funny way of showing it."

"What's that supposed to mean?"

"You told her us breaking up was not going to affect you being here for her, but she hasn't seen you since you left, Kegan."

Jaws clenching, he began to fumble with his hands as his shameful eyes gazed at me.

"I know, and I'm sorry about that, Sonya. I didn't keep my word."

"I don't want your apologies. You need to save them for Meena," I admonished.

Kegan stood, looking as sincere as he could.

"Sonya—"

"Six years you played a major role in my daughter's life. You were the father she never had, and she loved you, Kegan," I said, getting choked up. "Do you know how many nights that girl has cried for you? Do you know how many times she's waited on your call? But you never came by. You never called. You even missed her birthday."

"I said I was worry."

"The only thing I've ever asked of you was to not break my daughter's heart, and you couldn't even manage to do that. You crushed my baby, Kegan," I told him as tears formed.

"I can't even argue with you because you are right," he agreed.

"Why haven't you come before now? Did it have to take that bitch to tell you what happened for you to darken our doorstep?" I asked angrily.

"No . . . Look . . . I don't know," he floundered.

"You know, Kegan. Man up and admit it. Imani doesn't want you playing daddy to a child that's not yours biologically, right? Not my child anyway, but I guarantee you she has you playing daddy of the year with hers."

"Sonya, please."

This was my opportunity to get everything off my chest. The fact he showed up now acting all concerned once he found out about Meena being involved in shoplifting pissed me off. He had ample time to see what was going on with her. Hell, maybe if he hadn't up and left my daughter like he did, she wouldn't be doing the things she was.

"You let a bitch come between you and your relationship with Meena," I said, looking at him with disdain. "You know Imani is petty as hell because she automatically blamed Meena for what happened all because she's my child. She's petty because she kept you from my daughter. She's petty because she took you from me. And she is petty because she sent me an invite to your wedding to rub in my face how you chose to marry her and not me."

Now I was visibly crying. Kegan looked at me for a long moment before lowering himself back down on my sofa, like his legs had weakened beneath him. Something was going on with him, but I couldn't put my finger on it. As mad as I was with him, I could see there was something else he was not telling me. Being with this man for over six years helped me understand him.

"Sonya, please sit down," he pleaded.

I wanted to yell no, get the hell out my house and never bring your black ass back over here, but I did as he asked and lowered myself back down on the love seat.

With his hands clasped in front of him, he looked heartbroken.

"Kegan, what's going on with you? Why are you really here?" I asked earnestly.

Rubbing his hands together he said, "I really did come over here to see about Meena. I really did. Why did I come at this time, I don't know."

"Does Imani know where you are?" I asked.

"No. We had a fight."

Smiling slightly, I said nothing, waiting for him to continue to tell me the reason he was here. I had to admit I was inwardly happy about their squabble, but I wasn't going to say that to him.

"I knew Meena was not responsible for what happened, not like Imani was trying to make it seem."

"Is that what your argument was over? Meena?"

"Yes. I just lost it on Imani. She had no right talking about Meena the way she was. And when she threw in my face how I shouldn't care about her because I had a new family, I thought how I hadn't seen her since the two of us broke up. I literally racked my mind trying to convince myself I couldn't have failed her like that . . . only to realize I had."

It felt good hearing Kegan say this. Who knew Meena getting caught for shoplifting would be the pivotal moment Kegan needed to realize how he'd left her without looking back.

"And now you are here to see her."

"Yes," he said looking at me with that look that melted my heart. "I tried to have fun at this party tonight, but all

I kept thinking about was how desperately I needed to see Meena and tell her how sorry I am."

I shifted uncomfortably as I clutched my robe tighter around me.

"Kegan, Meena is not here."

Frowning, he asked, "Where is she?"

"She's at Kellie's house. Kellie wanted to spend some time with Meena and talk to her about what's been going on with her. As much as I wanted to ground her behind this shoplifting incident, I thought talking with Kellie was what she needed. You know Meena doesn't talk to me like that. If anything, she'd come to you."

He nodded with a chuckle before saying, "I remember. We had a lot of conversations you still don't know about."

"It used to tick me off, because I felt like my daughter should be able to come to me about everything, but now I realize I'm not as approachable as I should be. Having you here with me made it easier to deal with Meena because when she felt like she couldn't come to me, you were that rock she leaned on when she needed a listening ear."

"Well, I'm glad Kellie can be there for you. But I'm not going to lie . . . I was quick to believe you let her go with Kellie so you could have some alone time with old boy."

Damn, this man knew me as well as I knew him. His knowing gaze unnerved me, but I would never admit it to him. What type of mother would I be?

"Please, leave old boy out of our conversation. Remember, *you* left *me*."

Again he nodded.

"Is it too late to tell you I made a mistake?"

Sonya

27

Was I hearing this man correctly? Was Kegan telling me he made a mistake? Nine months broken up and *now* he realizes he made a mistake? I truly didn't know how to receive this epiphany from him. I wanted to gloat. I wanted to laugh and rub it in his face he lost a good woman . . . but I couldn't. I was even mad I couldn't. What in the hell was wrong with me? I remember a time I would be whooping up on his ass just for the simple fact he had the audacity to show up at my house this time with some BS Imani told him, but I guess I was becoming a big girl. I'd matured, if only a little.

"Kegan, you are saying this to say what?" I asked for clarification.

He stood and began to cautiously approach me. I watched him as he towered over me and instantly my eyes fell to his crotch, remembering the dick this man use to lay down on me. He smirked before lowering himself next to me on the love seat. Being this close to him caused my center to quiver with desire. I hadn't been this close to him in what seemed like an eternity, and now he was inches away from me.

With a softened expression, Kegan stared pointedly at me.

"What are you doing?" I asked.

"Something I should have done months ago."

Kegan reached over and gripped the back of my neck, pulling me into him. He kissed me passionately. My body arched forward, aroused by his lips being on mine again. Bliss filled me as my breathing thickened from the pure exhilaration of this man being here with me. I didn't know what was happening or why it was happening, but I was definitely enjoying the moment. That was . . . until the sound of broken glass brought us back to reality.

Both of us disengaged, looking at each other with passion and confusion. The sound of more glass breaking caused us to both stand to our feet. I rushed over to the window to see Imani in my driveway taking a bat to my car.

"No, this bitch didn't!" I said hurrying to the door and jerking it open.

Kegan ran out behind me and saw what his fiancée was doing and yelled, "Imani, no!" before the clattering of another window being broken sounded as she swung the bat again into my ride.

"Bitch, get the hell off my property," I screamed. As pissed as I was, my first instinct was to rush out and grab that bat away from her. But I knew if she swung that bat and hit me, I would take that bat from her and beat her to death with it.

"So *this* is how we doing things now, Kegan?" Imani said swinging again and putting a dent in the hood of my car. "The first person you run to is this fat bitch?"

"Imani, put the bat down," Kegan demanded.

Ignoring his command, Imani swung again . . . and again, adding more dents in my ride.

I decided to call the police. She wanted to destroy my property—then she was going to deal with the repercussions from it. When I rushed back into my house to get my cell, Dempsey was standing in the living room looking at me with a hurtful expression on his face. I forgot he was even here.

"Where's my cell?" I asked frantically.

"It's on the nightstand in your room."

I hurried in my room with Dempsey following behind me. I called the cops to report the incident as he stood near listening. When I hung up, I attempted to leave my room and go back outside when he stopped me.

"What?" I asked in frustration.

"I know we're not that serious, but you don't have to do a brother like this, Sonya," he said, glaring accusingly.

"What are you talking about?" I asked, pissed that he had the nerve to come at me like this now.

"I'm still in your house and you making out with dude."

"So?"

"So, you just finished fucking me. Now, you eager to hop on this man's dick too?"

I couldn't believe this. I didn't have time for this. Imani was outside my house yelling like she'd lost her damn mind, and I had Dempsey in my face playing the role of a wounded animal and questioning me about my kiss with Kegan. Didn't he know we weren't an item like that?

"You do remember, we are *not* an item, Dempsey. You are just something to do to pass the time away."

I knew what I said sounded insensitive, but it was what it was. He knew it was just sex between us. Why he was acting like I hadn't told him this before was beyond me.

"Now, can you get out of my way? I need to be outside when the cops get here."

He didn't budge. He stood blocking my path with his eyes narrowed in anger.

"Move, Dempsey. Better yet, get your clothes on and leave my house. How about that?"

"I'm not going anywhere so you can slide this man in my place."

"You don't have a place. Not here, and not anywhere else because you still live with your mama."

I knew I went too far with that statement, but he was getting on my nerves. Damn, I had turmoil outside and drama inside. This was too much.

"You can't talk to me like that," he said inching forward like he was going to do something to me. Had everybody lost their minds tonight?

"Did you forget the cops are on their way? Now, I called them for Imani's crazy ass, but if you want charges brought up on you too, then go ahead and do something stupid," I threatened.

He halted as his scowl deepened. But my words were enough for him to move the hell out of my way. I ran past him to get back outside, hoping Dempsey would gather his belongings to get the hell out of Dodge.

Imani was too dumb to leave. When the cops arrived, she was still arguing with Kegan, swinging the bat at him and my car until the cops detained her crazy ass. To my dismay, one of the officers that showed up was none other than Officer Damon Ward. *Damn, this is a small world,* I thought.

Our eyes locked, and I felt embarrassed he was here to witness this travesty. My car was destroyed by a crazy woman, a man was standing in my front yard in a tux, I was in my robe damn near naked, and I had another man in my home getting ready to exit at any moment. Not to mention we met with charges being filed against my shoplifting daughter. Talk about a hot-ass mess.

"You going to let them arrest me, Kegan?" Imani yelled in a panic.

"You got yourself arrested, Imani."

"Really? You choosing this fat bitch over me?"

"Imani, please."

"I saw you, Kegan. I saw you kissing her. We suppose to get married in a few weeks, and you're over here cheating on me."

"You lose him how you get him, honey," I yelled.

"Bitch, you don't know me."

"Nor do I want to get to know your ghetto behind. Come over here again and see what happens."

Imani turned to Damon, who had her in handcuffs and said, "Arrest her. She just threatened me."

"That wasn't a threat. That was a warning. If I wanted to hurt you, I wouldn't have called the police. I would have handled it myself," I stated, catching a glimpse of Damon watching me, but I tried to ignore his look of concern.

"Kegan, are you going to let her talk to me like this?" she said, bursting into tears.

To my dismay, this is when Dempsey decided to exit my home. He was fully dressed and still appeared angry about the conversation we had in the bedroom. Kegan and Damon noticed him as he made his way to his car to leave.

"You see. I knew this bitch was a whore," Imani yelled. "Look, she has another man in her house."

Leave it to Imani to put me on blast and bring attention to Dempsey and my torrid situation. Neither Kegan nor Damon commented as they watched Dempsey start his car and drive away. I was glad he was gone, but I wasn't glad Damon saw him leaving.

"Kegan, baby, please . . . Tell the cops to let me go," she begged as she began to struggle with the officers.

The cops warned her to stop fighting them, but she was so busy concentrating on Kegan to care about what the cops were telling her.

"Stop resisting, Imani," Kegan told her.

"Help me, Kegan. Make the cops let me go."

This woman was delusional. Did she really think Kegan had the power to tell the cops to release her after they caught her destroying my car and damn near assaulting her very own fiancé? Even if he asked, I wasn't willing to let her go. I was pressing charges, not only for the destruction of my property but also for the destruction of my relationship with Kegan.

"Kegan, help me," was the last we heard Imani say as the officers placed her in the back of the squad car. And like the maniac I knew her to be, this trick lay down in the backseat and began kicking the windows to the car. The officers had to open the door and restrain her to the point she couldn't hardly move anything. Then she tried to spit on Damon, which, to me, was a major violation. I just knew he was going to tase her ass. And I wished he did. But instead, he placed a mesh covering over her face to shield from any saliva landing on them. After doing so, they closed the door and proceeded to leave with Kegan's distraught woman. Damon gave me one last look before getting in his cruiser and driving away.

Kegan approached me as he looked at me sincerely. "I'm so sorry for all of this."

I shook my head as I looked at my car which looked damn near totaled, and said, "Your wedding money is going to get me another car."

He chuckled saying, "I promise, I got you."

I felt like those words meant more than Kegan making sure I had my ride repaired. The loving way he was gazing at me let me know he wanted more from me. But I wondered after everything that happened, was I willing to give him a second chance.

Monica

28

With everything that's been happening in my marriage, I thought it as a great opportunity to show up at church, hoping I would hear something that would help me figure out how I was going to make my marriage work. I also wanted to see my mother in-law squirm when she saw me enter the sanctuary. She did not disappoint. As flawless as she portrayed herself to the congregation, I could see her uneasiness when she noticed me enter the sanctuary.

First Lady Isabelle sat in her usual space at the front of the church, and to my surprise, Ms. Georgiana was not next to her. Oh, I knew she was in the building, but she made it a point not to sit alongside Isabelle for fear of how it would look to these good old-fashioned Baptist people. *Hypocrites,* I thought. Just knowing how conniving they all were ticked me off. I felt guilty thinking such unholy thoughts in church, but God knew me. Thinking badly here or outside of here was wrong, regardless. Still, I made a mental note to ask my God for forgiveness and pray for him to guide me, because right now, I knew the devil was all in me.

I looked over and was happy my friends kept their word to come with me to church today. Not only did Sonya, Kellie, and Vivian show up, Kellie brought her brother Victor, and Sonya brought Meena. I knew Sonya was going to be looking some kind of evil because she liked to sleep in, but to my surprise, she seemed happy.

When the assistant minister stood at the podium, he said, "It's praise and worship time. I know everybody in here has a reason to give God praise. No testimony is better than someone else because in God's eyes, it's all good."

The church chuckled at the way he said it's all good, which brought a smile to my face as well. It was time to say what I needed to say. Isabelle thought she was squirming when I walked up in here . . . just wait until she saw me stand to give my testimony. Rising to my feet, I looked at my friends who clapped at my bravery.

"Now that's what I like to see. Someone who is eager to give God praise. Amen," the minister said.

Amens rang out, and I watched as the first lady looked back in utter shock to see me standing. I smiled graciously at her. Then I shifted my gaze to Mr. Woods, who also seemed taken aback by me standing. Then I made it a point to smile at my enemy, Georgiana, who was sitting in the pew section to my right.

"Now you all have a small window of time to give God praise. You know how it goes. I'm going to sit down and give you ample opportunity. Once I stand, that's the end of praise and worship. Now, my sister, you have the floor."

I watched the minister go back to his seat next to Mr. Woods and began to speak.

"Giving honor to my Lord and Savior Jesus Christ . . . To the ministers on the roster, First Lady, deacons, deaconesses, and congregation, good morning."

Good mornings rang out around me.

"It's so good to be in the house of the Lord one more time. I wish I could say I'm here every Sunday, but I'm not. I'm a sheep who strays sometimes, but I always return."

"Amen," some members shouted.

"What people need to understand is that there's a lot of individuals like me. Many of you were me. We want to come to church, but then we get lazy and decide not to come for one Sunday, which leads to many."

"My Lord," someone said.

"My mother called it a teeter tottering faith. I use to get mad when she said this to me, but it wasn't until I was on the brink of losing my mom that I understood what she was telling me. She raised me in the church. She hoped I would remain in church, but she knew I would run out into the world and do me because that's what most of us do. She told me she did it too. My mom's last day here on this earth, she smiled and told me she knew I would return."

"Amens," rang out louder.

"That was the prayer my mother had for me. She was dying, but she was still praying and ministering to my soul because her faith was anchored. She knew where she was going and was happy about seeing her forever home. She used her last breath to tell me never forget where my blessings came from. 'Put God first and go to the house of the Lord and praise him.'"

"My Lord, my Lord," someone said.

I paused, getting choked up at the thought of my mother who I missed tremendously.

"I didn't like coming to church because I saw so many so-called Christians sitting in the pews claiming to be doing God's work but sitting in judgment. Some talked about people. Some shunned people. I say some even tried to destroy people."

"My Lord!" someone exclaimed.

"And I'm not going to lie, it angered me. I've been on the receiving end of this, unfortunately," I said, looking at Pastor Woods who nodded but quickly averted his gaze. "I thought Christians were supposed to be trying to win souls, not degrade them to the point of them never wanting to come to church at all."

"Say so, child," an elderly woman said.

"I can easily point fingers at a few people in this church right now who claim to be Christians but have made me feel like church is the last place I want be."

I noticed the entire time, Mrs. Woods didn't bother to turn around anymore to face me. I really wish I could see her expression, but it was okay. I was going to do what I came here to do.

"I've been at the grocery store and saw a minister, in this church, who I spoke to, and the man didn't bother to part his lips to me."

Moans and groans reverberated throughout the sanctuary. I noticed each minister on the panel look around to each other, wondering who I was speaking about.

"But when I came to church, he was smiling and trying to shake my hand, welcoming me to the house of the Lord, and all I could think about was *now he can speak*. Was this all about appearance and putting on a show? Doesn't he know you can't put on performances for God because he sees through all?"

"Yes, he does," many said, nodding.

"I have several stories like this. I've even considered naming individuals today because I've truly become fed up with the deceitfulness of people. I thought if I put them on blast, maybe this would be the wake-up they needed to do better."

I looked again at Mr. Woods, who tried to look calm, but I knew he was sweating bullets under his robe.

"But what kind of person would I be?"

My friends clapped, and it wasn't until then that I was reminded they were here with me.

"I would be acting just like them. My mom was a wise woman who told me you are responsible for your actions and your soul. Never allow someone to take you out of your character. I know she's here with me today," I said, looking upward as my eyes brimmed with tears. "Even now, my mom is holding my hand and letting me know that God fights my battles."

Vivian was beside me and reached out, grabbing my hand.

"I'm sorry to take up so much time with my testimony, but I felt this needed to be said."

"That's all right, honey," another church member said.

"I stood, thinking this was going to go one way, but God intervened, leading me down another path. I know he's proud, and I know for sure my mother is proud of me too. Please, church, pray I don't allow my enemy to take me down. Pray I continue to grow, despite the negativity of others. Please pray for my strength in the Lord, and I will do the same. Thank you and God bless."

I sat down and sobbed like a child. I honestly could feel my mother's presence in this moment, and it rocked me to my core. It was like her hand was in the middle of my back, telling me you're better than this and the only thing I could think about doing was making her proud. Funny how you go into a situation thinking one thing, not knowing God could quickly steer things to go in another direction.

Needless to say, my in-laws were relieved I didn't spill the tea. The fact I tap-danced around the issue let them know this could have easily gone another way. Trying to be the bigger person was not an easy task, and after church, I went over and spoke to both of them. They smiled and awed about what a wonderful testimony I gave. Again, this was for show. Many members were around us, and I knew it was all lies. But again, I felt my mother's hand on my back, telling me to smile and keep it moving. God has this. As much as I knew this, I still had my doubts. I wanted immediate retribution. That was the human side of me, but I had to suck it up in this moment and allow my mother's spirit to guide me down a more righteous path.

What was going on in my marriage and my life right now was challenging. Still, it wasn't as challenging as the secrets I'd been keeping for far too long. Maybe it was time to really speak my truth. I was afraid. I knew this truth could set me free, but it was also going to possibly rain down the biggest storm in my life.

Sonya

29

After church, everyone decided we should go have lunch together. I wanted to decline due to the long night I'd had, but Monica talked me into joining them. All I wanted to do was figure out the next steps I needed to take to get my car fixed, but I knew there was nothing I could do since it was Sunday. Right now, I was driving Kegan's spare vehicle, an Audi, which was a lot nicer than my own car. I almost told him I couldn't take this car, but after taking another look at the damage his crazy fiancée caused to my ride, I gladly accepted. I would drive it until the wheels fell off. We were supposed to meet up later and talk about how we were going to proceed with things. What that meant, I didn't know. He was the one who was engaged to be married, so was he going to tell me the wedding was off? He also wanted to see Meena and talk to her about everything that's been going on. It was a conversation that was long overdue, so I was happy he was finally making an attempt to see her.

Meena decided she didn't want to go to lunch with a bunch of old people. That was fine with me because that would be less money I had to spend. Of course, she had all types of questions about the car I was driving, and I told her everything that happened. Well, almost everything. I excluded Dempsey coming over because I felt like that would be a different type of conversation I wasn't ready to talk about. She took everything in stride and was happy Kegan was coming over later to see her. The excitement I saw in my daughter made me happy. I just hoped Kegan wouldn't disappoint her again. If he did, I was going to go find him and drag him to my daughter myself.

After dropping Meena off, I went straight to the restaurant. Even making that quick run, I still beat Kellie to the restaurant. Monica and Vivian were already seated when I arrived, making this feel like déjà vu again.

"Here I'm thinking I'm running behind, and Kellie and her brother haven't got here yet," I said, sitting down.

"You know Kellie. I've given up on her ever arriving anywhere on time," Monica replied.

"Well, I tell you one thing. I'm not going to wait on her like we did the last time. We're going to order our drinks and food, and she's just going to have to get in where she fits in, because I have plans," I disclosed.

"What plans?" Monica asked.

Smirking, I said, "Kegan is coming over later."

Both Vivian's and Monica's eyes widened at this admission.

"Is that whose car you are driving?" Monica asked.

"You noticed," I giggled.

"Of course, I did. Now, spill the beans and tell us how that came about."

I told them the short version of everything that happened and watched as the two of them listened intently. Neither had questions until I was finished, ending it with me driving Kegan's car.

"I'm surprised you showed up to church at all," Vivian said.

"Trust me, I wanted to call and say I couldn't make it. I'm exhausted."

"Not too exhausted that you don't want to see Kegan," Monica joked.

All I could do was smile because I was excited about seeing him. Many scenarios about how his visit was going to be flashed through my mind, but I tried not to dwell on them. The main thing I tried not to do was get my hopes up about us getting back together. As much as I would like to think I would take him back, I knew things were a lot different. Especially since he had a crazy ex-fiancée in the midst.

Changing the subject I said, "Monica, your testimony today was on point."

"Thank you. I don't even know where it came from. Honestly, I stood up to say one thing, and I ended up saying something different. If you all would have known what I was really up to, I don't think any of you would have shown up at church today," Monica admitted.

"What do you mean by that?" I asked.

Sighing, Monica started to speak, but Kellie and her brother approached the table.

"We made it," she said, sitting next to me. Victor pulled up the chair beside her and had a seat.

"At least you are not as late as the last time," I said.

"I wouldn't let her," Victor said, arching his brows. "I can't stand being late somewhere."

"You sure you're kin to this woman, because Kellie is late to everything?" I stated.

"Yes, she's my sister. She's always been like that. Usually, if I'm going with her anywhere, I'll drive because I know as long as I'm behind the wheel, we *are* going to make it on time," he said.

"OK, I'm right here, you guys. No need to bash me," Kellie said.

"You should be glad we're bashing you in your face and not behind your back," Victor joked, and Kellie playfully hit her brother.

"I know we just came from the Lord's house, but can we please get some alcohol on this table? I'm waiting for the waiter to change this water into wine," Victor said, and we all burst into laughter.

Seeing Kellie, I could tell she was happy her brother was here. I could see why, because he was hilarious. I'd met him one other time before, but it was just for a quick moment. It was nice spending more time with him. He was very handsome, and if he wasn't gay, I think I would have tried to hit on him.

"Come to think about it, no one has come to ask us for anything. Are the waiters and waitresses on strike?" Monica asked.

"Not at all because I see a few right there huddled up together." Victor lifted his arm and began waving at the young women yelling, "Excuse me, waitress girls. Can one of you come take our orders?"

Placing her elbows on the table, Kellie dropped her face into the palms of her hands and began shaking her head in embarrassment. We all were laughing because we thought it was funny. Victor was right. They were huddled up and not doing their job. We should have at least had our drink orders taken, but no one had even done that. One waitress immediately came over and apologized for our wait, but she looked none too happy about assisting us. After she noticed the disgruntled look Victor was giving her, she quickly switched up her attitude as she took our drink orders and immediately scurried away.

"She's not getting a tip because she acts like she has a problem with us," Victor said.

"No, the problem is not with you all. The problem is with me," Vivian acknowledged.

"Why?" I asked.

"I basically threatened her when she kept hitting on my husband the last time I was in this restaurant. She unbuttoned her blouse and everything. Her breasts damn near fell onto Sheldon's plate."

"Oh, hell nawh. I would have checked her too, honey," Victor said. "Women these days don't care if the man got a ring on or sitting right beside your ass. They are daring enough to try to snatch your man away from you."

"You mad, Victor?" Kellie asked her brother.

"I'm getting there. I can't stand people like her. They think because they pretty, they can disrespect the next woman, or man, for that matter. I've had some women tell my ex they could turn him back straight."

"Get out of here," Monica belted.

"I'm serious. But Aaron made sure not to tell me that mess until we got home, because he knew I would have snatched that bitch bald."

Laughter erupted around the table as I reached across Kellie to give her brother a high five. We smacked hands as the waitress returned with our drinks and appetizers. Victor sat back with his arms crossed, looking at his nails, admiring them like he'd just got them done.

"Do you have a problem with us?" Victor asked.

Kellie swatted at him, mumbling for him to hush, but he frowned and turned his attention back to the waitress awaiting her answer. Hell, I was interested in hearing what she had to say too.

"Excuse me?" the waitress asked, looking confused.

"I'm just asking because you look like you not happy about serving us. It's either that, or you are unhappy with your job. Which is it?" he asked.

"Oh no. There isn't a problem," she said giving us a weak smile. "I like my job."

"If you say so. I hope the next time you return to this table, you come with a better attitude because if there is a problem, you can get one of your other waitress friends to serve us."

"Victor! Oh my goodness, I can't take you anywhere," Kellie reprimanded.

"What? She know she has a problem with us."

"Sir, I don't have a problem with any of you," the waitress countered.

"Uh-huh," Victor said, side eyeing her.

Clearing her throat, the waitress asked, "Can I take your lunch orders if you are ready?"

"Give us a minute, please. Better yet, make it ten," Victor answered.

The waitress walked away, and I burst into laughter, saying, "Victor, you are a man after my own heart."

"I just like to call it like I see it."

"I hope you calling it like you see it don't make that girl put something in our food," Kellie added.

"I swear to Jesus Christ if I find out that heifer messed with my food, she's going to visit Jesus quicker than she anticipated."

Again, I burst into laughter, looking over at Kellie saying, "I'm moving him in with me. Because I'm in love with him."

"I know you strictly dickly, which I have a large one, but you don't have the genitals I'm interested in. Now, if you were born a man, we may have some things to talk about," he said looking at me flirtatiously.

"I'm all woman, honey, all 240 pounds of me."

"I like my girls BBW," Victor said, rapping Drake's lyrics.

"The kind that suck you dry and cook some lunch for you," I finished, and we both high-fived again.

I noticed some other patrons looking our way, but I didn't care. I was really having a great time with Victor. The funny thing was, we hadn't had any alcohol yet, but that was going to change now.

"I can't take either of you anywhere," Kellie admitted.

"Whew, I need a drink. I've worked up a thirst." Taking a long sip of his wine, Victor said, "Yes, Jesus fixed it. I so needed that."

"Me too," Monica agreed. "Especially with what I have to tell you guys."

All eyes fell on her as she shifted nervously. I noticed she wasn't talking as much after Kellie and Victor arrived. She was always more engaging, but now she wasn't saying anything. Whatever she had to tell us must've been weighing on her heavy, because she looked like she was about to hyperventilate.

"Please don't tell us you getting ready to die or something, because I can't take any news like that," I said.

"No, Sonya. But I do want to say I haven't been up front with you at all."

"About what?" Kellie asked.

"One thing I want to confess to you all is Devin has asked me for a divorce."

All of us looked at Monica with sympathy, and Vivian was the first one to break the sudden silence that fell among us.

"Monica, I'm so sorry to hear that."

"It's okay. I'm still trying to come to terms with it," she said, forcing a smile. "I would love to spill my guts right now, but I want to talk to you all more about what's going on with me away from this restaurant. I hope you understand."

"So you expect me to wait after you dropped a bomb like that on me?" I asked, trying to be funny and break the tension.

"Let's just eat first, and then we can go somewhere to talk about this."

"We can go back to my house," Vivian suggested.

"Really?" I asked.

"Sure. You ladies and gentleman have welcomed me in with open arms, so I would be happy if you all came back to my home."

"Is your husband going to be okay with this?" Kellie asked.

"He's working today, unfortunately, but I know he wouldn't mind."

"On a Sunday?" I questioned.

"I thought the same thing, but again, he's new to the company, and they're trying to break him in right, I guess," she giggled.

"Nothing like a hardworking man," Monica added.

"Just as long as he's working," Victor chimed in.

"Victor, will you quit!" Kellie nudged him.

"I'm just saying working weekends is the best excuse to cheat. And, Vivian, I'm not saying your husband is. I'm speaking from experience," he expressed.

Vivian laughed as she picked up her wine and took a sip, but she paused when she noticed something across the room.

"Vivian, are you okay?"

Vivian

30

I *know* this man didn't walk up in here with some other woman with him. He told me he had to work. Here I was laughing at what Victor said, and the truth in what he said smacked me in the face. I did think it was odd Sheldon had to go in on a Sunday but thought nothing of it since he never lied to me about anything. I guess there was a first time for everything, but I would have loved his lies not to play out in front of my new friends.

I stared in disbelief as Sheldon escorted some chest-nut-complected woman with long, lustrous hair to a table for two. Her face was oval-shaped and flawlessly made up. Her body was slim and tone as she wore a light grey pantsuit which hugged her curves in all the right places. On her feet were what looked like Jimmy Choos. I surmised her up in one quick glance and before I knew it, I was standing to my feet.

"Vivian, what's wrong?" I heard Monica ask.

I couldn't say anything. All I wanted to know was who this woman was walking in with my husband. I left the table with the ladies calling out to me. I ignored them as I made my way to my husband who was smiling at some woman I didn't know anything about. He didn't seem like he was flirting with her, but still, the appearance of how this looked upset me.

When I approached, Sheldon and the woman were picking up their menu trying to figure out what they were going to order. When he saw me, his eyes became as big as saucers. The nervous expression on his face only added to me thinking he was up to no good.

"Hon . . . Honey. Hey, what are you doing here?" he asked fearfully.

Smiling dryly, I said, "I'm having lunch with my friends."

I gestured toward the table I was sitting at, only to see them all looking in our direction. Sheldon smiled weakly at them before turning his attention back to me.

"Now, let me ask you what are *you* doing here? I thought you told me you had to work."

"I am. I'm having a meeting," he stammered.

Did he really think that short answer was going to suffice? There was no introducing me to the woman with whom he was having a meeting, and I thought this was odd. I'd met several people from his job, and this woman I hadn't seen before. So, I decided to take matters into my own hands.

"And she is . . .?" I asked, looking at the docile woman.

"This is Nina Alexander. Nina, this is Vivian."

With eyes narrowed, I looked at Sheldon with contempt, wondering why he introduced me by my name and not by my damn title. Even if he said my name, he could have at least said it in combination with the title of his wife. I kept smiling, trying to keep my temper under control. I could feel my face getting hot and decided to take a deep breath so I wouldn't act a damn fool up in this establishment.

Being the bigger person, I held my hand out and shook Nina's hand saying, "It's nice to meet you."

At that moment, the waitress Hailey approached the table asking, "Should I bring another chair over for you to join them?"

This bitch knew damn well I wouldn't be joining them. I knew she asked this in order to be funny. I could tell by the smug expression on her face.

"That won't be necessary. My husband is having a lunch meeting, and I thought I would come over and speak. Is something wrong with that?" I asked, scowling at the waitress.

She shifted uneasily, hopefully remembering the last time she came at me wrong. She should have learned from her previous experience with me. I was not the one she wanted to come for.

"Please, give them a few more minutes, okay?" I told the waitress, and she hastily walked away, leaving us to finish up our tête-à-tête.

I returned to talking with my husband and his companion. Sheldon looked at me perplexed, like he didn't know what to say or how to act, and this was very unusual for him. Nothing shook my husband, but I guess I had that effect on him, after all.

"So, you work with Sheldon?" I asked.

Her eyes darted as she looked to him for answers.

"Yes, we work together," she answered.

Lies, I thought as I glared at him, noticing his nervous energy which hadn't ended.

"What do you do?"

"I'm the executive assistant to our boss," she revealed.

"How nice. I wish Sheldon made it a point to tell me about you, but I guess it slipped his mind," I said glowering at him.

An awkward silence fell upon us, and I broke it by speaking again.

"Well, I'm going to leave you two to get back to your 'business.' It was a pleasure meeting you," I said, reaching out and shaking her hand again. "Sheldon."

I beamed as I confidently walked away from their table. Little did they know I was struggling to maintain my composure. All I wanted to do was walk out of this place, but I knew if I did that, then it would have looked obvious that something was wrong, and I couldn't have that, not after we'd just had a discussion about men cheating. So I returned to my place at the table, making sure to look unfazed. Of course, when I sat back down at the table, questions were being fired in my direction.

"Vivian, are you okay?" Monica asked, looking at me suspiciously.

Smiling weakly, I said, "Yes, I'm fine."

"Aw, hell, this bitch is about to explode," Sonya surmised.

"Sonya, I've told you about calling women bitches," Monica chastised.

"I'm sorry. I didn't mean it like that," she said, looking at me sincerely.

"I didn't take it that way," I told her.

"But Sonya's right. Vivian, girl, you look five shades lighter. All the blood has drained from your face," Victor added.

"I promise you I'm fine," I lied.

Victor looked at me sideways as he picked up his drink and took a sip.

"Who is that?" Kellie asked.

"That's my husband. And before you ask, the woman with him is his coworker," I answered, noticing each of them were raring to ask me who the woman was.

"Vivian, if you don't mind me saying, your husband is fine as hell," Sonya complimented.

I smiled knowing he was, which was why I had an issue seeing him with another woman. I honestly felt threatened in a sense this woman could take my husband away from me. Losing him to someone else was my biggest fear. I always wondered why he was with me anyway. I was plus size. I hated thinking being a bodacious woman was a bad thing, because in my heart, I knew it wasn't. I tried to accept there was nothing wrong with me, but it was an uphill battle. Now that this woman, who I thought was perfect, was with my husband, I could see why he would be interested in her and easily fall out of love with me.

"Vivian, I know I shouldn't be looking at your husband like that, but Sonya ain't never lied. Your husband is scrumptious," Victor added.

"Please don't think we're coming for your husband like that, because we are not," Sonya said.

"I know. At least you tell me to my face and are not disrespectful with it."

"I can see why this waitress was hitting on him," Victor said. "You are a lucky woman."

"And don't look now, but he's coming over here," Kellie added.

Instantly, everyone at the table turned their attention to him as he approached our table. None of their eyes left him until he was standing by my side.

"Hello, ladies and gentleman," Sheldon greeted.

Everyone spoke in unison as Sheldon turned his full attention to me.

"Babe, can I talk to you for a minute?"

"Sure, but let me introduce you first."

I did making a point to tell everyone this was my husband. I hoped Sheldon caught it but wasn't sure he did. Reaching out for me, I took my husband's hand and followed him to the area where the restrooms were. They were tucked in a corner away from patrons. We were out of eyesight and earshot of everyone, giving us a moment of privacy to speak to one another.

"Babe, I'm sorry."

"Sorry for what?" I asked ignorantly as I crossed my arms and looked at him menacingly.

"It's clear I said or did something to upset you."

"*Did* you?" I asked curtly.

"Look, I don't like to see you mad."

"Then you should have thought about that before you walked up in here with another woman," I shot back.

"Vivian—"

"Do you really think I believe you work with that woman?"

He dropped his gaze as I continued.

"I can't believe you lied to me like that."

Right then, a Caucasian man walked up wanting to enter the men's restroom, which I was standing in front of. I moved out of his pathway, allowing him to enter before we spoke again.

"Look, now is not the time, nor the place. We can talk about this when we get home."

Sheldon stared bleakly at me while I eyed him sternly.

"Baby, I am sorry."

"Okay," I answered snappily. "And by the way, I invited my friends over to our home after lunch. But that shouldn't be a problem with you *since you are working*."

He closed his eyes wearily as I walked past him to go back to the table. Sheldon coming over should have meant something to me, but right now, it didn't. I still couldn't get over the fact of how he lied *and* introduced me. It may be small to him, but to me, it was a huge problem, taking our relationship in the wrong direction. Nothing made a woman feel more loved than a man announcing his wife or woman to people, but Sheldon didn't do that. It was obvious he was embarrassed by me. One thing was for sure . . . I was going to find out what was going on, and I prayed my suspicions weren't right, because that would mean the end to our marriage.

Monica

31

Vivian's house was absolutely beautiful. I'm not going to lie, I didn't expect her to live in a house this nice. She was very stylish, but this home was far beyond what I'd dreamed for myself. I was happy her house was taking my mind off what I was about to do. Now that it was getting closer to me telling my friends everything, my nerves were shaken. I couldn't figure out, after all this time, why I was choosing now to spill the tea on my life. Maybe it was my testimony today. Maybe I wasn't only speaking to the hypocrites in the church, I was also speaking to myself.

"Sis, I know I asked to stay with you for a while, but I'm getting ready to leave you and make Vivian my new sister, honey," Victor said standing by the fireplace in the living room. "I mean, look at these ceilings, will you? I haven't seen anything like this."

"It's gorgeous. Vivian, you have a very beautiful home," Kellie agreed.

"Thank you."

"I mean, seriously, y'all must be bringing in the chips to be living like this," Victor assumed.

"Actually, this house is not as much as people think it is. We got a pretty good deal on it. The buyers were in a hurry to sell," Vivian explained.

"Well, I'm glad someone like you is living here," Victor said.

"Why? So you can come over here all the time?" Sonya asked.

"Exactly. I'm back in the Carolinas now. You ladies need to get used to seeing my pretty face around here."

As everyone chatted amongst each other getting comfortable in the space, Vivian asked me if I could come with her to the adjacent kitchen to help, which I happily obliged.

"Monica, what's wrong? You don't seem yourself," she asked with concern as she cupped my elbow gently.

I smiled weakly before responding with, "I'm nervous."

"About what?"

"What I have to tell you all. I've done some things, Vivian."

"Look, whatever you have to say, it's not going to change the friendship we've developed. We've all done things we are not proud of, trust me. There is not enough time in a day to tell you what I've been through."

"But—"

"No buts, Monica. You are an awesome person. Look how you accepted me into this circle. You didn't have to do that. So stop worrying yourself. Besides, from what I know about these ladies and Victor, I don't think you have anything to worry about. They aren't going to treat you any differently. So, spill your truth. God has brought you this far. He's not about to leave you now."

Grinning with appreciation, I reached out and hugged Vivian tenderly saying, "Thank you so much."

"Anytime, girl. I'm here for you," she comforted rubbing my back.

"All right, you two. That's enough of that. Where's the bubbly?" Victor interrupted and all Vivian and I could do was laugh at his flamboyant behind.

We both helped Vivian gather the wineglasses and bottles of wine and took it into the living room. Victor did the honors of popping the cork and pouring each of us a drink. After we all nestled back into Vivian's comfortable seating, Sonya turned to me to ask what this little get-together was about.

"Okay, Monica, what do you have to tell us? You've kept me hanging all afternoon now."

"I thought you didn't like to hear about people's drama," I countered.

"We never get to hear anything going on with you. But some people, who shall remain nameless, we know their entire life story," she said, cutting her eyes at Kellie.

"Excuse me? Are you throwing shade my way?"

"I wasn't trying to be shady. I'm just saying out of this bunch, the only person we know a lot about is you."

"You *are* my friend, right?" Kellie asked Sonya.

"Yes."

"Then why do you have a problem with me venting what's going on with me every now and then?" Kellie asked.

I could feel the mood in the room beginning to change and felt like this situation was going to get worse.

"You see, that's where you're wrong. It's not every now and then. It's *every time* we see you."

"Sonya, what have I said today?"

"Nothing. And I'm surprised. Maybe it's because Victor is here and the fact you've already vented to him. I don't know, but you are right. You haven't said anything today."

Here I was trying to speak my truth, and these two were getting into it. I swear if I didn't know any better, I wouldn't think they weren't friends at all. One minute they are fine, and the next, they are going back and forth. Unfortunately, the negativity was always coming from Sonya. She always found a reason to antagonize Kellie. As much as I loved her, she really needed to give Kellie a break. Especially after she told Vivian and I what happened to her last night.

"Sonya, come on. Leave Kellie alone," I pleaded, hoping I could somehow get back to the subject of me and what I needed to tell them.

"She came at me."

I started to tell Sonya that she was the one who threw shade first, but before I could say anything, Kellie erupted.

"You act like I was supposed to ignore your slick comment, Sonya. I'm getting tired of you ragging on me all the time."

"Please," Sonya dismissed her as she took another sip of her wine.

"No, I'm really tired of it. I would think of all of us, *you* would be the one who could relate."

The room fell silent as we were watching this scene unfold. Vivian placed her wineglass down as Victor turned his up. Our gazes shifted from one to the other as we waited for Sonya to respond. It was in her nature to defend herself, but it wasn't in Kellie's nature to get as angry as she was getting. I guess when you poked someone for too long, they eventually snap back.

"What does that mean?" Sonya asked, giving Kellie a cold stare.

"Your life is not all peaches and cream."

"I never said it was. Just because I don't tell everything going on with me doesn't mean everything is good," Sonya said, getting heated.

"I'm not you, though. I release my pressure. You, you let it build up while you play bully."

"Kellie, you better back off before you step to something you can't handle," Sonya warned.

"Okay, ladies, this is getting out of control," Victor said, scooting to the edge of the sofa, trying to minimize the confrontation. "We did not come over here for this. We are here to support Monica and hear what she has to say."

"Victor, no. I'm sick of Sonya and her damn mouth. I have never done anything but try to be her friend."

"Kellie . . ." Sonya cautioned.

"She's a single mother whose daughter is crying out for attention that she can't get from her own mother. But she worries about what I'm talking about. She needs to take that energy she's using to pick on me and figure out a way to be there for Meena."

Sonya jumped up and lunged for Kellie. Vivian was quick on her feet and jumped in between the two and blocked Sonya before she could put her hands on Kellie.

"Don't you ever talk about my daughter," Sonya bellowed as she struggled to get at Kellie.

"I'm not talking about your daughter. I'm talking about *you* and how you need to step your game up when it concerns her."

"Kellie, please. Stop it," I said. Of course, she ignored me and continued with her tirade.

"You don't think I know you only allowed Meena to come over to my house last night so you could sleep with Dempsey?"

"And?"

"Do you ever wonder how that makes *her* feel?"

"Kellie, when you have kids, then maybe you can give me advice on how to be a mother."

The room went silent again, this time knowing the level of things being spoken was being taken way too far.

"Sonya, no," Vivian advised.

"No, what? She needs to have kids of her own before she goes telling me how to raise mine."

I don't know if Sonya forgot about Kellie's possible inability to have kids, or she just didn't care. Either way, her saying this made this squabble a lot worse.

Kellie dropped her head as her eyes filled with tears, and Victor came to his sister's rescue.

"Okay, Sonya. You've taken this too far now. You know what my sister is dealing with, and you didn't have to say that," Victor said, wrapping his arm around Kellie's shoulders.

"She didn't have to bring Meena into this conversation. You don't talk about somebody's child," Sonya argued.

"Did you even listen to what she said? She wasn't talking about Meena. She was talking *for* Meena," Victor informed.

Those words caused Sonya to think twice. She literally stood motionless as she allowed his words to filter through her mind. Hell, we all did. I could appreciate Victor's way of saying this to my friend because it did make her stop and listen.

"My sister would never say anything negative about Meena, and you know it. She loves that girl like a sister. That's why she wanted her to stay last night, so she could see where her head was at."

Sonya stepped back from Vivian who was still blocking her path, and we watched as Sonya settled down on the sofa. She seemed taken aback, like she knew she handled this situation wrong, or at least that was what I was hoping. Her lips didn't part, which was a clear sign, as she allowed Victor to continue.

"Not only was Kellie being a friend to Meena, she was also being a friend to you by being there for your daughter. But you couldn't see that. All you heard was her bringing your daughter into this conversation, and you couldn't do anything but become defensive. My sister knows you are trying to be the best mom you can be. But she also knows some things you can do to improve communication with Meena, that's all. Your daughter is beautiful and smart. But she's also lonely, Sonya. But I don't think you needed me to tell you that," Victor finished.

I almost gave that man a round of applause. He spoke truth with compassion, and that was what was missing when Sonya and Kellie were going back and forth with each other. He definitely accomplished a miracle, and that was shutting Sonya down but in a respectful way.

"Umm," Kellie said, clearing her throat. "I think it's time for me to leave." She looked up at Victor who still had her in his embrace, and he nodded.

"Kellie, please. You don't have to leave," Vivian urged.

"It's evident Sonya feels some kind of way about me. I'm not sure why, but it has definitely become clear to me today that she really hasn't been a friend of mine."

"That's not true," I said, looking at Sonya to fix this, or at least say she was Kellie's friend. All she had to say was she was sorry and that could possibly fix this, but Sonya sat there and didn't say anything. Now, she was pissing *me* off.

"Sonya, say something," I urged. We all stared at her to say something, but she kept her lips sealed.

Removing herself from Victor's embrace, Kellie walked over and picked up her purse, saying, "Vivian, thank you for inviting me to your beautiful home. I'm sorry all of this happened."

I could tell Victor wasn't ready to go, but his loyalty lay with his sister, and I loved that about him. He gulped down the last of his wine and followed Kellie out of Vivian's home.

Seeming unfazed about Kellie leaving, Sonya picked up her wineglass, took a sip from it and leaned back like things were cool. I eyed Vivian, who looked just as confused as I was. I didn't know if this was a sign to keep quiet about what I wanted to say, but it was evident today was not going to be the day for me to say anything, and I had Sonya to thank for that.

Sonya

32

I was boiling inside. The nerve of Kellie thinking she could tell me how to raise my daughter when she wasn't even a mother to start with. Not saying she couldn't give me advice, but why wait until we have a disagreement to bring it up. If she was any type of friend like she claimed to be, she would have talked to me about Meena way before now instead of waiting to use my daughter against me. And that's why I kept my mouth shut. I really wasn't worried about how she felt or her damn tears right now.

"Sonya, *really?*" Monica asked furiously.

"Did you hear the things Kellie said?"

"Did you hear the things that *Victor* said? What? Did that go complete over your head?"

"I heard what he said."

"And that didn't warrant a response?"

"What was I supposed to say?" I asked with frustration.

"How about 'I'm sorry'?" Monica shot back.

"This was not my fault," she retorted. "Vivian, you are neutral to this. Do you feel like this was my fault?"

Vivian looked back and forth between the two of us before answering with a "Yes. I felt like you started this."

"How?"

Vivian sat down, sighing before saying, "By talking about Kellie always talking about her problems."

"It's true. Y'all act like I'm supposed to have sympathy for the ignorant decisions she's made." I couldn't believe the two of them were not on my side.

"Yes, she was the one who chose to love her husband and trust him," Monica explained.

"Which is why she's in the situation she's in. If she would have left him like I advised, then maybe she wouldn't be in the predicament she's in right now."

Monica sighed in disappointment as she walked away from me. She turned and looked at me like she couldn't believe what I was saying to her.

"She may not be able to have children, Sonya. Did you remember *that* when you said what you said?"

"Yes, but—"

"Do you like Kellie?" Monica interrupted by asking.

"Do you want the truth?"

"Please. I asked," Monica countered.

"No, I don't care for her. I put up with her for you."

There. It was finally out. I didn't care too much for Kellie. Maybe if I would have told this truth earlier in our relationship, there wouldn't be this confusion now.

"That doesn't make any sense, Sonya. You don't like her, but you use her as a babysitter to Meena?"

"Monica, I would recommend you not go there. You saw what happened when Kellie brought my daughter into this conversation."

"I don't care, Sonya. I've known you a lot longer than Kellie has. These ladies may not know how much you've struggled, but I do."

"I didn't *use* Kellie."

"Where was Meena last night?" Monica asked.

I hesitated.

"Where?" she yelled.

"She was with Kellie."

"And didn't Kellie bring her to church this morning?"

"Yes, but—"

"No buts. You were dead wrong, Sonya. Kellie cares for you. It's evident she cares for Meena also. I think you got mad because there was some truth in what Kellie was saying."

Now it was my turn to get up and walk away from Monica. I didn't feel like hearing this nonsense. I walked into Vivian's kitchen and placed my wineglass on the counter. I placed my palms down on the cold granite and leaned forward, lowering my head. I needed to calm down because this afternoon had become way too much for me to deal with.

"Why did you leave?" she said, entering the kitchen. "Was there some truth in what Kellie said?"

"I know what's going on with my daughter," I said firmly.

"You think you do. Even the best mother doesn't know everything going on with their child."

I stood upright and turned to face Monica. Vivian was standing to the side, leaning against the sink with her arms crossed, watching us intently.

"Look, the fact still remains I don't care for Kellie. That's it. Why can't you leave this alone?" I asked.

"Because I think there's more to it than that. What? You jealous of her or something?"

"Jealous of what?" I asked with a grimace.

"She's gorgeous and is married," Monica named.

"I'm not a toad or nothing. I look good too. And as for being married, she's with a man who keeps cheating on her and infects her with diseases. You think I'm supposed to be jealous of *that?*" I laughed.

Monica inched toward me, her shoes echoing off the tile floors as she said, "She's skinnier than you."

That hit a nerve with me. I stared defiantly at Monica, not saying a word.

"I see I've hit a hot button with you."

"Skinny women . . . they . . . They make me sick," I muttered tersely.

"So you hate all skinny women, is that it?"

"Yes. I can't stand them bitches. Flaunting their toned bodies, around looking at me like I'm beneath them. It makes me sick."

"You sure that's not in your imagination?"

"I'm not crazy. I know how I've been treated."

"Has Kellie treated you like you are beneath her?" Monica asked.

"No, but—"

"Sonya, come on. You know Kellie is not that type of person. You shouldn't punish a group of individuals for the ignorance of some."

I actually hadn't thought about it like that.

"If Kellie was fat like us, then you would like her better?" Monica asked.

"Maybe," I mumbled.

"So all this time, you've picked on her and been mean to her, not because she speaks her mind and tells us all her business, it's because she's skinny?"

"I wouldn't expect you to understand," I told Monica.

"Then what about me?" Vivian finally interrupted.

She'd patiently sat back and allowed me and Monica to talk about this situation. I glanced at her, forgetting we were still in her house.

"Sonya, I've kept my distance and comments to myself because I didn't want to overstep my bounds, but now I'm going to say something."

"Please do," Monica replied.

"It does seem like you've been really hard on Kellie. When I first met you two, I didn't know you were friends at all. I know Kellie sees you as her friend, but you acted like you didn't like her. To hear now it's because she's skinny, it makes sense."

"How does it make sense?" Monica asked in confusion.

"I have five sisters. Well, now four. One has passed, and one is in jail."

I was surprised because Vivian had yet to allow us into her business, not until now. To hear she's lost a sibling and another is in jail was a lot to take in and made my issues seem like nothing. With as much sympathy as I could muster, I said, "I'm sorry, Vivian."

"It's okay. I can't say it's not difficult, but I'm learning to deal with it. The point I wanted to make is out of all my sisters, I was the fat one. I was the chunky one, the fluffy one, the jolly one—hell, the biggest one, and I didn't like it. I used to get 'she's cute for a big girl' or 'she's stylish for a big girl.' For years, I wondered what that meant. Why did all the sentences have to end in 'for a big girl'? There were times I didn't like my sisters because they were skinnier than me. None of them know I've felt this way, but I have. I just kept it to myself. "

Monica and I were concentrating deeply on what Vivian was saying.

"I felt like I was the black sheep in my family, even though I was the oldest. I felt like I had to try extra hard in everything I did because I'd already lost when it came to body image. My sisters had that category locked. Did it build resentment within me? Absolutely. Did it make me dislike women who were a lot skinner than I was? Hell yeah. But I've learned to live with it."

"That's the problem. Why do we have to learn to live with it?" I asked.

"Maybe those weren't the best choice of words to use. There's a lot that goes on in the world we all have to learn to live with. Weight just happens to be a subject that's sensitive to us because being skinny is something we want to be. Television pushes weight loss and images of having the 'perfect' body. Magazines seem to celebrate women who are not as voluptuous as us. Even society gives us the side eye because they may think we don't fit the mode in what's beautiful, not realizing we are just as fantastic as the next person."

"I don't want to be skinny," I admitted.

"I wouldn't want to be Kellie's size. She looks amazing, but I don't think I would look right being as small as she is. A couple of sizes lower, I would be happy. But until I can get fully happy with me and love me in the body I'm in, I'm going to always find wrong with the world because I'm finding so much wrong with me."

Vivian was speaking to my soul. It was like she was in my head telling me everything I had been feeling for years. And if I would have stepped back and looked at the life God dealt me, I would have recognized my insecurities started with my mother and the lifestyle she led, only to include me in it later. When had I had the opportunity to love me when life, along with me being a single mother, overshadowed the love I should have been giving to myself?

"I wish I can tell you ladies I've learned to love myself, but I haven't yet. Not fully. This is why I have a problem accepting the fact my husband loves me."

"But I do," a deep voice said, causing all of us to turn in the direction it came from.

Vivian's husband was walking in the kitchen looking fine as hell. I knew it was rude to stare, but I could gawk at that man forever. He walked over to Vivian and pulled her into him.

"Did you hear me? I said I love you. There is never going to be another woman who can take your place, Viv."

He leaned down and kissed her tenderly, and in that moment, I became jealous of Vivian too. Not like that. I was happy for her. Seeing them together only reminded me of a love I once had with Kegan.

"I guess this is our cue to leave," Monica hinted.

"Oh no, please. Don't leave," Sheldon urged as he turned to us. "You ladies continue with your discussion. I didn't mean to interrupt. I just wanted my wife to know I do love her just the way she is, and I'm not going anywhere for nobody."

"Girl, if you don't want him, I'll take him," I said chuckling.

"You are one lucky woman," Monica added.

"I know. And so are you, Sonya, to have a true friend like Kellie."

"I know you are right."

"You don't have to call her tonight. Think about what I said, but try to fix this. The feelings you have toward her really don't have anything to do with her. It's your insecurities trying to ruin a good thing. Don't you allow that devil to come in and steal her from you."

Kellie

33

In the park swinging on the swing set, I let the mulch beneath my feet be my cushion as I pushed off to fluctuate back and forth. I enjoyed the wind caressing my face with its coolness which aided in extinguishing my sweltering rage. I needed this quiet moment to myself. It gave me an opportunity to think in peace without any interruptions. That's why I dropped Vic off at my house, telling him I would be back after a while. He didn't bother to question me, knowing I was going somewhere to clear my head. He kissed me on my forehead and told me he loved me before going into the house.

Usually the park was bustling with people walking their dogs or jogging, trying to get a workout in. Or there was some mom or dad pushing their child on the swing or tossing a ball back and forth, but for some reason, the park seemed empty. There were a few individuals, but not as many as I was used to seeing, which I thoroughly enjoyed. Why couldn't I go back to times like this when life was so much easier?

The park was a place I found comfort in because my dad used to bring me to the park all the time when I was a little girl. I smiled at the memory of him pushing me on the swing and catching me when I slid down a sliding board. Nothing felt better than knowing he was always there to catch me. I thought about him all the time and wished he was here to talk with me. He would know the exact words to say to me about dealing with any turmoil I was going through. Looking up at the arctic-blue sky, I closed my eyes and began to talk to him.

"Dad, I miss you so much. I wish you were here to tell me what I need to do. I'm hurt. I'm confused. I'm angry, and I don't want to do anything I will regret. I've tried to make you proud and do things the right way, like you taught me, Dad, but, it's getting so hard," I said, getting choked up. "I miss you so much. I just need you to hold me in your arms one more time and tell me it's going to be okay."

I paused, thinking of his round face, and the reflection in my mind made me smile.

"All I have is memories now, which I will cherish for as long as I live. I know you are my guardian angel looking over me. I love you more than my words can say."

A tear streamed down my face, and I reached up to swipe it away. More tears began to fall, and before I knew it, I was covering my face and weeping like a baby. The weight of everything that was going on in my life came spilling out. My marriage, the cheating, my husband's lover, the sexually transmitted disease, the possibility of me not being able to have children, and my failing friendship with Sonya were all too much to handle.

"Are you okay?" a husky voice startled me, causing me to jump slightly as I opened my eyes.

In front of me stood a tall, mahogany brother who had a concerned look on his face as he stared at me. By his side stood a little girl who was gawking at me too with her little hand in his.

"I'm okay," I said swiping at my tears.

I knew I looked a hot mess. Looking at my tear-drenched hands, I could see my mascara was ruining everything. Using the back of my hand, I did my best to get my appearance back on point, but it was no use. This man had already seen me look my worst.

"Are you sure?" he asked.

"I'm just having a moment," I giggled weakly.

"I didn't mean to interrupt you," his baritone voice said.

"No, you are fine. I was just talking to my dad."

The man looked around like he was searching for my father, and I instantly felt embarrassed. He looked at me like I was crazy.

"My father has passed. The park was our favorite place together. So, I come here to talk to him when I'm going through some difficult times," I explained with a nervous chuckle.

His sincere expression let me know he understood.

"It's good to know men like your dad exist."

"Thank you," I said.

"I lost my mother a year ago, so I completely understand where you're coming from."

"It's crazy how hard it still is."

"I know, right? My mother was my rock. I still pick up the phone to call her, realizing she's no longer here. I feel like an idiot when I do that."

"Just like I do now. I mean, look at me," I said wiping my hands on my black-pleated skirt. "I look like a crazy woman."

"You look fine to me," he said tenderly.

The way he said it caused me to gaze at him, only to notice he was looking at me compassionately. The handsome man smiled, causing my stomach to flutter.

"Daddy, can I swing now?" the little girl asked him.

"Oh, I'm sorry," I said, getting off the swing. "Here you go, sweetie. Aren't you a cutie-pie."

"Thank you," she said sweetly.

I watched as the little girl let go of his hand and ran over to the swing I was just in.

"How old is she?" I asked.

"She just turned five. I can't believe she's starting elementary school in September," he said as we both watched her rock back and forth to make the swing sway.

"By the way, my name is Landon," he said holding his hand out. "And that's Gabrielle."

I looked at my hand, which had smears of mascara, and hesitated shaking his. He reached over and took my hands into his, letting me know it was okay.

Smiling genuinely, I said, "My name is Kellie."

"It's nice to meet you, Kellie."

I don't know what it was about this man, but I really found him attractive. I was always leery of men I came in contact with because most were always gawking at me like I was a piece of steak. I didn't get that from Landon. For some reason, this man made me feel comfortable around him. But most killers did, didn't they? *Damn, I've watched too much Wendy Williams,* I thought. She always said the killer is lurking.

"Daddy, come push me," his daughter demanded in her cute squeaky voice.

"I'm coming, honey. Give Daddy one second."

"Let me leave so you can get back to your sweetie pie," I said.

"Are you sure you're okay? You don't have to leave if you don't want to."

"I am. Thanks for asking. Besides, I don't want to intrude."

"You are not intruding at all. This is an open park. You are more than welcome to join us."

"I don't know," I said with hesitance.

"Please. Stay. Do you see that young lady," he said pointing to Gabrielle. "She's going to wear me out. We can be out here an hour swinging, and she would still want to stay. As much as I love this quality time with her, a brother needs a break and sometimes a little adult conversation. You would be amazed at the things my daughter brings up to talk about sometimes. It scares me."

I laughed at Landon, thinking I loved his sense of humor. I decided to join in the fun.

"So, what you are saying is you want to use me for a break?" I asked jokingly.

Chuckling, he said, "Of course."

I laughed, asking, "Then how can I say no to that?"

Landon nodded with a smile as his daughter called out to him.

"Daddy, come push me."

"Stay right here," he said as he scurried over to his daughter.

I stood and watched, happy he'd invited me to be a part of his father-daughter moment. The little girl squealed with laughter as Landon pushed her. She grinned as that same wind that was caressing my face was now embracing hers. Her daddy made sure she went high, and it looked like she enjoyed every bit of it. He smiled at me as he pushed his daughter who screamed, "Higher, Daddy, higher."

Remembering my father doing the same thing, I beamed, knowing he was here with me. I knew that was my father's way of letting me know *you are going to be just fine*. I was going to take it as that because seeing this dad and daughter together gave me a comforting feeling that I hadn't felt in a long while.

I wasn't sure how long I was in the park with Landon and his daughter, but I knew it was long enough for my brother to call me several times to make sure I was okay. I ignored the first three calls, but I finally answered him, letting him know I was okay.

When I hung up, Landon asked, "Your boyfriend?"

"No, that was my brother. He's worried about me."

"You don't look like you should have any worries," Landon said, watching his daughter climb the jungle gym in the park as we sat on a nearby picnic table.

"You would be amazed."

Gabrielle ran over to her dad and asked, "Daddy, are you ever going to tell me where babies come from?"

"I've told you already."

"Babies don't come from bakeries, Daddy. I asked Mom."

"Then where did your mother tell you babies come from?" Landon asked his daughter.

"She told me to ask you again."

Smiling warmly, Landon said, "Babies come from a special garden where people plant seeds."

"Can we go find some of those seeds, because I want a brother or sister? I can help plant them," Gabrielle said.

Landon sighed nervously, mumbling, "I want you to stay away from those seeds."

"Why?" she asked, tilting her little head.

"You weren't supposed to hear that young lady," he said.

"Why?" she asked again.

"Gabrielle, we will talk about this later, sweetie. We are going home in a little bit. So, go have a little more fun before we go, okay?"

"Okay, Daddy," she said running back over to the jungle gym to have more fun.

With his hands clasped in front of him, he dropped his head, blowing out a deep sigh. All I could do was giggle at him.

"You see what I'm talking about? She stopped everything she was doing to ask me that. Where do kids get these questions from?"

"She sounds like a smart little girl," I complimented.

"She's too smart. And I wasn't playing when I said I wanted her to stay away from seeds," he said, shaking like the image disturbed him. "My daughter may not ever be planting any seeds of her own if I have anything to do with it."

I laughed to myself, realizing he was a lot like my dad. My father didn't want me having any kids either. Not any time soon. Little did he know I may not ever be able to have any.

"There you go again. What's on your mind?" Landon asked, noticing I'd drifted off a bit.

"Just things," I answered hopelessly.

"I hope you know whatever you're going through, it's going to work itself out."

"How do you know?" I asked.

"Faith."

His answered stunned me. Not because it wasn't correct, but because it was something my father talked to me about when he was alive.

"You do have faith, don't you?" Landon asked warmly.

"I would like to think I do, but sometimes, I feel like I have none," I said honestly.

"It's okay."

"But it's not okay. I need to have faith things will work out . . . but I don't. The way things have been going in my life, I'm waiting for the next negative moment to happen to me."

"If you are looking for it to come, then it's going to come. Bad things or negative things will always happen, because that's life. Unfortunately, we are not living in heaven. I pray I make it there."

I chuckled at his humor.

"There's always going to be bad times, but there are going to be good times as well. There is no reason for you to sit and be unhappy about the bad things that may happen when you can concentrate on the good things that are."

"Can you say that again?"

"No. That was a mouthful," he chuckled.

"I know you're right, but it's easier said than done," I disputed.

"True, but you have to smile your way through."

"Is that what you do?" I asked.

"Not all the time. Giving you advice is a lot easier than me taking my own."

Remembering my conversation with Sonya earlier, I knew that all too well.

"I tried to give a friend advice today, and I believe it ruined our friendship," I told him.

"It didn't sound like she was a friend to start with," Landon surmised.

I looked at him with a puzzled expression. He understood my look and went on to explain. "If you were truly friends, something as simple as advice shouldn't ruin a friendship. That's what friends do . . . advise one another, especially when we see our friends maybe doing something that could hurt them in the long run."

"I would like to think we were friends. I was definitely a friend to her," I said.

"But was she a friend to you?" Landon asked.

That was one of the things I'd been racking my mind about all day. To know we'd been hanging out with each other this long and her allowing her daughter to stay with me, how could Sonya not be my friend? It was very difficult to think she never was one.

"Sometimes, we force relationships to work in our lives. Whether friendships or partnerships, it doesn't take one person to make these things work. All parties have to be a part of making any relationship work."

I looked at Landon who watched his daughter enjoy herself wondering where this man came from.

"Daddy, I'm hungry," Gabrielle said, running back over to Landon.

"Me too, honey. What do you want to eat?"

"Pizza," she said with excitement.

"I think Daddy can make that happen."

Landon stood to his feet and scooped his daughter into his arms.

"I'm tired too, Daddy," Gabrielle told him, laying her head on his broad shoulder.

"Good. Maybe Daddy can get some rest when you take a nap."

"I'm too big to take a nap. Remember, I'm five."

"Nobody is ever too big to take a nap, sweetie. Your daddy might take one himself."

"But after pizza, okay?" his daughter said sweetly.

"Okay," he said chuckling.

Landon turned to me and said, "You are welcome to join us if you like."

"No, I think I better get home before my brother sends out a search party for me."

"It was really good talking with you, Kellie. Don't get me wrong, I love being here with Gabrielle, but having you here made this outing even better."

"I enjoyed being with you and Gabrielle as well."

"Do you think I can 'use' you again?" Landon asked, smirking.

"Um, I don't know . . ." I said with hesitancy.

"I'm not twisting your arm or nothing," he joked.

"I know. It's just—"

"You have a boyfriend?"

I didn't answer. I didn't want to tell him I was married. I saw him peep at my left hand, I guess checking to see if I was wearing a wedding ring. I was glad I was no longer wearing them. I took my rings off the day I found Jeffrey together with Kyle. Those rings were supposed to be a symbol of a loving union which Jeffrey and I didn't have.

"Look, put my number in your phone," Landon suggested.

I pulled out my cell and entered the number he recited to me.

"This way, you can call me if you would like to have lunch or something. We can even do the park again, if you like. I can push you real high on the swing next time."

I giggled saying, "I'll let you know."

"Good."

"Daddy, come on. Let's go. My tummy hurts."

Smirking, he said, "I better get out of here before I be in trouble."

I watched Landon walk away with his daughter as I thought about the wonderful afternoon I had with him. My cell phone rang, and I knew it was Vic calling me again, but when I answered, Vic's voice was not the one on the other end of my phone.

It was Dr. Hoffman.

Vivian

34

I was in the kitchen preparing dinner for Sheldon and me, acting like things were okay with us when clearly it wasn't. Just because he came in earlier and professed his love to me in front of our friends didn't mean I didn't have a problem with him showing up at that restaurant with another woman. I still felt some type of way about him introducing me by my name and not my title. I yearned to get to the bottom of it at once, but I had to wait until my company left first.

"Dinner smells great, babe," Sheldon complimented as he walked over and kissed me on the cheek.

He'd gotten comfortable and changed into a pair of his basketball shorts and a tank. I could tell he'd showered also and wondered if he did this to wash away any remnants of the woman he was with.

A cold "Thanks" passed my lips.

He pulled out a stool from the island to sit down. He knew I was still pissed, which was why I kept my back turned to him. I stirred his favorite dish, gumbo, which I made for him and my sisters all the time.

"You still mad at me?" he asked.

"What do you think?"

He sighed as he said, "Vivian, I'm really sorry about earlier."

I said nothing.

"I should have told you about the meeting I was having, but I didn't know how you would take it."

That was my cue to turn to him and engage in this conversation.

"Why? Did you think I would lose it?" I asked with an attitude.

"Yes, in a way, I did. I didn't want you to think I was interested in another woman," he explained.

"You see how that worked out, don't you?"

"Yes," he said dejectedly.

"Like you being with that woman wasn't bad enough, you introduced me as 'Vivian' and not your 'wife.' How would you feel if I did that to you?"

He closed his eyes, now realizing why I was so upset with him.

"Viv, I didn't realize I introduced you like that. I thought you were mad because I didn't tell you about the meeting with Nina."

"You know what? There's a lot of things you don't realize anymore. You seemed to pay more attention when you were my best friend than now that I've become your wife. You have fallen into the same category with the rest of the men who fail to pay attention to the woman they claim to love."

"Please, Viv, don't put me in a category with anybody else," he warned. "I'm my own man."

"Then act like one. If you haven't noticed, I think our marriage is in trouble," I informed him as I turned back to the pot of gumbo and began stirring it again.

"Are you regretting you married me?" he asked probingly.

"Yes. Yes, sometimes I regret marrying you, Sheldon," I answered clicking the stove off as I removed the pot from the heat. Then I turned back to face him.

Disappointment was etched on his face, and for a moment, I wondered if I had made a mistake by telling him that.

"Babe, you know my biggest fear was our intimate relationship with each other, and I feel marriage changed that. I miss the friendship we once had," I said, speaking in a softer tone, hoping this would relieve some of the tension that was building.

"Come on, Viv, that's not fair."

"Why isn't it? Can't you see things have changed?"

"It happens when people get married sometimes," he countered.

"Did you forget we were friends first?"

"No, Viv."

"You don't think I've noticed the man you've become is all of a sudden holding back from me?" I conveyed. "You always could be yourself with me. But these past few months, something has changed with you."

"I wish you would stop saying that," he belted out.

"What else am I supposed to think other than you are not attracted to me and maybe you regret marrying me?"

"I don't regret marrying you—unlike yourself," he deflected.

"You act like you don't want to be around me. You don't have sex with me as much as you used to. Hell, you act like you don't want me to suck your dick anymore."

"What I'm going through has nothing to do with you."

"Then tell me what's wrong."

Sheldon searched his mind for what to say. I could see his wall going up, and this unnerved me. He never used to be this way with me. He was always an open book with me, but now, he was starting to hide chapters in his life, like I was not important enough to know his full story.

"I can see you shutting down now."

My husband lowered his gaze. I stepped toward him and watched as he pinched the bridge of his nose. I could tell he wanted to say something, but he wouldn't allow his thoughts to part his lips.

"You know as well as I do, this marriage can't work with only one of us willing to give our all. And right now, I'm tired of trying to pull things out of you, when this was never you in the first place."

"Viv, you keep pushing me," he said with frustration. "Why can't you allow me to choose the time to tell you what's going on with me? As my friend, you never pushed me, but now, that's all you do."

"I've let you have your space. If I see something wrong, of course, I'm going to ask you what's wrong, but when you say nothing, I've left it at that, Sheldon. So, how in the hell am I pushing you? This is the only time I've really come at you like this, so I'm confused," I said, growing agitated.

"Please, just leave this alone for now, okay?"

"Okay," I blurted. "You want to leave that alone, then how about this? Who was the bitch you had lunch with?"

"Now, we are back to this," he sighed loudly. "Make up your mind what you want to talk about. Damn."

"I'll talk about whatever the hell I want to talk about," I said angrily. "So tell me who the hell she is!"

"She's a coworker, Viv!" he yelled.

"I can't believe you are lying to my face," I murmured, looking at him with disdain. "I called your job this afternoon and asked to speak to Nina Alexander, and guess what they told me?"

His eyes grew as large as billiard balls as I stood across from him on the other side of the island and watched his face become flushed.

"Guess?" I said again, but Sheldon said nothing. "I was told that a Nina Alexander doesn't work at your firm."

He continued to remain tight-lipped, looking at me blankly.

"What? You don't have anything to say now that I caught you in a lie? I was giving you an opportunity to tell me the truth, but you said nothing."

"You are checking up on me now?" he muttered.

"You damn right I'm checking on you. Especially when I could tell both of you were lying to me at that lunch today. I mean, why else would she look to you to see how to answer me."

The look of torment covered him as he rubbed his hands down his face in frustration.

"I can't believe you would do this to me. I trusted you."

"I haven't done anything," he defended.

"Like hell you haven't. You standing there not saying nothing, but you expect me to believe what you are saying, when you know I've caught you in a lie. It explains your change. It explains you not fucking me."

"Viv, chill, please."

I walked around the island and watched as he looked up to the ceiling. Swiveling his stool around to face me, I poked him in his chest.

"Viv, please back up off me," he warned.

"Or what? What are you doing to do?" I taunted poking him in his chest again.

He looked down at my hand touching him and chuckled dryly. He pressed his lips together as he brought his eyes up to meet mine, giving me an icy glare. He stood up, but I didn't move, causing him to push the stool back so he could step back from me. I inched forward, getting close to him again, and he blew an exasperated breath as he grimaced at me.

"Viv, please, leave this alone. You know how I am."

"And that's supposed to scare me?" I frowned.

"I don't want to scare you, but you are pissing me off."

"You pissed off? No! *I'm* pissed off because I caught your ass with another woman, and you have the audacity to not give me an explanation. Do you *really* think that's going to fly?" I yelled, pushing him as hard as I could in his chest. I pushed him over and over, letting the hurt of the day come out in a physical altercation.

Sheldon snatched me by my shoulders and shook me violently, yelling, "Is this what you want?"

"Sheldon!" I screamed, surprised he'd put his hands on me.

"You satisfied now? Is *this* the Sheldon you want?"

"No!"

"You want to know who Nina is? She's my psychiatrist. Are you happy now?"

She shoved me hard, causing me to fall against the kitchen sink.

His abrupt outburst scared me more so than him shaking me like he did. He frantically paced back and forth, rubbing his head and breathing erratically as his hands were clinched into a tight fist. I didn't know what to do. I felt bad I'd pushed him this far, but what else was I supposed to do? I'd already left this alone for way too long. How long did Sheldon expect me to deal with this?

He jetted toward me, and I raised my arms to block him. With a guarded stance he stared at me with rage in his eyes before he realized I was cowering like he was going to hit me. And as if a switch was flipped within him, Sheldon's expression suddenly turned sullen. His hardened eyes softened, commanding sympathy for a situation I had no clue about, but how could I? The strong man I knew all of sudden was emaciated and shattered; looking defeated and hurt by whatever happened to him, which was the reason why he had to see a shrink. For the first time, I looked into the eyes of a man who was afraid, and that, alone, made me wonder if I wanted to know why he needed to see this woman.

A tear rolled down Sheldon's face as he dropped to the floor and leaned against the kitchen cabinets. He brought his knees up, resting his elbows on them, and lowered his head as he began to sob. I dropped down on my knees beside him and wrapped my arms around him. I'd never seen him like this before. He leaned his head on me, and before I knew it, he pulled me onto his lap and nestled his face in the crook of my neck holding me tight.

"I'm sorry, Viv."

"Babe, it's okay," I told him as I cried with him.

"I . . . I . . . wanted to tell you, but I didn't know how. I thought you would leave me."

His words caused more tears to fall, and I knew in that moment, this man had to love me if he feared I'd leave him.

"I'm here for you, babe. I'm not leaving you."

Sheldon gripped me tighter, if that was possible, and I gladly consoled my husband. I still didn't know what had him so upset, but I knew I wasn't going to push now. Whatever it was, it was devastating for him to break down like this. I was going to back off and give him time to come around. We couldn't have another evening like this one because it might destroy our relationship.

Sonya

35

The first thing I did when I walked through my door was take my church shoes off. My feet were hurting some kind of terrible. As much as I loved heels, my feet hated them. I sat on the couch and rubbed them bad boys, wishing I had a man here to rub them for me. I was concentrating so much on the pain radiating through my feet that the music from Meena's room didn't hit me until the pain subsided.

"I told that girl to keep her music down."

Aggravated by Meena's total disrespect of my rules, I looked up at the ceiling, wishing I could click my heels three times and transport myself to Jamaica. Then Kellie entered my mind, and I calmed myself. As much as I hated to admit it, I knew how I communicated with Meena wasn't the best. Maybe I could handle it differently this time. I did tend to snap more than talk. This was probably why I had a teen who had so much attitude.

Standing outside her door, I prayed this girl didn't give me any attitude because things would go left real quick. It was one thing to try, but it was another to be disrespected.

I opened her door saying, "Meena, honey, I thought I told you—"

My words got caught in my throat. There was Meena with some guy drilling her from behind while beside them on the same bed were two females tonguing each other down. All of them were butter ball naked, intertwined like a damn pretzel while August Alsina's music played in the background.

"Meena!" I screamed, storming into the room like a raging bull.

The boy jumped off of her, falling against the wall, causing her curtains to come crashing down over his head. The two girls jumped over Meena to get as far away from me as possible. That's when I noticed the boy was her drug-dealing friend, Corbin. And the two girls were none other than Asha and Shannon.

"Mama!" Meena yelped.

I scurried over to the dresser where the blaring speaker was and swiped everything to the floor. The music stopped as all of them looked at me in panic.

"What are you doing in my room? You don't know how to knock?" Meena had the nerve to ask like I was disturbing her.

I looked around to make sure there was nobody else behind me because I *knew* she *wasn't* talking to *me* like this.

When I saw no one else I asked, "Who . . . do you think you are you talking to?"

"Mom, I'm talking to you," she snapped.

I giggled calling Jesus in my mind before I lunged for my daughter. Meena scuffled to the headboard to get away from me, but I snatched her by her hair and yanked her to the floor. The sheet she had covering herself fell from around her naked frame and she shrieked. Asha, Corbin, and Shannon were cowering nearby as they watched me whoop Meena's ass.

"Mom, stop! You're hurting me," she pleaded.

I couldn't stop swinging on her I was so pissed. Her screams snapped me back from my rampage as I heard her friends also plead for me to stop. I let her go, stumbling back to observe the scene before me.

Asha was struggling to put her clothes on as Shannon looked at me fearfully. Corbin stood there cockily with his dick still swinging like he didn't have a care in the damn world. I couldn't help but look at it, which was a nice size for someone his age. I actually hated admiring it like I did. Then I realized his dick was not covered by any protection whatsoever.

"Lord, you better come back now before I commit a murder," I belted out. The kid's eyes *really* bulged when I said that.

Meena struggled to stand to her feet as she reached for the sheet to wrap around herself.

"Really, Meena . . . Not only did you disrespect my house, but you disrespect yourself by sleeping with this boy with no condom?" I said in disappointment.

"Mom, please. We don't have to use condoms because he pulls out," she said ignorantly.

"What about herpes, gonorrhea, and AIDS?" I asked.

"We're clean," she argued.

"How do y'all know? Did you exchange medical records before fucking?" I asked.

None of them said a word.

"What about babies?" I asked. "Females get pregnant all the time with the pullout method. Either of you ever heard of precome?"

Both of them eyed each other as they thought about what I was saying. And then I knew they didn't care. All they wanted to do was have sex, not really thinking about the consequences of their actions . . . as usual. Damn, I felt like this was a reoccurring thing with her. I knew she wasn't this stupid.

"I want all of you to get dressed while I call your parents. And if any of you are confused about what's getting ready to happen next, *I'm calling your parents*," I threatened.

I heard all of them say no, but I wasn't going to deal with this by myself. When they made this my problem, they also made it a problem for their parents.

"For real, Mama, you don't have to call them."

"You know what's real?" I said walking toward her. "That ass whooping I gave you. *That's* real. The fact he's not wearing a condom . . . *That's* real. You all being too young and dumb to be doing anything like this . . . Now *that's* real. I'm so about this situation I want to jump on your ass again."

When I said that, Meena stepped back cautiously. I shook my head at her as I turned to exit the room.

"Ms. Gordon, please don't do that," Asha pleaded.

"Does your mother know you are here?" I asked her.

She shook her head.

"How did you get here?"

She looked at Corbin who was pulling his shirt over his head.

"All y'all's parents need to know," I broke down.

"All my mom is going to do is take my car for a day or two," Corbin said, unconcerned.

I could tell from the first time I met this boy he had his parents wrapped around his little finger. It sickened me to see kids play their parents like a string instrument in an orchestra, but I wasn't that type of parent. Granted, my daughter and I had issues, but I was trying to guide her down the right path.

I stood here not understanding if I went wrong as a parent for her to do something like this. Then Kellie entered my mind again. Ignoring my thoughts, I asked, "What is your parents' number?"

The only number I needed was Corbin's parents because I had Abigail's number, and I was going to call Kegan for Asha because Imani wasn't allowed on my property due to the restraining order I put on her after she destroyed my car.

Corbin didn't answer. For somebody who was so nonchalant about not getting much punishment, I couldn't figure out why he was hesitating at all.

"Either you tell me or you tell the cops. Either way, I'm calling somebody."

That got Corbin's attention. He was nineteen years old having had sex with a minor. He shifted nervously as I glared at him with disdain.

"You pick," I told him.

And just like that, I had the number.

Sonya

36

All three kids sat in the living room waiting for their parents to arrive. I made Meena be present as well since it was her room she decided to have this little orgy in. I still couldn't believe her audacity. What in the world was she thinking? I knew we had a great day earlier, but did she take that as her cue to do what she wanted to do? She had to know I wouldn't condone anything like this. She sat on the sofa with her arms crossed, wearing a tan jogging suit she'd finally managed to put on. None of them were saying a word as I paced the floor awaiting the first knock at my door. Corbin leaned back with his eyes closed, like he was tired. I guess he was. I gawked at him, and then at Meena, who looked at him before hunching him awake. He peered through squinted eyes at her but quickly closed them, to resume his catnap.

I shook my head as a knock sounded at my door. When I swung the door open, Abigail didn't bother to speak as she rushed past me into my home and over to Shannon who was sitting on the sofa with the other three guilty culprits.

"Honey, are you okay?" Abigail asked as she kneeled in front of her daughter.

"Mom, I'm fine," Shannon said with embarrassment as she glanced at her crew. This was different than the innocent little girl persona she put on at Macy's the other day.

"I thought I told you to stay away from these people. They are nothing but trouble."

"Abigail, please, don't start. Not here. Not now. And *not* in my house," I warned.

"You will not tell me how to talk to my daughter. I'm trying to find out what happened."

"Then talk to me. *I'm* the parent."

"An unfit one, if you ask me," Abigail shot back.

I stepped toward her saying, "You don't have a police officer here to keep me off your ass this time. So stop with your insults and let's try to talk about this situation like adults."

"You can put your hands on me if you want to, but I promise you, I will have your ghetto behind placed in jail."

"Mom, will you stop!" Shannon urged.

"I told you to stay away from them. Do you see why? As soon as you get with them, I get a call that something else has gone wrong."

"Are you going to tell her, Shannon, or am I?" I said, looking at her sternly.

Shannon gaped at me as her mother asked, "What is she talking about?"

"Ms. Gordon caught all of us in a compromising position."

"What does that mean, a 'compromising position'?" Abigail asked.

"We were all having sex," Shannon admitted.

Abigail whirled around and unleashed her fury onto me saying, "You *told* my daughter to say this horrible thing."

"*Excuse me?* I didn't tell her to say or do anything. I caught them all having sex in Meena's bedroom."

"Stop lying on my child. She wouldn't do such a thing." Turning to Shannon she asked, "Honey, who made you do this? Did they rape you?"

"Rape?" I belted along with Meena and Asha.

Abigail continued her dramatics saying, "Honey, we can go to the police station and file a report on these people."

"Mom, I was not raped."

"I know you are scared, but you don't have to be anymore. Mommy is here to protect you," Abigail pushed.

"Mom, I said there's nothing to report," Shannon asserted.

There was another knock at the door. When I opened it this time, it was Officer Damon Ward. I didn't want to call him after last night's fiasco, but I figured I needed a police officer here to make sure things went according to plan. Especially with this bunch. Abigail was already screaming rape, and I knew with Asha being here, Imani was going to show. There was no restraining order big enough to keep her from her daughter. Plus, I would be able to have her behind arrested again for trespassing.

"Corbin," Damon called out.

I looked as the arrogant young man scuffled to his feet like he was in the army and his sergeant just called him out. The sight of Damon put the fear of God in this boy. His eyes bulged as he put his hands in his pocket before he answered.

"Da . . . Dad. What are you doing here?"

"*Dad?*" I repeated, looking at the two of them in shock.

"Yes, Corbin is my son."

I honestly didn't think this situation could get any worse, but it did at the mention of him making this declaration.

"What are you doing here in Ms. Gordon's house?"

Corbin's mouth opened and closed like he wanted to explain, but he knew if he did, the man standing before him would probably whoop his ass like I did Meena's earlier.

"Answer me, boy!" Damon roared.

"I don't know," he muttered with terror dripping from his answer.

"Did you forget who I was and what I represent?"

"No."

"No *what?*"

"No, sir," Corbin corrected.

"You thought your mother was going to show up, huh?"

"Yes, sir."

"Don't worry. She's on her way. Not that it matters."

I looked on in astonishment as Damon scolded his son. You could have never convinced me Corbin belonged to him. But looking at them standing across from each other, I could see the resemblance now. Corbin looked just like his father.

"Oh my goodness, what has the world come to? Now the police has a criminal for a son," Abigail assumed.

"Abigail, please," I chided.

With her nose heisted high in the air, she said, "Please *what?* This young man had sex with all these young ladies, and I know he's too old to be doing so with them."

Hearing Abigail say this made me nervous now. I know I threatened Corbin with the cops, but I figured Damon would help this situation. I never figured Abigail would try to use this against the young man.

"Abigail, Shannon didn't have sex with this boy," I advised her.

"But you said—"

"Your *daughter* said I caught all of them in a compromising situation. You were too busy trying to make your daughter out as the victim again."

"She is."

"No, she isn't. Corbin was sleeping with my daughter and Shannon was sleeping with Asha."

Abigail stumbled back as she clutched her chest. Her breathing became labored, and she looked like she was about to hyperventilate.

"My daughter is not gay," Abigail yelled.

"You can say what you want, but I know what I saw."

"You sure you were seeing things clearly after the night you had last night?" she smiled wickedly.

I gazed at Meena who was watching everything unfold. I'd told her part of the story, but I hadn't told her everything because I didn't want her to know.

"I heard about you sleeping with an engaged man."

"I didn't sleep with him. Kegan came by to see Meena. Get your facts *straight*," I snapped.

"Did you sleep with the other man that exited your cozy home?" she snarled, looking around at my home like it was beneath her.

"I sure did. Maybe if you parted your legs for someone and got you some good dick, you wouldn't be so stuck up."

"I have respect for myself—unlike you. Police officers, a scorned woman, damaged property, you have naked, and handcuffs. You had your own episodes of *Cops*, or would that be *Cheaters?* Either way, you are trifling. I guess the apple doesn't fall too far from the tree," she condemned as she eyeballed Meena.

I traipsed over to Abigail and slapped the hell out of her. She gasped, grabbing her cheek in shock as she yelled, "Arrest this woman, Officer. She assaulted me."

"I don't know what you are talking about," Damon feigned.

"She slapped me. You need to do your damn job and arrest her."

Damon didn't move. Abigail looked at everyone in the room saying, "I'll have your badge. I have a room full of witness who saw what she did."

It was clear no one was going to vouch for Abigail, and she saw this.

"Shannon, you see what happens when you get involved with people like this? They will assault you and lie on you to try to destroy your good character."

"You deserved it."

"Shannon!"

"You do what you do all the time, and that's blame everybody for things you are weak in. I'm your gay daughter, and instead of confronting me about this, you decide to jump on Ms. Gordon."

"I *know* you are covering for this boy. You don't want him to go to jail, so you'll say anything for that not to happen."

"Mom, please. Stop with your dramatics. Why can't you be like normal moms? I didn't sleep with Corbin because I'm not into boys. He's with Meena. I was with Asha because she's my girlfriend," Shannon make known.

"Girlfriend?" Abigail shouted.

"And Asha and Meena didn't make me shoplift. It was my idea. Like you said, you know the vice president of the store. He's been over for dinner with you, remember?" Shannon divulged, and Abigail shifted uneasily. "I stole the contraption because it was that easy. He trusted me in the store, which made it easy for me to rob him blind."

"Why would you do that?" she asked.

"Why wouldn't I? You teach me every day I can have anything I want by any means necessary. There's never any repercussions because you always come to my rescue. That's how you live your life. Are you mad because I admitted it, or are you mad because I stole from your lover?"

You could hear a pin drop as Abigail stood there speechless.

"Tell them, Mother. You're busy standing here judging Ms. Gordon. Why don't you tell everyone how my father left you because he caught you in bed with the vice president of Macys?"

I wanted to clap my hands and rag on this woman, but I couldn't. As much as it would have given me pleasure, I wasn't going to take Shannon's moment away from her. This was something that needed to happen between them, and I was going to allow it to play out.

"I think it's time for us to go."

"As much as you pride yourself in being the best mother ever, you're not. If anything, you are teaching me how to end up in jail, kill myself because I won't be able to accept the fact I'm not perfect, or worse, turn out to be a whore like you."

Abigail slapped Shannon across her face saying, "Don't you ever speak to me like that again."

"Truth hurts, don't it, Mother? Well, here's another truth for you. I'm moving in with my dad."

With that, Shannon brushed past her mother and walked out of my home, leaving Abigail standing there emotionally fractured.

She looked at each one of us saying, "I guess you're happy."

"Abigail, I'm not ever happy to see another parent have issues with their child. Just because you can easily degrade people and their children, I'm not going to do that to you."

Abigail stared at me before cautiously walking out my door and past Kegan. And he wasn't alone.

Sonya

37

I knew regardless of the restraining order I put on Imani, she was going to show her face up in my house. She looked like she came for battle wearing a pair of sneakers, grey sweatpants, and a tee. Her hair was pulled back away from her face, and the only piece of jewelry she had on was the engagement ring Kegan gave to her.

"Asha, let's go," was all I heard when Imani pushed her way into my home.

"You know you aren't supposed to be here," I reminded her.

"I'm here to get my daughter," she responded angrily.

"Did you forget about the restraining order I have on you?"

"Do you think I care about a piece of paper? I don't care if the president was here himself; no one is going to keep me from my child."

"Kegan is more than capable of getting Asha, and you know this," I said, looking at him.

"No, I don't. Not after the last time I saw you two together. Wouldn't want you to fall into another lip-lock," she said snidely.

"You need to leave," I demanded.

"Not without my child."

"Mom, chill," Asha said.

"I heard what that other little girl said. You like eating carpets now?"

"Imani, come on. You don't have to come at her like this," Kegan interjected.

"The last time I checked, this was *my* daughter, not *yours*," she snapped.

Asha looked so defeated. She dropped her head in shame as tears streamed down her cheeks. Seeing how Imani was talking to her made me realize I acted like this woman toward my own daughter. I know I embarrassed the hell out of Meena earlier. As parents, we don't always know how to act. I was grateful for this moment because it helped me see that my approach wasn't the best one. I was looking at a mirrored image of myself, and I didn't like it, especially seeing the pain in Asha's eyes.

"Get your ass up and come the hell on," Imani hissed.

Asha stood with an attitude, and Imani jumped in her face.

"You got a problem?"

"No."

"Then you better check that attitude of yours before I beat it out of you. You got me coming over this woman's house over some bull when you know I can't stand her ass."

"The feeling is mutual," I blurted.

Imani turned her antagonizing demeanor to me.

"You just mad I got your man."

"Do you?" I disputed.

"Who is he with?" she retorted, throwing her hand up to show her ring.

"But is he going with you?" I asked.

"Oh, he's going with me, all right."

"Okay," I said smirking. "I'm not going to go back and forth with you. You need to get out of my house and look at this as me allowing you to be a mother to your child and not having you arrested for violating your restraining order."

"How's *your* mother, by the way?" Putting her index finger on her chin, she looked up, saying, "Oh, that's right, she's dead."

Her words really caught me off guard. I turned to look at Kegan wondering how this bitch knew anything about my mother. Had he been talking to her about my life? He looked stunned himself, like he didn't know what was going on. My gut was saying he had nothing to do with this, but at the same time, this was the man I never thought would cheat on me with another woman. I then looked into my daughter's pleading eyes which were telling me she wanted me to leave this alone. As mad as I was, I didn't like acting this way around her. Crazy to think this after I whooped her ass. But this was different. I was allowing Imani to take me out of my character, which was easy for her to do since I couldn't stand the ground she walked on.

So, I took a deep breath and smiled at my enemy saying, "Imani, please take your daughter home. She needs you," I told her.

Ignoring me, she continued with, "What did she die from again? That's right . . . That whore got AIDS."

Those words caused the room to erupt in chaos. Meena came out of nowhere punching Imani, screaming. Imani didn't see it coming, catching a fist to her right jaw, causing her to stumble. The force of Meena caused both of them to tumble to the floor with Meena falling on top of her. Imani began swinging, hitting my daughter in her face, and that's when I got involved. I too began pounding on Imani for putting her hands on my daughter. I knew she was defending herself, but this was still my child. I wasn't going to allow anybody to put their hands on her.

Kegan jerked me off of her by pulling me around my waist. I watched Corbin grab Meena the same way, trying to get her to the other side of the living room. As Imani got her footing to lunge for Meena, Damon restrained her. The coffee table was turned over. My lamp crashed to the floor, and Asha stood frozen, watching the madness unfold.

"Arrest her," Imani shrieked, pointing to Meena.

Kegan looked at Damon before saying, "No one is getting arrested, Imani."

"That little bitch put her hands on me."

I attempted to charge Imani again for calling my daughter out of her name, but Kegan's hold was too tight.

"Have you forgotten *you* are the one in the wrong here?" Kegan said as Imani's face scrunched up. "You are violating your restraining order. If Meena is arrested, then you will be too."

"I'll gladly go to jail if it means she's going too," Imani said contemptuously.

"It's called self-defense," Kegan told her. "You forget you are trespassing on our property."

Confusion blanketed Imani's face as she asked, "*Our* property, Kegan?"

I caught what he said as well.

"I meant, their property," he backpedaled.

Imani's baffled expression turned to hurt. Now glaring at Kegan, she pushed Damon away from her and calmly said, "Asha, let's go." Asha did as she was told and rushed out the door. Imani leisurely walked to the door, never taking her scornful eyes off Kegan until she was out of my home. I wasn't sure what that look was about, but knowing Imani, I knew this was just the beginning.

Sonya

38

All I could do was clean up the mess that was made in the struggle as I went over everything in my mind. The only sound being made was me sweeping up the shattered lamp. Kegan was kneeling with the dustpan as I pushed the pieces into it. Damon repositioned my table back to its original spot. Corbin and Meena returned to their place on the sofa, this time sitting apart from each other. Meena was hugging herself while Corbin was biting his nails. This was not how I pictured this evening going.

After Kegan went to the kitchen to dump the dustpan, he returned to the living room asking, "Sonya, do you think I can have a moment to speak to Meena privately?"

"If it's okay with Meena, I don't mind."

We both looked at her waiting to see how she was going to respond.

"Can we talk, Meena?" Kegan asked.

She nodded, standing to her feet and walking over to him.

"You can go in my room. I don't think you want to go into hers. Not until we change those sheets."

The two of them disappeared, leaving me with Damon and his son. Damon was standing, still looking a little upset about everything.

"Damon, I'm sorry all of this happened," I apologized.

"What did you do wrong?"

"I should have been here. Then none of this mess would have happened."

"These kids know right from wrong. They thought they could get away with it and got caught. I still can't believe my son had the audacity to do something like this," he said giving his son a stern look. Corbin lowered his head and said nothing as someone knocked at the door.

My stomach fell because each time I opened my door tonight, chaos ensued, and I wasn't in the mood to deal with any more drama. I didn't want to answer. I didn't know who it could be. What if that crazy ass Imani was returning? I swear I couldn't deal with her. The person knocked again, and Damon looked at me to see if I was going to get it.

"Do you want me to answer it?" he asked.

Sighing, I said, "No, I'll get it."

Opening the door, I saw it was Corbin's mom, Leann. I forgot I called her. I wasn't sure if I was happy to see her or afraid it was going to be a repeat of how this night went so far.

"Damon, what are you doing here?" she asked when she saw him.

"I was called by Ms. Gordon."

"Oh my goodness, is everything okay?" she asked frantically.

"He's not hurt, if that's what you're wondering. Not yet anyway," Damon said cutting his eye at his son.

"Please, tell me what's going on."

Damon took it upon himself to tell her everything, which I was grateful for because I was tired of talking about it. Leann look appalled as she gaped at her son with disappointment in her eyes.

"Corbin, honey, what were you thinking?" she asked.

"That's just it. He wasn't," Damon said.

Clearing my throat, both parents turned to look at me as I struggled to tell them the one thing that wasn't said tonight. I didn't want to say anything but felt it was something they needed to know.

"I failed to tell you Corbin did not use protection."

"Corbin, no," his mother cried.

Damon went over to his son and snatched him up yelling, "How many times have I told you to strap it up."

"Dad—"

"I've bought you enough condoms to last years, and you still too stupid enough to use them?"

"I'm sorry."

"Your mother and I are not the ones you need to be apologizing to. You need to apologize to Ms. Gordon and her daughter."

Damon let him go, and Corbin backed away from him. Corbin did as his father suggested and apologized to me. I nodded as Damon began to speak again.

"Turn around and face me, Corbin."

His son did as he was told, looking deflated and afraid at the same time.

Pointing his finger, Damon said, "Do you think because your mother married John and you got some money in your life now, you can act a damn fool?"

"No, sir."

"That's what you're showing us. Yes, you have a nicer house, nicer clothes, and a nicer car, but that doesn't give you the right to become this arrogant, defiant person."

Corbin dropped his head in shame.

"I didn't raise you like this, and you know it."

"Neither did I," Leann added.

The scowl Damon gave her spoke a thousand words. With his forehead creased and eyes narrowed in anger, he looked at her with so much disdain that she nervously recoiled. She took that as her cue to be quiet.

Turning back to Corbin he said, "I'm going to deal with you when we get home. Now, apologize to Ms. Gordon again."

"I'm sorry—" he started to murmur before Damon reprimanded him.

"Speak up, boy. Hold your head up and address her like a man."

Corbin did as his father demanded and apologized, looking at me with the first signs of sincerity I'd seen from this young man.

"I accept your apology," I said, not sure if I wanted to, but right now, Damon scared me, and I felt I had no choice but to accept.

"Now, go to the Jeep and wait for me."

Corbin scurried past everyone, leaving the parents alone to talk. Once his son was out of earshot, Leann began to speak.

"Why are you not allowing me to take my son home?"

"What, so you can baby him and tell him it's going to be okay?"

"Damon, you know I'm going to punish him for this."

"How? By taking away his car and video games, Leann? That's not punishment for that boy. Ever since you married John, you've spoiled him by giving him everything he wants. What is that teaching him?"

"He's a good boy, Damon."

"So, you think having unprotected sex with Ms. Gordon's daughter is being a good boy?"

"Kids make mistakes," she defended.

"He's not a kid anymore. He's a grown-ass man sleeping with an underage girl. And if you expect me to believe this is his first time doing this, you crazy."

I thought the same thing but dared not put my two cents in.

"Damon, I've talked to him about being safe. You know I have because of what happened to us. We did the same thing they did, which is why we have Corbin in the first place."

Damon shifted uneasily.

"You know I'm a good mother to him."

"I know, Leann, but you need to pull back some. Corbin should be working and getting ready to go to college. Not sleeping around and partying like he's been doing."

"You're right. I'll do better with that. But please understand I'm not happy about this either. Nor am I placing blame. We all need to help our children and figure out where we go from here since the act has been done now."

I nodded, agreeing with Leann and liking this woman even more. Honestly, I thought since she was rich, she would be acting like Abigail and pointing the finger at me.

"Ms. Gordon?"

"Leann, please, call me Sonya."

Smiling weakly, she said, "Sonya, I'm so sorry for this. I didn't raise my son to act this way."

"Please believe me, I get it. I didn't raise my daughter to act like this either."

"Whatever you need from me, please don't hesitate to call me," Leann said, walking to the door.

"Leann," Damon called. "I'll bring Corbin home in the morning, okay? Just let me have a man-to-man talk with him tonight."

Smiling, she nodded saying, "Don't hurt him, Damon."

Both chuckled.

"I know you. Try to keep your foot out of that boy's ass."

"I'll try, Leann. Go kiss our son and I'll see you in the morning."

Leann said good night and exited my home.

It was just me and Damon now. This was the first time we'd been alone.

"You really must think I'm a bad parent," I said feeling responsible for all of this.

"Not at all."

"Between the shoplifting, the destruction of property, and now this, you have to look at me with some skepticism."

"Well, now that you've reminded me, I do thing . . ." He trailed off before chuckling.

"I didn't think our next encounter was going to be like this," I said.

"Neither did I. I'm starting to get scared because we keep meeting under bad circumstances. Maybe we need to do something about that to break this bad-luck streak."

"What do you mean, Officer Ward?"

Smirking, he said, "Let me take you out to dinner next weekend."

"You want to go with me after all you've seen?" I asked suspiciously.

"I wouldn't have asked if I didn't want to be with you."

Well, damn, I thought. *He wants to be with me.*

"I would love to go to dinner with you, Damon."

"Great. I'll call you with further details, if that's okay with you?"

"I look forward to hearing from you."

Damon reached out to shake my hand, and I gripped it. The sexual attraction between us was undeniable. Saying good night, I was happy I finally was getting with someone I was interested in. That was . . . until I turned to see Kegan standing there. From the expression on his face, I knew he'd heard everything.

Vivian

39

Today was the first day of my job, and to say I enjoyed it was an understatement. I think I found my calling in fashion. Don't get me wrong, when I arrived, the staff, or should I say Julia's aunt Meredith, wasn't happy about me joining the team. But after having meetings with Julia and seeing her plan and location for the new store she was opening she wanted me to run, I was ecstatic and could care less what Meredith thought. What would have made this day better would have been if my husband wished me luck or even kissed me good-bye this morning. Sheldon didn't do either. After he had his breakdown, he must've thought about it because he seemed mad at me. Sheldon had very little to say to me, and it bothered me. It wasn't often we were mad at each other, but I knew I was wrong . . . well, partially, and I would do what it took for us to get back in a good place.

The table was set. The lighting was low. Smooth music played in the background as the candles flickered, illuminating the dinner I'd prepared for us this evening. I was showered, moisturized, and sitting on the sofa in a sexy number waiting patiently for Sheldon to come home.

As soon as Sheldon laid his eyes on me, he smiled lovingly. To my surprise, he was holding a dozen long-stemmed yellow roses. We both laughed, realizing each of us was working hard to get back in a better place.

He walked over and handed me the flowers.

"Thank you, babe. They are beautiful."

"Beautiful like you," he said, sitting next to me.

He leaned in and kissed me passionately.

As we disconnected, Sheldon said, "I don't like when we don't get along."

"Me either. I'm so sorry for jumping on you like I did. I shouldn't have overreacted and provoked you the way I did."

"I'm sorry also. I thought about it, and if I found you in a restaurant with another man without me knowing about it, I think I wouldn't have waited until we got home to act a fool."

"I know you wouldn't have waited. I know you crazy."

"I should have told you what was up," he said.

"Babe, I want you to feel like you can come to me anytime," I reassured.

"Viv, I can on most things. But what I'm going through right now, I feel like only a psychiatrist can help me with."

I lowered my head wondering if it was something I did to trigger his issue.

"Don't do that," he said.

"Do what?"

"Stop blaming yourself. Sometimes, Viv, it's not about you," he smirked.

I nodded, agreeing with him.

"You have to understand, concerning emotions and deep suffering, men move at a slower pace. We think we can get over any tragedy, not knowing things that have happened to us affects the man we become."

I didn't know if I should respond or continue to listen. What I wanted to ask was what happen to him, but I was

afraid I would push him away again. So I decided to stay quiet.

"I want to tell you why I've been seeing a psychiatrist."

He paused like he was trying to get his courage up to tell me, which scared me a bit. I grabbed his hand and held it tightly, smiling at him to let him know it was going to be okay.

Clearing this throat he said, "When I was sixteen, my family had a party which consisted of a lot of drinking. Really, they had many parties that consisted of drinking. Yes, I was underage, but I got twisted also, to the point of passing out in my room. When I woke up . . ."

He hesitated, biting his lower lip as he squeezed my hand.

"When I woke up, I found someone performing oral sex on me."

I sat and listened, not saying a word.

"That someone was my cousin."

With his forehead knitted, he went from biting his lips to tapping his foot anxiously.

"My cousin is a male."

I didn't move. I don't know if I even breathed. What I tried to do was keep the same loving expression on my face and not looked shocked by what he was telling me.

"I didn't get him off me soon enough," he eyed me, and I understood. "I damn near beat him to death. Family members broke it up, but the damage was done. It caused major friction in my family. People looked at me differently because my cousin bragged about how I enjoyed it. He could care less at how it looked on his end, but I guess that's how demented his mind was. He had everybody thinking I was some kind of man on the down low."

I let go of his hand and began rubbing his shoulders.

"It took awhile for everybody to forget about what happened. Unfortunately for me, I never forgot about it. If anything, the incident made me an angrier man."

"It's okay," I consoled him.

"How did he think it was okay to do something like that to me? I wondered if I gave off something that made him think I would be okay with it. And the fact I actually climaxed, did that make me like what he was doing to me, or even like men for that matter?"

"You didn't know, Sheldon."

"I climaxed, Viv," he said in a raised tone, clinching his hands into fists. "The fact I did that has fucked me up. I thought I was having a wet dream, but to find my cousin giving me head fucked me up on the real."

"This's why you jump when I touch you in the middle of the night?" I asked.

"Yes, because I'm afraid someone else is going to violate me like that again."

"You do understand it's not your fault."

"That's what my psychiatrist said. She told me my body reacted to its natural urges which I had no control over. But the fact I was hard and enjoyed it, and then finished, made me question my manhood."

"You're human. You are a handsome, heterosexual male. And your cousin is a rapist."

Sheldon held his head lower, shaking it as his fisted hands returned to a relaxed position.

"If you don't mind me asking, whatever happened with your cousin?"

"He's okay, far as I know. I heard he married his partner and was living somewhere in Florida."

We sat for a long moment without saying anything until Sheldon spoke again.

"Viv, what I've been going through has been difficult for me. I was afraid if I told you, you would stop loving me or look at me differently as a man."

I frowned saying, "Nothing will change the way I see you, babe. You are my man, and I love you."

"A part of me doesn't know that, like a part of you wonders why I love you so much. Maybe we are more alike than we think."

"Look at you, Sheldon. What's not to love?"

"Looks aren't everything, Viv, and you know this."

"I do but—"

"Stop with the buts already. You are an intelligent, beautiful woman. I feel like you try to push me away because you're afraid I will eventually leave you for something better. I'm here to put your negative thoughts to rest and tell you no one will ever be better than you." Looking squarely in my eyes, Sheldon said, "I love you more than myself."

"I love you too, babe," I replied, cupping his face.

We kissed each other deeply.

"Make love to me," I moaned, and my husband didn't hesitate as he stood, took my hand into his, and led me to our bedroom.

Kellie

40

I was a nervous wreck. I sat on the examination table in the room, foot bouncing from the waiting. Vic sat in one of the two chairs in the room watching me as I tried not to have a nervous breakdown.

"Kell, chill. Everything is going to turn out fine."

"How do you know that?"

"I just do. So, will you please be still and stop acting like ants are in your pants."

This caused me to giggle. I was happy my brother was here for moral support because I didn't think I could do this on my own.

It wasn't long before Dr. Hoffman walked in holding her tablet. Following her was a young woman also in a white lab coat.

"Hello, Kellie."

"Hi, Dr. Hoffman."

"This is Amanda. She's a med student who will be shadowing me today. Is this okay with you?"

"Of course," I responding thinking she could have twenty students following her as long as I got the news I wanted.

"I see you brought your brother. Wow, I haven't seen you in quite some time," Dr. Hoffman greeted.

"It's good to see you again. You look good. You haven't changed a bit," Vic complimented.

"Thank you."

All this chitchat was good, but I really wanted to get to why we were here in the first place. We could socialize after the results.

"So, I guess we should get down to why you are here."

"Yes, please," I said anxiously.

Swiping across the tablet, Dr. Hoffman scanned the screen before looking back at me.

"Kellie, you are fine."

I sighed the biggest sigh of relief. My hands were covering the biggest grin ever. Tears began to form as Vic clapped his hands with elation.

"I told you, Kell."

"Dr. Hoffman, are you sure? I will be able to have children?"

"Yes, your reproductive organs look wonderful. The pains you were having were a complication from the STD."

"I never thought I would be happy to hear that," I said giggling. "You've made me the happiest woman ever."

"I'm glad I could give you this good news."

"Will she need to have any more tests done?" Vic asked.

"Not right now. As long as she continues to take her meds, her STD should clear up."

"I'm taking that faithfully," I told her.

"As long as she's having safe sex and doesn't expose herself to someone who's infected, Kellie should be fine," Dr. Hoffman explained.

I was on cloud nine, but noticed my brother's happiness dwindle a bit.

"So she's clear. She's good?" Vic asked.

"Victor, stop. Dr. Hoffman said I'm good. I'm soon going to be STD free, as crazy as that sounds. All of my other tests came out clear. So stop worrying."

"I'm asking, Kell, because I have a reason to worry."

"What do you mean?" I asked, frowning.

"I wanted to hear from Dr. Hoffman you were good with everything before I told you something."

"Should I step out while you two talk?" Dr. Hoffman asked.

"No, please stay, because you may be able to help me understand this as well, or let me know I'm right," Vic said.

"Vic, what is it?"

"Do you remember when we had that 'guest' stop by the other night?" he asked.

I thought back to what he was talking about and remembered Kyle.

"Yes."

"Remember you asked me what was wrong?"

"Victor, spit it out already," I urged.

"Kell, I know him."

"What do you mean you know him?"

"Kyle and I use to have a thing back in the day," he revealed.

"What?"

"No sex was involved, thank goodness. Just some smooching and rubbing . . . you know."

"Why didn't you tell me?"

"That was when I first came out as a gay man. Many years have passed, and it's been rumored that Kyle . . . has . . . AIDS."

"Wha . . . What?" I said breathlessly.

I looked at Dr. Hoffman whose face remained stoic, but her student looked at me with wide eyes. I could feel my stomach churning at this news.

"I didn't say anything, because I didn't want to worry you. That's why I asked Dr. Hoffman all these questions about you being clear because I was afraid your husband . . ." he paused.

"AIDS!" I repeated.

"It was a rumor, but later, I found out from a reliable source it's true."

I sat there dumbfounded. I felt like I could not win.

"Dr. Hoffman, I know you tested my sister for AIDS as well, and she's clear. Does this mean she's good even if she could have been exposed to this disease?"

My brother was asking these questions, which I knew I needed to know, but I couldn't grasp the fact I could have been exposed to AIDS. Victor should have told me. I wanted to understand he was looking out for my best interest, but regardless of everything, I still needed to know. Here I was happy about being able to have children . . . only to have that dream taken away from me again. Was that why Kyle showed up on my doorstep to talk to me? He wanted to tell me to get tested because my husband had exposed me to this? I wanted to leave so badly, but I needed to hear what Dr. Hoffman had to say.

"Kellie's HIV test did come up negative, which is great. But based on the fact she may have been exposed, she should come back in three months to get tested again. We call this a window period. More likely than not, if you test negative three months later, you can feel safe assuming you do not have the virus. Me, personally, I have my patients come back six months later to get tested once more due to the fact if your immune system has been compromised for any reason, you could still test positive."

"I can't believe this," I murmured.

"I'm sorry, Kell."

"You could have told me before now," I yelled.

"I didn't want you to worry."

"What am I doing now? What do you think I'm going to do for the next nine months, Vic? If you would have told me, at least I would have gone into this knowing what I was facing. But you allowed me to rejoice before ripping that sense of relief away from me."

"Kell, I said I'm sorry. You know I didn't do this to hurt you. I didn't know how to bring this up. I thought now was a good time to talk about it since Dr. Hoffman could help us understand."

"Oh, I understand. I could be dying and the hopes of me ever having children could be gone as well," I said, jumping down from the table with tears streaming down my face.

"Kell, please," Vic pleaded.

I ignored my brother as I brushed past Dr. Hoffman, leaving the examining room. I'd had enough of everybody, and all I wanted to do was be alone.

Monica

41

Not only did Devin not attend church with me on Sunday, he didn't bother to come home either. I called him several times, but all my calls were sent to voice mail. I called his parents' house, and no one bothered to answer there either. I even went by his parents' house, but no one answered the door. Talk about pushing me to the limit. Here I was trying, by not divulging the negative behavior of his parents in church in front of the entire congregation, and now they all were treating me like I didn't exist.

Since Devin refused to deal with me by phone, I went by his job, only to be told by the security check-in officer I wasn't allowed on the premises. All I could do was look at the officer in disbelief. My husband had me banned from the property.

I can't say I didn't sulk in my emotions the last few nights waiting for him to get home. I could tell he'd come home while I was at work by the glass being left in the sink or a few more of his clothes going missing. I was so upset this morning I called into work, telling them I wasn't feeling well. I did not feel up to dealing with anyone. I hadn't slept in days, waiting to hear from him. I did hope Devin would come home, thinking I was at work. I knew if he saw my car in the garage, he would probably turn around and leave. This was why I parked my car on a neighboring street. I knew it was drastic, but I was willing to do whatever it took to have this conversation with my husband once and for all.

Devin never suspected anything until he entered the room he'd been staying in, to find me sitting on the bed holding one of the pillows. He was dressed down in a pair of jeans, a white tee, and a dark blazer. He looked like he'd been sleeping just fine.

"What are you doing here?" he asked, holding a large folder.

"I was waiting to see if you would show up."

"I thought you had to work."

"I can say the same for you."

"I had some business I needed to handle," he said looking down at the paperwork.

"Is that for me?" I asked calmly.

"Actually, it is," he said stepping forward and passing me the folder.

Without opening it, I asked, "Is it what I think it is?"

"If you think it's divorce papers, then, yes. That's exactly what it is. That's your copy."

I tossed the folder on the bed and continued to glare at my husband.

"So you are really serious about leaving me and being with Georgiana?" I asked.

"Monica, I wasn't playing when I told you this."

"And you expect me to let this happen so you can move on?"

"Yes. I think it's best for both of us."

I looked over at the folder and opened it. *Petition for Dissolution of Marriage* was in bold print at the top of the document.

"You didn't come home. Were you with Georgiana?"

Tucking his hands in his pockets he answered with, "I don't think that matters."

"I'll take that as a yes then. Did you fuck her?"

"Monica."

"Answer the damn question."

"Look, I came to get my things and leave you with those papers. We need to move on with our lives," he said walking over to the guest closet which housed most of his clothes.

"You want to move on with your life, but I want to make our marriage work," I said.

"Let this go, Monica," Devin said, taking out one of his suitcases. He brought it over and plopped it on the bed. Opening it, he proceeded to empty one of the top drawers like I wasn't in the room with him.

"Do you know your mother had me investigated?" I asked.

"She mentioned it to me," he said, stuffing his underwear into the suitcase.

"She found nothing. I guess I've done a great job hiding my secrets."

"What are you talking about, Monica?"

"I'm telling you your mother was right to have concerns about who I was," I glared at him as I continued to hug the pillow.

Devin looked at me cautiously as his packing became slower. With a knitted brow he asked, "Monica, say what you need to say."

"Do you remember me telling you my parents passed away along with my brother Michael?"

"Yes," he answered.

"Well, I lied. My parents are alive and well, and my brother, he's not dead either."

Devin peered at me asking, "What do you mean they are not dead?"

"They are very much alive."

"Are you serious right now?" he reacted.

"As a heart attack."

"This is just another reason why I should leave you, because you've lied to me all this time. But you want to get on me about how you gave your all and I didn't. Looks like we both are guilty of the same thing."

Ignoring him, I said, "My brother lives right here in Greensboro."

Devin stared at me in utter shock. He wasn't packing much of anything now. He seemed taken aback by this conversation, looking at me like he was trying to figure out where I was going with this. Well, he was getting ready to find out.

"Your brother is here in Greensboro?" he inquired.

"He lives in this house."

Devin chuckled saying, "Now you are crazy. Something is *definitely* wrong with you."

He walked over to his closet and took out an armful of his slacks and brought them over to the suitcases, placing them all in there like he was trying to get out of here sooner rather than later.

"It's the truth," I professed.

"I don't think you would know the truth if it smacked you in the face."

"Well, here's another truth for you. I'm my brother, Michael."

Devin halted. With narrowed eyes, he stared at me with a frown, trying to figure out what I was saying.

"Excuse me?"

"I'm Michael."

"Wait . . . wait . . . wait . . ." he repeated, rubbing his head as he walked unsteadily to the closet and back to the bed in confusion.

"My name is Monica, but I used to be Michael," I revealed.

Devin's face contorted in agony as he leaned forward to balance himself by holding his knees. He looked at me, like he was waiting for me to say I was joking, but I knew he understood the expression on my face, and he knew I was speaking the truth.

"Wait . . ." he whimpered, gripping his stomach as he stumbled back a few steps. "What . . . What are you saying?"

"I'm telling you I am a transgender man," I clarified.

"You're lying," he pointed, shifting from one foot to the other. "You're doing this to keep me from divorcing you."

"It's true, Devin."

"But . . . but, you don't . . ." he sighed like he was going to throw up. "You don't have a—"

"Dick?" I finished.

"Yes," he answered.

"I had the sex reassignment surgery before I met you."

"But you have tits, and ass, and a vagina. We've had sex, and you felt like a woman. You don't look like a man," he said in distress.

"I'm going to take that as a compliment. My surgeon is good at what he does."

Devin kept staring at me and turning away but looking back at me trying to see if I was lying. Then again, he could have been examining me to see if there were signs he missed. Either way, I had his full attention now.

"No. I don't believe you. I have not seen one sign to confirm what you're telling me," he argued.

"Remember the medication I take every morning. I told you it was because I had high blood pressure and hypothyroidism which caused my weight gain?"

"Yes . . . but—"

"Those are my hormone medication and other medication I need for my life as a woman."

"Oh my goodness. Oh my goodness," he kept repeating.

"This is also why I can't have children," I divulged. "Of course, I would have loved to give you a child, but it's medically impossible. Science hasn't figured out a way for transgender men to have children yet."

I watched Devin sort through his mind trying to understand what I was telling him. To further put the nail in the coffin, I got up from the bed and dropped to my knees to reach down and pulled a safe from under the bed. I had the key around my neck, which I usually kept in my jewelry box, but a part of me knew I would need it today. Sticking the key in the safe lock, I opened it, revealing all my personal and medical information about myself.

"If you don't believe me, here's the proof," I gestured toward the safe.

Devin took a few steps toward me but stopped like he didn't want to see what was in the safe. He probably knew once he had proof of what I was saying, he would have to face the fact I was born a man. Seeing he was not going to come any closer, I pulled out a picture of myself.

"This is me as Michael," I said holding up a picture when I was fifteen years old. "Here's a few more," I said holding up several more. "Here's the document showing when I changed my name from Michael to Monica," I showed him. "And here is the medial documents confirming the surgery I had done."

Tears formed in Devin's eyes. He backed away from me with his hands on his head until his back hit the wall.

"What have you done to me?" he asked, overcome by this revelation.

"I've done nothing but love you."

"But our love was based on a lie," he yelled.

"Would you have married me or even dated me if I told you I was once a man?" I asked.

"Hell no. I'm not gay."

"Devin, this does not make you gay," I tried to comfort.

"How the hell doesn't it? You are a fucking man, Monica, Michael—whoever the hell you are."

"I'm a woman. If I had never told you this, you wouldn't have thought any different."

"Then why did you tell me?" he asked.

"Because I thought you should know. I also didn't want you to leave me," I told him.

"What makes you think I'm going to be with you after what you've told me?"

"Because you don't want anyone to find out, do you?"

His entire demeanor changed. Anger quickly turned to dread as the fear of everybody finding out raced through his mind.

"You wouldn't," he murmured.

"Why wouldn't I? Your parents wanted to know the truth about me. I would be more than happy to tell them, especially that mother of yours. I wonder how she's going to take this," I kidded.

"You can't do that."

"Why not?" I asked cockily.

"They will disown me. My parents . . . they . . . They will not understand. Hell, *I* don't understand."

"You've left me with no other choice, honey," I told him.

"So, you are trying to blackmail me?"

"You call it blackmail. I call it trying to keep our marriage together."

Devin slid down the wall landing on his behind. I went to him and crouched down beside him. He moved away from me slightly, looking at me like he didn't know who I was.

"Devin, I love you so much. I'm still the woman you married."

"Why are you doing this?"

"I just told you. I love you with everything in me. Look at the life we have together. Look what we've accomplished. We have a nice home, nice cars, great jobs, nice clothes, and money in the bank. Many people would kill to have the life we have. I never once stepped out on you. Georgiana can't say that. Even if you slept with her while you were gone these past few days, I'll forgive you so we can move on. But this does mean you can't have any contact with that woman ever again. She's blatantly trying to take you away from me. She had her chance and messed up. Now, you are mine."

"I can't believe you are doing this to me."

"I'm doing this for us."

"You will not get away with this."

"Devin, the ball is in your court. If you still want to divorce me, then sign the papers and leave them on the kitchen counter. I will sign them and get them to you. But please keep in mind what the aftermath of your decision may be. I have no reason to keep my truth to myself anymore. I will tell everyone. Your parents, your job, the church, Georgiana—everyone. Because if I have to live my life without you in misery, then it will be a misery accompanied by your own misery."

Devin stared at me as I stood to my feet. I went over to the bed and gathered my safe, locking it again. I picked it up, looked at my crumpled husband, and exited the room.

One Month Later

Monica

42

As my guests arrived, I allowed them to arrange their items on the tables I had set up. Each table had an item for them to sort their things out. One table was for shoes, one for jewelry, then tops, bottoms, bags, and then jackets. Each table was running over with items, which I was excited about.

"Ladies, ladies, calm down. We have enough items for everybody, plus some," I said looking at the women rummaging through all the pieces brought for the clothing swap party.

Not only did my girls show up, they came with their hands full of nice things. Vivian was here, and she brought her boss Julia, who also brought items with her. Kellie was here with Victor, and the two of them brought bags, jewelry, and shoes. Sonya was here and brought a new friend, and both of them came with a lot. I also invited a few other ladies to be a part of this day, thinking, the more, the merrier.

"We have some really nice items here," Sonya said, picking up a silver necklace.

"I know, right? I'm excited," Vivian added.

"We are not going to fight, push, shove, or scratch each other's eyes out for these items, ladies. Do you hear me, Kellie and Sonya," I said, pointing.

"No, you didn't bring the shade," Sonya joked.

"Just making sure you ladies are good."

"I told you, we've made up. We've hashed out our issues," Kellie said.

"I know we've told her this before, Kellie, but Monica doesn't want to believe we are good," Sonya said, holding a pair of silver Stuart Weitzman stilettos.

"You know you can't walk in them," I told Sonya.

"I can learn because these bad boys are hot," she retorted, sticking them in the ecofriendly bag I provided for all the ladies.

I was happy to see my friends were back to being friends again.

"I got food in the kitchen, along with drinks, if you all want some," I announced.

"Please, tell me you have some wine, honey," Victor said.

"Now, what would a party be without wine, Victor?"

"I knew I loved you for some reason," he declared.

"You love anybody who will supply anything free," Kellie added.

"That too," Victor said, laughing. "While you ladies get your rummage on, I'm going to the kitchen to make myself at home."

Looking around at everyone in my home made me feel like things were back to normal. My event was a success. I knew these past few weeks had been difficult for all of us. As many things that happened, we had no other choice but to vent to one another or we were going to explode. I believe even Sonya was happy to get some things off her chest.

Vivian and her husband Sheldon were in a great place. She told us that the woman her husband was with that day in the restaurant was a psychiatrist he was seeing, but she didn't want to go into the details of why, and we all respected that. We were happy they were happy. Vivian was bragging about all the good sex she was getting now. In that area, I was jealous.

Kellie did finally file for divorce from Jeffrey who was fighting really hard to get her back. Why, I don't know. We thought he just messed up giving her the STD, but boy, there was more. Kellie told us everything that happened, down to finding him with another man and Victor telling her this man had AIDS. We were all shocked by this news and afraid for our friend. Kellie's situation could have been any of ours, so we supported her in what she was going through. Kellie confronted Jeffrey on this bit of news, and he said he was in the clear. This was the same man who denied giving her gonorrhea, so nothing he said could be believed. He wasn't ready to make his marriage work because if he was, he still wouldn't be playing those games with Kellie. All that mattered was my friend was healthy. I knew further tests would show she's okay also. I was praying that over her life. Kellie was a strong woman, who, I believe, was keeping a secret of her own from us in the form of a man. Each time we asked her if she was seeing someone, she blushed. As long as she was happy, I was happy for her.

As for Sonya, she was going back and forth between two men, Kegan and Damon. As handsome as both of these men were, I felt like Sonya needed to choose one and stop playing with both of their emotions. She, of all people, knew going back and forth between two individuals was going to have some repercussions eventually. Kegan called off his wedding from Imani, who was still threatening Sonya for being the reason why he called off the wedding. Sonya was unfazed and happy about her situation because she felt wonderful for the first time in a long time. Two men wanting her and both vying for her attention . . . what more could a woman want? Maybe to be a grandma. That's right, Sonya was about to be somebody's grandma. Meena was expecting. Sonya took her to get checked out after she caught Meena sleeping with some boy. Sonya was rightfully upset, like any mother would be, but a part of her was excited about this little one who would be arriving in six months. One thing for sure, this pregnancy brought her and Meena closer.

As for me, my identity was still a secret. I'm glad, because that afternoon when Sonya and Kellie got into it after we went to church that Sunday morning, I was planning on telling my friends who I really was. I felt like I needed to. But fate wouldn't allow that to happen, which worked for me in the end.

I got what I wanted. Devin was still living with me. He decided not to sign the divorce papers, but I knew he would make that decision. He didn't want everyone to find out he'd been sleeping with a man all this time. Who would ever believe he didn't know? Everyone would look at him like he also played a part in this farce of a marriage and went along with it to satisfy his Christian parents. I knew when he married me, he thought I was a woman. I knew he loved me too, but somewhere in our marriage that changed. I've known this for a while but convinced myself we were going to be okay. That was, until he verbally expressed not loving me anymore. Then it was real, and something I had to face head-on. I could no longer hide behind my own delusion of what I thought our marriage to be.

Finally understanding what he wanted was devastating. Devin thought he could divorce me and move on with his life with Georgiana, but I wasn't going to have that. Was I wrong for blackmailing him? Yes, I was. Did I still believe he loved me? I knew he didn't. But that didn't matter to me anymore. As long as Georgiana couldn't have him, I was happy. I knew that was crazy, but I'd rather him be unhappily stuck with me than happy with her. Served him right for breaking my heart and thinking he could treat me any kind of way.

Now, Georgiana was out of the picture. That poor woman was devastated when Devin had to break it off with her. I made him put the conversation on speaker so I could hear it. He didn't want to, but he had no choice in the matter. Georgiana wept uncontrollably as she pleaded for him to take her back. I could see the internal struggle he was having with himself, but he had to do what was best for the sake of our marriage.

When his parents found out, all hell broke loose. They could not believe Devin chose me over Georgiana. I knew they were ticked off by his decision, especially his mother, Isabelle. I have to say, Devin was very convincing when he told them why he was staying in his marriage. He told them his vows meant something to him, and as Christians, they should understand that. Little did they know their son was trying to spare them the embarrassment of a scandal. Was I afraid Devin would do something to me? No. You had to have a backup plan to your backup plan. If anything ever happened to me, you best believe this big girl would be the talk of the town.

ORDER FORM
URBAN BOOKS, LLC
97 N. 18th Street
Wyandanch, NY 11798

Name (please print):_______________________________

Address: _______________________________

City/State: _______________________________

Zip: _______________________________

QTY	TITLES	PRICE

Shipping and handling-add $3.50 for 1st book, then $1.75 for each additional book.

Please send a check payable to:

Urban Books, LLC

Please allow 4–6 weeks for delivery